EX LIBRIS
VINTAGE CLASSICS

MR PYE

Mervyn Peake was born in 1911 in Kuling, Central Southern China, where his father was a medical missionary. His education began in China and then continued at Eltham College in South East London, followed by the Croydon School of Art and the Royal Academy Schools. Subsequently he became an artist, married the painter Maeve Gilmore in 1937 and had three children. During the Second World War he established a reputation as a gifted book illustrator for *Ride a Cock Horse* (1940), *The Hunting of the Snark* (1941), and *The Rime of The Ancient Mariner* (1943).Other books include *Alice's Adventure's in Wonderland* and Grimm's *Household Tales* (both 1946) and *Treasure Island* (1949). *Titus Groan* was published in 1946, followed by *Gormenghast* in 1950 and *Titus Alone* in 1959. Peake had planned to write more about Titus, but the onslaught of a protracted illness made that impossible. Mervyn Peake died in 1968.

ALSO BY MERVYN PEAKE

Titus Groan

Gormenghast

Titus Alone

Shapes and Sounds

The Craft of the Lead Pencil

Letters from a Lost Uncle

Peake's Progress

Poems

Rhymes Without Reason

The Glassblowers

The Rhyme of the Flying Bomb

For Children

Captain Slaughterboard Drops Anchor

MERVYN PEAKE

Mr Pye

VINTAGE BOOKS
London

Published by Vintage 1999

10

First published in Great Britain in 1953 by William Heinemann
Methuen edition 1985
Interior illustrations by Mervyn Peake

Vintage
Random House, 20 Vauxhall Bridge Road,
London SW1V 2SA

www.vintage-classics.info

Addresses for companies within The Random House Group Limited can be found at: www.randomhouse.co.uk/offices.htm

The Random House Group Limited Reg. No. 954009

A CIP catalogue record for this book is available from the British Library

ISBN 9780099283263

The Random House Group Limited supports the Forest Stewardship Council® (FSC®), the leading international forest certification organisation. All our titles that are printed on Greenpeace approved FSC® certified paper carry the FSC® logo. Our paper procurement policy can be found at www.randomhouse.co.uk/environment

Printed and bound in Great Britain by
CPI Bookmarque, Croydon CR0 4TD

Mr Pye

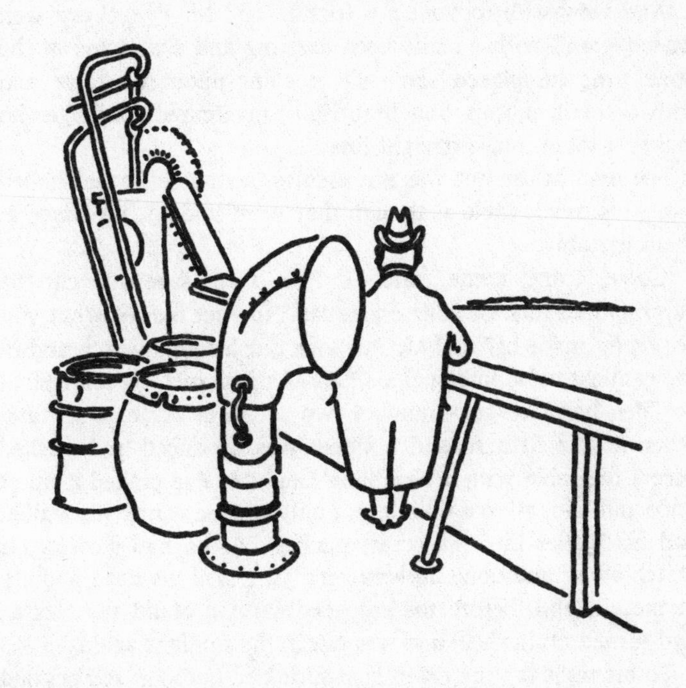

ONE

'SARK.'

'Yes, sir,' said the man in the little quayside hut. 'A return fare. Six shillings.'

'A single, my friend,' said Mr Harold Pye.

The man in the little hut looked up and frowned at the unfamiliar face.

'Did you say a "*single*", sir?'

'I believe so.'

The man in the hut frowned again as though he were still not satisfied. Why should this fat little stranger be so sure he wanted a 'single'? He was obviously only a visitor. A return ticket would last him for three months and would save him two shillings. Some people, he reflected, were beyond hope.

'Very well,' he said, shrugging his shoulders.

'And very well to *you*, my friend,' said Mr Pye. 'Very well *indeed*–' and with a smile both dazzling and abstracted at the same time he placed some silver coins upon the table and with a small, plump, and beautifully manicured forefinger he jockey'd them into a straight line.

The man in the hut was not used to having coins marshalled along his trestle table as though they were soldiers. He stared at them irritably.

'Come, come, come,' said Mr Pye. 'I am sure you can be quicker than this. Of course you can. Now let me see what you are *really* made of,' and Mr Pye took out his gold watch and in the gentlest voice imaginable: 'Shall I time you?' he said. 'Shall I? Then here we go – one ... two ... three ... four ...' and when at the fifth second a ticket was produced and pushed across the table with a trembling hand, Mr Pye picked it up at once and had, all in a breath, not only slipped it into his wallet, and his wallet into his breast pocket, but he had stowed his watch away and done up his overcoat, tossed his head happily in the air, and, before the stupefied Sarnian could say 'knife', had turned on his heel and was out in the sunlight again.

To his right lay the green boat-sprinkled harbour and beyond it the town of St Peter Port on its terraced hill.

An hour before sunrise the wind had dropped abruptly and now at eleven o'clock in the morning, as Mr Pye pattered confidently along the Guernsey quayside, there was not a wave to be seen. The air was mild and golden and the sky stainless, save for a single wisp of cloud that hung like a hammock, high above Peter Port.

Of course the *Ormer* was late in sailing. Last minute passengers found as usual that they had hurried themselves for nothing. Little more than half the cargo had been stowed away. The small crane swung out its iron arm, lowered its latest burden into the hold where the straining ropes went limp and the murderous hooks were released, only to soar again, out of the shadow of the harbour wall, and into the upper sunlight.

But there was no hurry, for the sea was motionless and the passengers were in good humour. The climbing town of Peter Port gazed down at them benevolently across the inner harbour from a hundred gleaming windows.

For some while Mr Pye stood on the quayside, his small hands grasping the lapels of his light overcoat, a short spruce gentleman whose paunch, both neat and benign, was both contradicted and emphasized by the straightness of his spine. It was a spine that suggested boundless vitality.

He watched with an alert and knowledgeable satisfaction the work in progress, and seemed in a quite indefinable way to be giving it his blessing.

When, after several minutes of silent 'supervision', he turned upon his heel and took a dozen crisp paces along the quay, it was as though, by the mere fact of his motivity, something significant had taken place.

Of the passengers who loitered on the quayside there was not one who had not stared at the stranger. It is true that it was not unusual for visitors to take the Sark boat in March, but there was something rather different about Mr Pye. He did not quite fit into any of the categories. It was quite obvious that he was not a schoolmistress, or a commercial traveller, or a scoutmaster, or a fugitive, or a painter, or a remittance man – and it was apparent from his two suitcases and one large haversack that he was no day-tripper. Who was he, and where would he be staying on the island?

And so, from time to time, by way of diversion, the passengers turned their gaze from the cargo-loading and stared at the enigmatic stranger, and noted the little smile upon his face. It was a curious little smile, both charming and secretive. It was as though he had private knowledge of something very droll denied not only to those who watched him but to mankind in general.

To and fro walked Mr Pye along the quayside, with his private smile on his face. One or two of the waiting passengers, on catching his eye, said: 'Good morning,' but Mr Pye did not reply in any way beyond intensifying that smile of his. It was as though he were saying: 'Yes, yes ... there is time for all that, later: we will be friends before long, no doubt (for the future is big with promise) . . . but for the moment, my friends, be patient – the time is not yet ripe.'

By now the cargo had been stowed away, and the passengers began to file down the harbour steps that are so vile a green. The pilot climbed to his nautical pulpit. Ropes, loosened from the bollards, splashed into the water and were hauled aboard, dripping. The car tyres that were used as 'fenders' were pulled over the sides, and the screw began to turn; and, with a shout or two, and one sudden and quite extraordinarily offensive oath from one of the sailors who had suddenly slipped and broken his leg, the *Ormer* began to nose her way out of the harbour.

It takes about an hour from St Peter Port to the little Creux Harbour in Sark. The *Ormer* put on steam and throbbed her way eastwards. The passengers stood in knots on the deck, or leaned on the railings, watching the familiar landmarks of Guernsey grow gradually smaller while the gulls circled and cried peevishly in the wake.

But Mr Pye was not the kind of man to look backwards. With never a glance for Guernsey he gave his whole attention to that far strip of land that by slow degrees grew ever closer, while the cormorants winged rapidly across the surface of the breathless sea, or stood in groups upon the passing rocks like members of the clergy who have agreed, with bad grace, to differ.

It was hard to believe, on such a morning, in the black gales that could so whip the sea into a mania – that could heave up into such horrid hills and sink again into such piebald hollows and make, between Guernsey and Sark, so dire a stretch of foam.

Lucky Mr Pye. Was ever a voyage more conducive to happy speculation? His spherical face was positively aglow. His sharp nose, not unlike the beak of a bird, trembled as though on the scent of some Olympian quarry. His glasses twinkled.

Herm and Jethou, the half-way islands, passed by unnoticed as far as Mr Pye was concerned. It was that other island that he craved.

And there she lay at full stretch upon the skyline, her attenuated and coruscated body reaching from north to south, the morning sunbeams playing along her spine and flickering upon the crests and ridges of her precipitous flanks.

Mr Pye, who had for the last fifteen minutes been staring fixedly at the approaching island, joined his hands together beneath his chin, turned his round face to the sky, closed his eyes, stood upon the tips of his toes, and breathed deeply.

'It is just the right size,' he murmured. 'It will do very nicely.'

TWO

MISS DREDGER was a resident of long standing in Sark, and it is by no means an easy thing to be promoted from the rank of 'visitor' to that of 'resident'. It has been known to take many years. It is difficult to understand quite how the transference comes about. It is an almost mystical procedure and is, of course, in the hands of the natives – that basic layer in the triple sandwich of island life.

Miss Dredger had not been to England for over fifteen years, and very seldom went to Guernsey. But the longer she stayed in Sark the more English she became.

Every summer she took in visitors at Clôs de Joi. It was a four-square house with a gable and an upstairs veranda, and a south view across the island to the sea with Jersey on the horizon.

Miss Dredger had ordered a carriage to take her down the harbour hill. Although it was a steep and broken decline, she would normally have taken it in her gaunt and purposeful stride, and what is more would have returned on foot up the long gradient, for Miss Dredger scorned all weakness of the flesh.

Nevertheless, in spite of her stamina, she had ordered a carriage on this particular morning, for she had a gentleman to meet at the harbour. Both he and his luggage must be got up the harbour hill. It was plain that the luggage could not walk up on its own and from what she knew about men it was ten to one that her new boarder would be as helpless as his luggage.

And so, as the carriage had to go down the hill before it could come up again, Miss Dredger, with her sharp sense of logic decided that, in order to make use of this fact, it would be as well to be called for at Clôs de Joi.

With unexpected punctuality and to the accompaniment of a crunching sound from the wheels, the decrepit carriage negotiated the short curve of her drive, the horse's hoofs cutting cruelly into the moist red gravel.

When Miss Dredger emerged from the house she frowned with momentary irritation at the furrows in the wake of the wheels, for she had had the gravel carefully raked on the previous day when a light rain had pocked it like goose-flesh. But she climbed into the carriage without a word. The driver, young Pépé, with that dreadful cast of the left eye, aloft on the driver's seat, whipped savagely at the large grey mare and, egging her forward and drawing her back alternately, was able to turn her about, with a creaking of harness and a squeaking of the axle, and a mangling of the soft red gravel.

Miss Dredger sat sternly on the mildewed leather of the seat, her feet astride on the rotting boards of the 'well', her hands on her angular knees.

The grey mare, taking her own time, mooched through the gate, dropping her heavy hoofs as if they were deadweights, or as though her tendons had been cut. Every few yards she would toss her head up in the air as though to free herself from some irritation or other. Young Pépé whistled tunelessly between his teeth and scratched himself almost without pause.

Down they trundled, past the Old Manoir with its view across the meadows to the two hotels ... round the bend of the road where the grey two-roomed school stood cheek-by-jowl with a pocket-sized prison like a stone sea-chest ... down the Avenue that was no longer an avenue, for all that remained was the great stub ends of the massacred trees ... and so, past the butcher's shed and the general stores and the gift shop, and two or three houses, to the end of the 'Avenue' where the Colinette basked in the sun.

The Colinette is the cross-roads at the top of the harbour-hill where a few houses – too few to call a village – form a little cluster and trail away to the north.

It is at the Colinette that the day-trippers, exhausted by their climb up the harbour-hill, come to a halt, mop their brows and inquire which way to go. It is usual to send them down the dipping path to the south, which leads eventually to a small, rather ordinary bay. There they find themselves in a stone pocket and as it is too much trouble to trudge back to the main body of the island, they spend the day wondering why they ever came to Sark.

It is at the Colinette that the dogs of Sark can best be studied – supposing that anyone wished to study them – as they lounge in the white dust, or snap at flies, or molest one another or scratch their ears with the claws of one of their back legs, their muzzles pointing at the sky, or while they lie in the warm dust meditating on the vicissitudes of life, and how mean a fortune is theirs with never a bitch to woo, for none, by law, are allowed on the island.

It is here at the Colinette that the carriages congregate before they rumble their way down the steep hill to the harbour, and the horses are tied by their reins to the stunted trees.

Straight over the cross-roads jogged Miss Dredger. Some carriages had already started and were taking the first slope of the hill. Others were still tied to the trees. In one of them an old man was fast asleep, a cat in his arms. There was no hurry. Nothing was ever on time.

Down the long hill until the trees closed overhead and the high ferny banks slid by, bruised with bluebells, and in the dappled shadows at the foot of the banks a rivulet sparkled in the ditch.

Down plodded the horses, straining their traces, and leaning backwards against the weight of the carriage, with young Pépé perched high like a monkey, with one hand on the brake and the other scratching at his little patch-work rump. There was no need for him to hold the reins. The old mare had made this same journey every morning for the last twelve years. She knew the way.

Every now and again the verge of the uneven road was punctuated by small stone basins where the water brimmed for the horses, and, sliding over, continued its loquacious way.

And all at once, they were out of the shadows and the sun shone down on the last stretch of empty looking road, and the ocean was before them standing up vertically like a back-drop, on whose blue surface two fishing boats were stuck like coloured flies.

The leading carriages had turned to the right and were already in the short echoing rock-tunnel whose seaward opening, like a proscenium arch, contained this morning a harbour-set, as lovely and inventive as you could wish. The props were all in place. Boats upon their sides, lobster pots, nets hung up to dry, all the stock-in-trade of harbour life.

When Miss Dredger's carriage drew up alongside the high harbour wall, she descended and stood for a moment with her hands on her hips, gazing at the horse as though waiting for it to say something. Then she consulted her watch. Were the *Ormer* to have been on time, she should have been rounding the bluff by the Cat Rock at that moment, but of course she wasn't.

A few children and the local painter, who was supposed to be colour-blind, were the only ones sitting on the long sea wall. It was as wide as a table top. Miss Dredger turned her back to the wall and took four slow, purposeful steps to the edge of the little enclosed harbour and stared down into the water. A small lilac jellyfish was floating in the depths, innocently, unaffectedly, minding its own business, but she turned her eyes from it with a gesture of irritation. It was really too absurd. What Miss Dredger insisted on was purpose, backbone, and common sense with no frills. Some things were too feeble.

Above Miss Dredger, above the green water, above and all but surrounding them, were the precipitous walls of coloured rock that glowed this historic morning with blends of lichen green and honey colour, with a long section of old rose that slanted for two hundred feet across the southern face. All this was reflected in the still water of the harbour for those who were interested in reflections. No one was.

Thorpe, the painter, gazed ruminatively at the sea, his legs dangling over the sea-wall. He propped his thinly bearded chin on his hand. His eyes were out of focus, like his painting. To him, *atmosphere*, for the moment, was everything.

What is more delicious, he thought, than sitting on a harbour wall with all the time in the world to waste with the brain as bland and empty as ether. The eyes can watch a puffin on a rock, if they so wish – it is their affair – but for the brain, oh no, there's nothing doing there. Nothing can draw the brain out, short of a corkscrew, on a day like this.

Far away, perhaps, there was a hint of melancholy, a sense of the heroic deeds, the golden pilgrimages, the splendid dreams that had passed him by. Somewhere or other a mistake had been made. A mistake as vast as the sky, but, mercifully, as intangible. And yet there was always that flicker of hope. Of hope that a moment would arrive – a centrifugal moment when all becomes possible – but not today. Today was so lovely as it was, waiting for the *Ormer*, with the sun gloating on the unrippled water and the blank and zoneless bliss of an empty mind.

Thorpe re-crossed his legs. His vague reverie was not shared by Miss Dredger. She would have agreed that it was a mild morning, there was no disputing *that*, but would have added that it was unseasonable. 'Everything in its place,' she would have said, 'and a place for everything.'

She drew a packet of 'Three Star' from the pocket of her tweed skirt and lit a cigarette. Then she struck a match on the sole of her brogues. She inhaled deeply and slowly, her tough unpainted lips apart, and her large teeth clenched and shining in an almost oriental grimace. When at last the two white jets of smoke sprang simultaneously from her equine nostrils it was as though they were competing in a race.

And then, suddenly, one of the boys on the wall shouted, 'Here she comes.' Had he been able to gaze into the future and appreciate how pregnant with fate was this innocent-seeming morning, then surely he must have cried not, 'Here *she* comes', but here *he* comes, for it was not the *Ormer*, but Mr Pye who was so soon to turn the island inside-out like a salted leech.

Mr Pye, standing at the bows, gazed up at the high sea-wall and he found it good. He loved each block of stone that went to its making. He saw the children running along the top of the wall, and Thorpe the painter getting to his feet. He noted the high coloured cliffs that towered above the harbour on three sides, and he extended his benison to them also and to the ivy that patched them. The lanky Mr Stitchwater, standing with his large freckled hands on the rail, a few feet from Mr Pye, could hear the stranger humming gently to himself. 'From Earth's wide bounds, from Ocean's farthest coast, Through gates of pearl streams in the countless host.'

And now the *Ormer* was moving into the narrow harbour mouth and the group on the quay turned their backs on the sea-wall and mooched to the verge of the imprisoned harbour where the emerald water had become rippled with expectancy. A horse stamped. A seagull wheeled and settled on a ledge of rock. A figure, the size of a halma-man, high up on the cliff top whistled shrilly, and waved.

It was easier for Miss Dredger to conclude which of the passengers must be Mr Pye than for Mr Pye to guess which of the figures who lined the quay above him, was Miss Dredger. For Mr Pye was the only stranger on the *Ormer*. But his eyes moved to and fro in contented and unhurried speculation, and when eventually, standing very upright, with his hands as usual clasping the lapels of his coat, he allowed his gaze to rest a little longer than usual on Miss Dredger's seasoned face, and found that he was himself being unblushingly scrutinized – he lifted his hat a few inches from his head and bowed very slightly from the hips. This simple gesture was performed with such simple and unostentatious dignity that it set him apart from anyone else who had ever prepared to set foot on the island. But beyond raising his hat and inclining his spruce and portly body, he made no other sign. His heart was full of love, but he was at the same time a man of exemplary control. He knew how to hold his horses, and to lead them, ever so gently, to those pastures of his choice. He knew how goodness can be as disrupting as evil. How all things must be insinuated.

He was on the threshold of a new world. A world of some three hundred of God's creatures. A world that measured three miles by one-and-a-half – but ah, how immeasurable in terms of the human soul.

'Gently does it,' he murmured to himself. 'Gently does it, my friend.'

THREE

DIRECTLY Mr Pye stepped ashore he heard her voice. 'The name is Dredger,' it said.

Mr Pye lifted his head again, his thorn-shaped nose veering towards her and the rest of his round face following it, as a ship must follow its bowsprit. His little mouth continued to smile gently but it gave nothing away.

As he remained silent, Miss Dredger raised her voice as though to establish the fact of her forthright nature from the outset. 'Mr Pye, I imagine!'

Her new acquaintance removed his glasses, wiped them carefully, and re-set them on his nose.

'Who else?' he murmured. 'Who else, dear lady?'

As Miss Dredger could not think *who* else could possibly be Mr Pye, and had no wish to follow so foolish a train of conjecture, she blew some smoke out of her nostrils.

Mr Pye watched the smoke-jets with interest, and then, as though he were suggesting an alternative attitude to life, he drew a little box from his waistcoat pocket and helped himself to a fruit-drop.

At this, Miss Dredger raised one of her black eyebrows, and as she did so she caught sight of young Pépé – and seeing him reminded her of Mr Pye's luggage. She turned to Mr Pye, her scrubbed hands on her tweed hips.

'What have you brought with you?' she said. Mr Pye turned his gaze upon her. 'Love,' he said. 'Just . . . Love . . .' and then he transferred the fruit-drop from one cheek to the other with a flick of his experienced tongue. His fat little hands that held the lapels of his coat were quite green with the light reflected from the harbour water.

Miss Dredger's face had turned the most dreadful colour and she had shut her eyes. The smoke drifted out of her nostrils with no enthusiam. There were some things that simply are not mentioned – unless one wishes to be offensive and embarrassing. Religion, Art, and now this new horror – Love. What on earth did the man mean?

When she opened her eyes and found herself gazing into a face so brimming with dispassionate affection she found that her anger ebbed out of her.

'What *else*?' she muttered. 'Have you brought anything *else*?'

All at once Mr Pye was as alert as a bird.

'Two suitcases and a haversack.'

'Did you hear what the gentleman said?' Miss Dredger had turned to young Pépé, who was standing close by scratching himself as usual.

'That will be quite all right, miss,' said Pépé, without looking up.

'Very good. Get them off the boat as quickly as you can. How will he *know* them?' She turned to Mr Pye.

He addressed the youth. 'My initials are H.P., my good friend – and my belongings are so marked.'

'Fair enough. Now if you will come with me,' said Miss Dredger, turning to her guest, 'we will find our carriage.'

'Undoubtedly,' said Mr Pye.

Miss Dredger, marching along the quay at his side, frowned

darkly. What had he done to put her off her balance? Everything he did or said seemed curiously out of focus.

It was not long after they had reached the carriage that young Pépé arrived with Mr Pye's luggage, and he was soon climbing up to his seat. While doing so he was at the same time shouting down to a large pale-faced woman in a purple hat, half-way between a busby and a tea-cosy, 'No, miss, this carriage is ordered, miss, you should have phoned from Guernsey, miss.'

'Phoned from Guernsey!' muttered the large woman, 'do you think I'm made of money?'

'Might be made of almost anything,' thought young Pépé, squinting at her vast marmoreal face, but he said, 'Don't know about *that*, miss,' and then, 'Whoa; there – whoa!' as the grey mare moved sideways and out of line.

Now Miss Dredger and Miss George had not spoken to each other for over a year. They had ceased to be fond of one another. There had been the question of a right of way across a corner of Miss Dredger's garden. (This short cut would have saved Miss George's legs at least a mile a day, but would have meant that for three hundred and sixty-five days out of the year Miss Dredger would have been liable to see the purple busby in her grounds.) The ugly argument had erupted a year ago and alienated the two of them. So that when Mr Pye suggested that Miss George might like to ride in the carriage while he walked, the effect was horrible.

In the stunned silence which followed his ignorant suggestion, Mr Pye turned his head sharply from one to the other. What had he said? Was he already being sucked into the quicksands of island life? It seemed for a moment that he was at a loss: but only for a moment.

'But, ladies! ladies,' he said. 'We are here to help one another, are we not? What else is there in life?'

This was evidently a new approach to the art of living as far as Miss George and Miss Dredger were concerned, and an even longer silence throbbed its way to completion.

'I don't know anything about *that*,' said Miss George at last, 'but you are evidently a gentleman': at which she heaved herself grotesquely into the carriage and lowered her enormous rear to the mildewed seat.

'I would prefer to walk,' said Mr Pye; 'but there is room for both you ladies in the carriage – where you can chatter happily together.'

Young Pépé shook his little monkey-head.

'We can't have 'em both in the carriage, sir. Miss George is all the horse can manage, *up* the hill, with the baggage, 'n' everything. She's not as young as she was, sir.'

'What has my age got to do with it?' muttered Miss George, adjusting her purple busby.

'I was talking about the *horse*,' said young Pépé.

Miss Dredger had gone perfectly white. When at last she spoke she brought out each separate word as though it were a thing on its own, self-sufficient and divorced from the other words in the sentence 'I ... have ... no ... intention ... of ... sharing ... the ... vehicle ... with ... Miss ... George. It appears ... that ... she ... has ... done ... very ... well for ... herself, *I* ... order ... the ... carriage – but ... *she* ... squats ... in ... it. However ... she ... can ... pay ... for ... it.'

'Oh no!' said Miss George. 'Not with *your* luggage around my feet. Oh, no! That wouldn't do at all.'

Mr Pye joined his hands together. Here, already, within a minute or two of his landing, was an ugly knot for him to untie. A positive thrill ran through his trim little penguin body. What splendour, what beauty there was in smoothing out the crumpled sheets of passion, in fusing seemingly allergic souls. Oh the lubrication of it all!

He popped a fruit-drop into his mouth. Then he turned to them each in turn.

'I would have offered you a sweet, Miss George – and, Miss Dredger, my dear, I would have offered *you* a sweet as well, but I will not offer them. You are not worthy of the gesture in your present mood. See, here are the two sweets in my hand, but they are not for you – they are for Dobbin –' and Mr Pye spread out the palm of his hand and held the fruit-drops under the nose of the grey horse.

All that happened was that the huge black wrinkled lips of the horse curled back to reveal two rows of such dreadful yellow tombstones that Mr Pye withdrew his hand at once, and tossed the sweets into the harbour.

'You notice I do not return them to my little box,' he said. 'They are tainted. Tainted by the unpleasant tone which you two ladies have used to one another. I will speak to you both later. You have distressed me. Is all my luggage here, my young friend?'

Pépé, who had his mouth and his eyes so wide open that his head appeared to have been swallowed by his face, took some time to shake himself out of his amazement, and even then all he could do was to nod his head.

As he began to pull at the reins and edge the old horse out of alignment, Mr Pye plucked the whip from the metal quiver near the driver's seat and cracked it in the still, sunny air. Then he handed it up to the dumbfounded youth.

'Away with you, charioteer,' he said. 'We have wasted enough time as it is.' He glanced at Miss Dredger. She turned her head from him at once. What a profile the lady had. It was authority personified – the large aquiline nose; the eloquent eyes incarcerated like prisoners beneath the beetling brows – the stern, uncoloured, male mouth – the determined chin with its three long hairs that could so easily have been snipped off, every morning.

It was obvious that she was gathering herself together. But she said nothing, and now that the carriage had freed itself of the long line of vehicles and was beginning to roll towards the tunnel in the rock, she strode behind it, quite ignoring Mr Pye, who kept abreast of her, nevertheless, his eyes taking in all that lay about him with that same expression of inner satisfaction.

It was a far longer climb than Mr Pye had anticipated, but he was not the man to drop behind Miss Dredger's tireless raking stride.

A few yards ahead of them the huge rounded back of Miss George was all too visible, the thick white waxen neck and the monstrous purple busby. Miss Dredger was experiencing that ungovernable distaste that comes from the contemplation of the very stuff of which an enemy is composed; that thick, white neck of lard, those doming and abominable shoulders.

The humiliation of it was too dreadful – this following in the wake of Miss George – it was as though she and Mr Pye were that woman's retinue.

When half the climb had been completed, the horse drew to the side of the road where a brick-built basin was filled to brimming by the thin stream – and the large grey head lowered itself into the wet ferny shadows and the ripples ran vertically up the gulping throat.

Mr Pye came to a halt beside the carriage and mopped his brow. From where he stood he could not see Miss Dredger, but he heard her voice on the other side of the carriage.

'You will deposit Miss George at the top of the harbour hill. She has unfortunate legs. You will then continue to Clôs de Joi with Mr Harold Pye. I shall be waiting for you and will settle with you. Do you understand?'

'Yes, miss.'

Without another word Miss Dredger, leaning slightly forward from the hips but with her head held high, began to stride inexorably forward and upward, her long, thin, iron-muscled legs working like pistons.

By the time the grey horse had quenched its thirst Miss Dredger was round the bend – and by the time the carriage had reached the Colinette she was almost home.

When young Pépé stopped at the cross-roads where the dogs foregathered, Miss George was fast asleep in the carriage. To many the question of how to rouse her, or even *whether* to rouse her, might have proved a difficult problem – but Mr Pye had no hesitation in reaching for the whip and cracking it with the authority of a ring-master.

Miss George opened her eyes. For a little while she stared at Mr Pye with a face as expressionless as the top of a mushroom, but when she remembered what had happened, and particularly how it was through Mr Pye that she had been able to ascend the hill in comfort, she pushed the hairy brim of her purple busby a little farther from her eyes, and lifting the ends of her mouth, smirked. There was something so horrible about this that Mr Pye helped himself to a fruit-drop.

'Out you get,' he said. 'Did you not hear Miss Dredger's instruction? You must not be greedy, you know, must you?'

'I wish to be taken to my house,' said Miss George.

Mr Pye put one foot on the mounting step and leaned over into the carriage so that his sharp nose was within the shadow of the purple busby.

'Do you want me to be cross with you?' he whispered.

There was such intensity in the inquiring whisper that, almost like a reflex, the great doming body began to heave itself inch by inch to the rickety door, and then down to the ground.

Mr Pye climbed into the carriage at once. 'Away we go,' he cried to young Pépé, and as the horse began to canter down the avenue, and before the stranded Miss George was out of earshot:

'Au revoir, dear lady,' he cried. 'I can see that I shall have to *talk* to you!' Then he rested his round head against the warm leather at his back, closed his eyes, and smiled.

FOUR

NEVER had Miss Dredger smoked so immoderately, or absorbed more nicotine into her system in so short a time. Her head, like Scaw Fell Pike, was all but lost in cloud, from which white haze the twin jets of exhalation sprang forth like an eternal renewal of life. Her anger and mortification so unsettled her that she paced from one room to another like a caged creature, as she waited for the carriage to arrive, and in each room the white wreaths billowed and coiled and eventually found their way out of the open windows.

Sometimes she would come to a dead halt, her hands on her hips, her feet astride, and her chin thrust forward as an access of irritation precluded even the use of her legs.

The insufferable nerve of the little man had caught her unawares, but that sort of thing must end immediately. Here, on her own ground, she would stand no nonsense.

She marched to the kitchen where Ka-Ka, a very old woman, was stirring up the wrong ingredients in the wrong bowl at the wrong time. Old Ka-Ka's idea of a *vol-au-vent* was entirely her own. She was blind in one eye, completely deaf, and had a cleft palate.

This was very sad, but Miss Dredger could not be sympathetic all the time. The milk of human kindness has a way of turning when things go wrong, and Miss Dredger plucked the pastry-board from the old woman and threw the dreadful contents out of the window.

Immediately, a black-backed gull landed beside the jetsam, straddled its way around it, squinting at the mess from every direction, and then, in spite of its hunger and the jaded condition of its palate, flapped away peevishly.

Miss Dredger raised her hands to the level of Ka-Ka's one remaining eye and spelt out in deaf-and-dumb language the uncompromising message, which after several attempts was interpreted eventually as 'Go home'.

She would have to prepare another kind of lunch altogether and, if it was late Mr Pye could bally well wait for it. She returned to the front door and stared at the palm tree on the lawn ahead of her. It was an ugly thing with a hairy bole like a baboon's hide. The fingers of its outstretched hands were in dreadful condition – not a grey-green finger protruded in the right direction and half of them were either torn or broken. No tree had ever been in direr need of a manicure.

The palm tree gave her no solace. To do her justice she was not looking for solace. That would have been *too* feeble. She was simply gazing at one of nature's less fortunate manifestations because her face happened to be set in that direction.

Oh, she would show him! Either he toed the line or he must go! She shifted her gaze to the gravel at her feet and blew some smoke at it. Its ravaged condition reminded her that she should waylay the carriage at the gate to prevent yet another eruption of ruts and hoof-marks.

But on reflection she was damned if she would be seen waiting for Mr Pye at her own gate as though she were interested in his miserable existence. No! Let the drive look like the Pennine Range! What did she care? If Mr Pye objected he could take the next boat back to England, or find somewhere else on the island.

As she brooded darkly she heard the sound of wheels on the road, and she lifted her eyes and stared across the lawn to where a few bamboos, mixed incongruously with a high screen of laurel, formed the southern margin of her garden. Beyond this hedge there was a steep decline to the flanking road, so that the passing carriages and horses were invisible from her front door, but the heads of the drivers could be seen with difficulty through the gaps in her hedge.

When it came in sight – in this case the monkey-like head of young Pépé – she lit a fresh 'Three Star' from the stub of her old one and made a rectangle of her tough mouth. Then she inhaled as though to fill not only her lungs, but her entire body with smoke. At last she launched the jets across the drive, in a stern propulsion of release, like steam from a kettle.

With a crunching of hoofs and wheels and the noise of an axle screaming for oil, the old carriage rounded the bend of the drive, and there was Mr Pye, his sharp nose scenting the air and his face radiant.

Even before the horse had stopped he had jumped neatly from the well of the carriage. 'My *dear*,' he said with a quietness that contrasted oddly with the nimble speed of his descent. 'My dear – is this *it*? Is this the house I have so dreamed about? Oh, but perfect, perfect. It is as it ought to be – and an upstairs veranda where we can sit together, you and I, and discuss all kinds of things – from goldfish to the nature of Limbo, and, incidentally,' he added, his eyes on the roof and with a note in his voice of almost clandestine confidence – 'I will repair your guttering this afternoon – and *now*, just settle with our charioteer, will you?' (holding up a ten-shilling note), 'and tell me where the garden-rake is kept.'

'Well, *really*!' said Miss Dredger, in a voice which she hardly recognized. 'I am not used to . . .'

'No one is. No one is. . . .' said Mr Pye, quick as an echo. 'But don't keep me waiting, will you? I *know* you won't. Come, come, my dear . . . the rake?'

His gently chiding voice and the sweetness of his smile unnerved her, and Miss Dredger lifted a trembling hand and pointed to an old shed, half hidden by the house.

Between her outstretched fingers he slipped the ten-shilling note – and then all at once he was gone from her side and could be seen pacing away towards the shed with his back as straight as a penguin's and his paunch as benevolent and purposeful, and his nose as sharp as a beak.

Almost in a state of coma, Miss Dredger paid young Pépé, who made his slow departure from the garden with his head dangerously screwed back over his shoulder and his eyes fastened on Mr Pye and his little walnut of a brain inflamed with conjecture – while the old grey mare found her own way down the drive and through the garden gate.

'First things first,' said Mr Pye. 'I positively am not coming intoi your beautiful house until I have furnished you with the finest drive in the Channel Islands.' He took off his coat, folded it, handed it to Miss Dredger, undid his gold cuff-links, stowed them away in his waistcoat pocket, rolled up his sleeves, popped a fruit-drop into his mouth and began to smooth the tortured drive, and rake it this way and that, while leaving behind him as he moved the most ingenious herring-bone striations that Miss Dredger's rake had ever brought to birth.

'Would it not be *best*,' said Mr Pye, stopping for a moment, 'if you ran in, to see whether all is well with your arrangements for lunch? In twenty minutes I would like you to take me to my room.'

He bridled back his round and gentle head and drew a deep breath of island air. For a moment or two he held the rake at his side like a guardsman at attention.

Then, breaking out of his momentary reverie with a gay little toss of his head, he returned to the raking of the drive in a manner both swift and meticulous, the prongs of the rake leaving the most charming patterns in their seven-pronged wake.

Miss Dredger was by now trembling from head to foot. The suddenness with which all this had happened had produced in her a state of mind and body which, had it been experienced by a woman of less will-power, less moral fibre, less traditional English phlegm and less physical strength, might well have proved shattering to nerve and spirit.

Miss Dredger found to her surprise that she was in the house and was climbing the stairs from the hall without having decided to do so. From the top landing she moved into her large, sparsely furnished bedroom – *moved* rather than strode, although her paces were just as long and just as gaunt. The way one foot followed another was no longer an affair of character, but an automatic operation drained of purpose.

Inevitably she found herself at the window and inevitably she gazed down at Mr Pye, her heart beating. She could hear him humming to himself and then as he stopped in his work for a moment with his head cocked on one side as he considered a particularly elegant whorl of rake-lines, she heard his humming break into a kind of singing. So clear it was, yet so private in the morning stillness. It was a voice so full of friendly gaiety that she thrust her hands into the pockets of her tweed skirt and shut her eyes in bewilderment.

'The purple headed mountain,
The river running by,
The sunset, and the morning
That brightens up the sky,
All things bright and beautiful
All creatures great and small,
All things wise ...'

At this point he broke off to pop a pear-drop in his mouth, and then he continued more musingly, as he turned to a new stretch of spoliated gravel:

'Each little flower that opens
Each little bird that sings,
He made their glowing colours
He made their tiny wings....

All things bright and ...'

Here he ended for the moment as he effected a particularly elegant flourish of his fanciful rake.

Miss Dredger, fighting down a desire to smash the window to let out her soul, clasped her head and moved across the room to where a tall mirror hung against the wall. There she examined her face as though to make sure that she was really in the room. Then she sat on the end of her bed and lit a cigarette.

A fresh surge of irritation, anger, and ire filled her. The humiliation of it all seemed almost to choke her and she started to her feet and, marching to the window, flung it open.

It was unkind of fate that it should have been that particular window which had been giving trouble, for the violence of her action broke both its hinges and it fell with a crash and a splintering of glass to the gravel below, dislodging on its way down a couple of flower-pots on the outside window-sill of the room beneath.

Mr Pye gazed up with not so much as a raised eyebrow.

'Miss Dredger,' he said, 'you look seedy!'

'How *dare* you!' cried Miss Dredger, finding her voice. 'What are you! I will have no more of you!'

Her features were as grim as a native mask, but there was also something strained and uncertain that hovered in her face.

Mr Pye moved a few steps nearer to the house so that he was immediately below her.

He lifted his right arm and crooked his index finger, and then to her consternation beckoned her as one might beckon a child, the last two joints of the digit vacillating to and fro with great rapidity.

They stared at one another while the beckoning proceeded and until she became aware of how his face was suffused with a glory of high purpose not to be gainsaid.

And then Miss Dredger, the indomitable Miss Dredger, turned from the window and, like a somnambulist, crossed the room and descended to the hall where she was met by her paying guest.

Just for a moment something of her independence returned and she folded her arms fiercely, but only for a fraction of time, for they fell like deadweights to her sides as he said in the gentlest voice she had ever heard:

'You are poorly, Miss Dredger, and you will now go to bed. I will bring you your lunch as soon as it is ready. There is no need for you to show me where things are. I understand houses.'

FIVE

For Miss Dredger to find herself in bed at twelve-thirty on a spring morning would have been unthinkable were it not that she could think of nothing else. It was as likely that she should be sitting there, bolt upright with the eiderdown drawn up to her chin, as for her to have suddenly found that she was performing the Dance of the Seven Veils in a Belgian fruit shop.

But to plunge still farther into the nightmare, she was at this very moment having her lunch prepared for her, in her own kitchen, by a man. A man! A stranger whose acquaintance she had made within the last three hours. A man whose avuncular commands and soft admonitions had already undermined the formidable structure of her self-confidence.

The whole affair was monstrous; unthinkable – but she was thinking it. Unbearable – but, in her rigid way, she was bearing it. Un-arguable – perhaps; but she would argue it, if necessary, until her tongue became too hot to hold in her mouth. Oh, she would argue it all right! She would argue it if necessary with a poker in one hand and a meat-knife in the other. She would . . .

There was a knock at her door. A knock as discreet as the knuckle-tap of a connoisseur with his ear at the rim of a rare ceramic. It was a tap to which there could only be one answer. But she was shocked to realize how quickly she replied: 'Come in.'

'Come in', indeed! What had happened to her within the last three hours! Had she forgotten what it was to be a lady? Had she forgotten Tunbridge Wells and the advice of Lady Cork-power?

She began to blush.

Miss Dredger had not blushed for over twenty years; not because she was shameless, for she was manifestly a woman of rectitude, but because her way of life with its code of tough virginity, its insistence upon backbone, its detestation of all that was 'feeble', had created within her such an exclusive condition that nothing in the way of an irregular accident had a dog's chance of germination.

But she began to blush, the beetroot stain extending its boundaries every moment; and when the door opened and Mr Pye came in she bowed her gaunt and handsome head in shame.

And yet, at the very moment that she longed to sink into the island earth, never to reappear, she lifted her face at the sound of his voice.

'I have found my room, and what a charming room it is with its view across the island, and the daffodils on the table and the charming blue bedspread. And I found your kitchen with everything so well arranged that it has been the purest pleasure to prepare this little lunch for you – and I do hope you will enjoy it. I am a little late for I simply *had* to procure some wine, for you are evidently out of it – and, of course, not knowing the island, it took me a little while to find what I wanted – but la! la! I have made my first excursion and I could even now draw a little map of where we are and what lies close about us to the south and east. Is it not a lively, a mercurial feeling to be upon fresh soil? – but here we are, here we are! Perhaps if you lowered your knees, Miss Dredger, the tray could lie at a more convenient angle. There we are! The herbs took some finding, but I unearthed them, behind your little stable – what an odd place for them, my dear – and now I will put the finishing touches to the rather bizarre little course that is to follow . . .'

Mr Pye, who from the very first word of his gay run of babbling small-talk, had been drawing up a bedside table, positioning the tray, adjusting the curtains to deflect the glare of the sun, rearranging a bowl of primroses, now pattered away to the door which he opened and shut in a breath, and was gone suddenly from her, gone utterly, save for the happy modulated notes of his voice as he sang:

> 'Many giants great and tall
> Stalking through the land,
> Straightway to the earth would fall
> If met by Daniel's band. . . .
>
> Dare to be a Dan . . . iel
> Dare to . . .'

and his voice fainted away and was lost in the distance.

Yes, Miss Dredger had lifted her head and her eyes had remained fixed from the moment he had opened his mouth. She had no reason to withdraw her gaze, for no sooner had he opened the door than he had not only begun to talk, but had busied himself so concentratedly on this and that connected with Miss Dredger's comfort, that he had not once turned his eyes to her. Not for a single moment had he given her the least cause for embarrassment. He had come, and he had gone, and there she was with the tray on her legs. When she lifted the cover she found below her the most delicious omelette that ever spread itself across a shallow dish.

She lifted a glass of Sauterne, and poured a little down her throat. The tumbler glittered and shone in such a way that made her look at it twice to make sure that it *was* the one that she had bought many, many years ago, in Tunbridge Wells.

Then, turning to the omelette as though she had an old score to settle, she began very sternly to devour it. Receiving the seductive bloom of the aromatic miracle upon her all too opaque palate, and sensing rather than appreciating the quality of the thing, she heard the reflex voice within her, muttering from sheer habit: 'Really, this is too feeble.'

She broke a fresh crust, spread it with the veritable island butter, as yellow as the daffodils on Mr Pye's window-sill. She had tasted it for the last twenty years, but today it seemed different – bland yet briny, something that, with the splendid crust and the wine and the omelette, suggested to Miss Dredger, however vaguely, the possibility of another kind of world where the simplest of produce can combine into a kind of agrarian glory – where, dancing as it were hand-in-hand beneath her all but ruined palate the north cornfields and the southern vineyards can join in mutual praise, and the egg, that less romantic marvel, can really spread itself.

But it must not be supposed that Miss Dredger was to be seduced and vanquished by a mere lunch, however delectable. Not at all. Forty years of rectitude had not left her as vulnerable as all that. There was something in Miss Dredger that could not suddenly be dislodged by the blandishment of an egg. She was no pearl, but the grit was there.

'No! No! No!' she suddenly cried out, as a fresh wave of mortification swamped her. She had drawn herself bolt upright in bed and she sat, with her arms perfectly straight and rigid, her hands clenched at her sides. Then she stared at the empty plate and the wine-glass and wished she had never touched them. Why had she done what she was told? Why had she taken this compromising step? Was it not obvious that she was all but snared? There were no two ways about it. She was on the edge of ignominious serfdom. How could she simply go on sitting there, waiting like a parrot for her lump of sugar? He would be feeding her next, with a teaspoon – *she*, Connie Dredger who, wherever she had lived had become to be known as someone to be reckoned with.

At school, whether in work or play, she had been truly formidable. Her hockey had been of a ferocity to set her in a class apart; so much so, that she was generally, in spite of her belief in the team spirit, to be found practising by herself. When she had led her team to the green field, the small fry at St Winifred's had cheered themselves sick. With her jaw thrust forward almost to the point of dislocation she had scoured a score of meadows lashing at the ball as though possessed. Now she was here – now there, giving battle everywhere, and her own team-mates had been as much in fear of her lashing scythe as their opponents. But above all they knew she had been right, that one's heart must be in whatever one is doing and that she was a sport. When the twenty-one cripples limped off the field she had thumped them one and all upon the back; 'Rattling good, rattling good!' she had cried – while they grinned wanly and rubbed their shins, and those of them who had remained faithful in memory would have instantly recognized the forceful personality who was now sitting upright on a Channel Island bed. Perhaps they would have wondered at a certain apprehension in her eyes – and perhaps there was something to suggest that the Miss Dredger of these latter days was not a little disillusioned by the *feeble* quality which she had discovered in *homo sapiens*: perhaps, at forty she recognized that she was rather lonely in her championship of the virile virtues. But there was her fighting jaw – and it was no more brittle now than in the old days.

How, after all, would any of her bygone cronies have acted under the strain that she was, at this moment, sustaining? What would they have done?

Would they have stayed in bed and waited feebly for the second course? Perhaps they would – but not she. Oh, no. Not she.

But her integrity was stronger than her forethought for, when Miss Dredger thrust the tray aside and leapt out of bed and paced barbarically across the carpet, she had no formulated notion of what to do. She had obviously wasted time over the omelette, and it was more than likely that Mr Pye would return before she could get dressed again. And this was precisely what occurred.

At the very moment that Miss Dredger stood breathing deeply in the centre of the room she heard again that tactful tap upon the door.

There were two alternatives – or rather there were three, but the third one of staying where she was, in her night-dress, in the middle of the room, was, of course, grotesque beyond thought. Of the other two, Miss Dredger chose, in that hectic moment, the wrong one. It is true that she was closer to the hanging cupboard than the bed – but it is sometimes hard to be rational when the heart is beating like a tom-tom.

The morning had been outlandish – the mental climate so disconnected with anything she had ever experienced before, that Miss Dredger acted too fast for reason to follow.

She was all at once in the hanging cupboard among the dresses, and had closed the doors, and there she stood and realized that she had thrown herself upon his mercy.

Opening her eyes in her agony of spirit, she noted a point of light on the level of her breast-bone and she bent with difficulty, for it was a very narrow cupboard, and put her eye to the keyhole.

And then she heard his voice in the room. 'Here we are again.' His voice rang out like a clear little bell. Miss Dredger could not see him, but by his tone she could tell that, as on the previous occasion, he was doing everything except look at the bed.

'Was it acceptable, Miss Dredger? My little omelette?'

For a moment Miss Dredger imagined he was referring to her, and an unaccountable sensation affected her for the merest fraction of time – as though the wing of a bird had flapped beneath her ribs.

All at once Mr Pye was framed within the keyhole. He was standing quite still and was gazing down at the little brass tray in his hands with its pagoda of fruit.

It seemed some while before he raised his eyes from the tray, although it could not have been for more than a few moments. Then he began to sing very quietly to himself as he placed the tray, not on the crumpled bed, but on the table in the centre of the room. His movements were brisk, his singing clear and unhurried.

> 'The purple headed mountain ...
> The river running by....'

He was now at the bedside and was no longer within Miss Dredger's vision – but she could hear, if she could not see, that he was re-making the bed.

'The sunset and the morning
That brightens up the sky....

All things bright and beautiful...
All creatures...'

He was back again near the table, and now for a moment he allowed his gaze to move around the room, not inquisitively, but in a mood of affectionate interest. When his eyes fell upon the hanging cupboard they lingered there, and Miss Dredger could not help feeling that just as he was plainly visible to her, so she, in her dark cupboard, must be visible to him, and she jerked her eye from the keyhole, and in doing so her head struck upon a hanger, which, swinging wildly, dislodged from some shelf in the darkness a cascade of moth-balls – and as though this were not enough the cupboard door, responding to a convulsive movement of Miss Dredger's knee and shoulder, swung open – and there was her bedroom, shimmering in the morning sunlight, and empty as a desert. Her bedroom door was closed. Her second course sat neatly on its tray. Her bed was made, its counterpane folded back and, to reinforce the unexpected privacy in which she found herself, she could hear a gay and sprightly voice singing in the room below:

'Hobgoblin nor foul fiend
Shall daunt his spirit,
He knows he, at the end
Shall Life inherit;

Foul fancies fly away –
He'll fear not what men say,
He'll labour night and day
To be a Pilgrim.'

SIX

ON that very same day, towards dusk, a cold tremor ran across the island, and the water in the bays began to reflect a strange and unhealthy colour. Within the space of a few minutes the sky had changed its nature. All day there had been no cloud. But now, the Sarkese turning their faces to the sky could see that they were in for a dirty night.

Innumerable small clouds, each one more filthy than its neighbour, began to pour themselves over the northern horizon, the last of the sunbeams slanting between them and lighting up the sea in livid patches. Behind this scurrying vanguard, the great storm clouds gathered. Grey rulers of rain were already falling like smoke over Alderney.

Miss George in her bungalow to the north of the island where the land begins to fall away in a long narrowing peninsula, waddled to the window of her little stale sitting-room and faced the sky through the glass, curling her lip disdainfully at the particularly evil-looking weather. Safe behind the window-panes she munched ignorantly at a piece of buttered toast. Yet, in spite of her contempt for the forces of nature, the scene was not entirely without interest to Miss George, for her brother-in-law, now in his grave, had once painted a picture of a storm at sea. She had told him quite frankly that she had never seen a storm at sea, or anywhere else, look anything like his painting, and he had been angry. Ever since then Miss George was reminded of this contretemps whenever there was a storm, and, because her brother-in-law was in his grave, felt it her duty to give the deceased his due and to glance at the sea and sky to decide whether perhaps that picture had, after all, some connection with the elements. She stared fixedly, congratulating herself, as she always did, on the way she gave him every chance, but *no*. No. What faced her was nothing like that extraordinary picture. He was wrong again. She gave a wheeze of relief – a peculiar little sound to come from so vast a bulk – and it was with a glow of satisfaction that she returned to the fireside where a plate of buttered toast awaited her.

Thorpe, the painter, in his small Sark cottage with its witch's-seat half-way up the chimney, was also staring through the window. He had been caught in the first downpour as he made his way home from the 'Seaweed', where he had been sitting in a corner sipping his eternal rum-and-peppermint.

And while sitting there, with his eyes out of focus, he had brooded upon a curious thing he had discovered about himself. It had come to him as rather a shock to realize that he was essentially a jealous type. He had always thought that he moved in an atmosphere altogether too rarefied for that sort of thing. But on the previous evening, while turning over the pages of an old magazine, before screwing it up to light his fire with, he had suddenly experienced an unpleasant twinge of naked anger at the sight of that glossy group. There they sat at their night-club, the smirking playboys, each with his addle-headed flame, utterly happy: idiotically happy: their faces flattened out by the flash of the camera. It was their happiness that had angered Thorpe.

But he was intelligent enough to know that his anger was really jealousy. He could see that the glossy group had no need for art or the eternal verities. And suddenly he felt that he had no need for them either. He would like to sit in night-clubs with a group of friends, and share with them their horror of anything serious.

He looked down at his corduroy trousers: he looked at his thumb-nail. Neither were in very good condition.

And now, standing at his window, and staring out at a giant bulge of gun-grey cloud, he cursed its ominous grandeur that would once have so excited him. He cursed it because he knew he could do without it. This was a terrible acknowledgment. Was he a turncoat? Was he a failure? Was he a fake? He drew the blinds sharply across the splendid sky, and peeling off his wet rain-drenched jacket, flung it on the floor.

'...and he said to her,' said young Pépé, holding forth to a shivering conclave of young bloods who had been caught in the rain and were sheltering in Old Le Lourchat's cow-shed, '...he said, "Out of it, you bloody old bundle," he said ... "walk to your own bloody house yourself, on your own flat feet," he said.'

'No!' cried a large boy with a birthmark on his nose the shape of Australia. 'Did he say that? Cor! What did Miss George do?'

'What did she *do*?' shouted young Pépé, working himself up, and glorying in his status of sole witness. 'She said, "You can cut my legs off first," she said, "you silly fat 'something'," she said!'

'No!' shouted the boy with the birthmark. 'What happened then?'

'What happened *then*?' echoed young Pépé, scratching madly at his ribs – 'I'll tell you. He jumped into the carriage, right in the middle of the bloody Colinette, and he whipped her out of the carriage, with my dad's horsewhip, and then I drove him off to old Dredger's.'

'Cor,' said another voice, as though there were a rook in the cow-shed.

'"Cor" it is,' yelled young Pépé, 'and he shouted out to her from the avenue, "I'll be bloody well *seeing* you," he shouted, "and I'll beat the fat hide off you, you old bloater," he shouted, and then he grinned all over his face, he did, while Miss George stood howling in the road with her purple hat over one eye and her bum on fire.'

All about the island the darkening water heaved and broke upon the rocks. The tide rose momently. Along the tortuous passages of the caves the hollow echoes rumbled and the billows hissed and slapped the slimy walls.

High above the caves and the shrivelling beaches, on the island's rain-drenched back, the trees that slanted all one way from the prevailing winds creaked in the darkness.

It was no night for anyone to be walking abroad, let alone a stranger. It was a night to test one's belief in the reality of the bygone day, so far away it seemed, like some bland dream, or the golden weather of another world.

To Mr Pye the storm was no more nor less than a direct challenge, for in his view there was nothing that did not carry its own peculiar message. When he heard the first tapping of the rain on the glass of his bedroom window, he knew that he was being called.

No midwife is more at the mercy of being shaken from her bed than the man who follows the flights of his own soul : the man of private faith : the perfectionist : the sleuth of glory.

Mr Pye, as a matter of fact, had not retired to bed. He was unpacking his clothes and stowing them neatly away. It was no haphazard selection of garments that now hung on the hangers or were impeccably folded and laid one upon another in the chest of drawers. He had chosen his wardrobe with care and foresight, over the last year, while the preparations for his descent upon Sark proceeded, and it was, strangely enough, at the very moment that he was lifting his black oilskin coat and leggings from a suitcase that the first gust of rain spluttered against the window.

He stood up at once, the black oilskin in his arms. It was as though he was carrying a child, so carefully did he dandle it for a moment before setting it gently on the bed.

He stood perfectly still and upright. His eyes were shut. His lips were pressed in a contemplative love-knot. He drew himself up on tiptoe, his hands grasping the lapels of his jacket, and then, with his spherical head thrown back and his sharp nose pointing at the ceiling, he gave a little whistle; both a lively and a speculative sound.

Miss Dredger on the other side of the house was fast asleep. Deep in her subconscious she heard Mr Pye's whistle. All that happened was that her dream veered off down an unexpected alley so that she was no longer whacking unbreakable gull's eggs across the harbour, with a hockey stick, but was suddenly floating over Tunbridge Wells hand-in-hand with Miss George.

Mr Pye had spent the early evening in a heart-to-heart with his patient. He had restored to her a little of the self-confidence she had lost. By painful degrees he had re-orientated her outlook. Insisting on preparing her supper, he had laced her chicken soup with a strong sedative. It was plain that the good woman needed a full night's sleep. By tomorrow night she would surely be like clay on the wheel of his love.

As a potter with his medium, so he would throw her and fire her. The Kingdom of Love had need of her as it had need of him.

As Mr Pye whistled, a lashing and rattling at the window-panes caused him to open his eyes and he could see the water smothering the face of the glass.

In the short time that his eyes had been shut he had understood. It was for him to draw the island to his naked breast. To know her in all the vagaries of her flighty nature. To taste the sharp and the sweet of her; the warmth and the chill of her; to watch her melt like butter or congeal like frost. It was a challenge.

Outside the window a drama of salt water, rain water, wind, and darkness was being played out. It was for him to dress in his oilskins, tie his sou'wester under his chin, borrow Miss Dredger's storm lantern, and pace forth into the heart of it all.

And this is what he did, having carefully adjusted the wick of the lamp. How could he now begin to give true joy to the islands and bind them into a cosmos of love unless he knew the background of their lives? Sark was not only the three hundred odd inhabitants. It was the atmosphere they breathed and all that they shared in common. Who knew, it might be that only through their elemental heritage he could find the way to their hearts.

When Mr Pye had reached the gate at the end of the drive that was now swimming with the downpour, every vestige of his elegant rake-work washed away for ever, he directed his lantern on the bolt and drew it with some difficulty from its socket. Directly he had done this a rotten bough snapped off high above him, as though his withdrawal of the bolt had been a signal, and fell with a crash of tangled branches immediately in front of him, one of its outer branches flicking his ear with cruel accuracy.

Had he taken his first few steps forward it is doubtful if the tale of Mr Pye could ever have been told, for he would almost certainly have been killed by the heavy boughs.

The pain of his whipped ear seemed to have a strange effect upon him. It seemed that through the blow his whole body was whipped into a state of exultation. His radiant smile all but burned through the darkness.

'What splendid pain!' he whispered. 'What splendid pain! There is more truth in this than half the creeds.'

Pondering on the idea of how faith must be made plastic, he goose-trod over the spread-eagled branches that gleamed like a tangle of golden serpents in the light of his hurricane lamp. When he was free of the heavy snare that had so nearly struck him to the ground he turned his face to the wind and rain and forged an oilskin path into the night.

What did Mr Pye expect to get out of this voluntary soaking? It would be hard to put into words and Mr Pye would have felt the question unwarranted and crude. He would have told one, very gently, that he had no wish to *get* anything out of it. It was his purpose to *give*, not to get. He must give himself to the storm so that he might learn and thus be able to give what he had learned to others.

Every two or three hundred yards Mr Pye would halt and gather, by the light of his lamp, a few stones from the broken lanes, and these he would place together in a little group so that he could be sure of finding his way home. It was characteristic of the man that in forming these minute cairns he received pleasure in the very grouping of the stones, leaving not one of them unturned before he placed it artistically alongside its neighbours, for there is surely not a stone without at least *one* interesting face?

His love for perfection, his meticulous artistry, was in seeming contrast to the breadth of his vision and the intensity of his drive.

And so these little clusters of stones were left behind him, each one having been finally adjusted in the glow of his lamp, while the golden rain danced close about them, and spurted fiercely on their sides and crowns.

Turning to left and right as his fancy dictated, Mr Pye exulted. He had for the last mile been moving along a road comparatively straight; a road that was wide open to the sky. He guessed himself to be travelling along the backbone of the island for he sensed rather than saw that the land fell away on either side. And then quite suddenly the road dipped sharply, and at that same moment his face and body were freed from the force of the cross-wind. On either side of him, and flanking the decline, were walls of rock. He felt their harsh streaming surfaces with his little gloved hands. He approved of them and continued to the end of the decline, where the storm struck at him once more, and a roaring of waves was added to the sound of the wind.

And then suddenly the moon broke free and fled across the night, only to be lost immediately in the black surges of the sky. But in that moment of silver radiance Mr Pye had seen the Coupée.

Mr Pye had, of course, known as part of his general education that Sark was divided into two parts. There was Big Sark and there was Little Sark, and where the isthmus joined these Sarks together the island was waisted like a wasp. This was something that a child could have seen from a glance at a map. Mr Pye also knew that this bridge of rock went by the name of La Coupée – but what he did not know was that the moon would break out of the sky on this, his first night upon the island, and uncover such a scene as this.

Within a few feet of where he stood, and upon his right hand, a moonlit wall of rock fell in precipitous rhythm to a wilderness of dazzling foam. Out in the bay the waters heaved with an unearthly sheen. Equally close to him, upon his left, the cliff plunged down into the moonless shadows where the foam roared and tumbled in the darkness. Ahead of him the high, dangerously narrow track of La Coupée, curled through the night llke a white ribbon. It seemed to be suspended in the air. The iron railings on its either side shone balefully. And then the wild moon fused and Mr Pye was left in darkness.

He did not move for quite a little while and then he took two paces to the right-hand railing. His oilskins flapped about him, and when he lifted his head the rain lashed his face; but he did not flinch.

'This is where the wisdom begins,' he said, and his words were whipped away on the wind. 'This is what the soul has need of. Soak it in, my friend. Soak it in.'

SEVEN

It did not take Mr Pye very long to acquaint himself with the main features of the island. Within the first month he had made a reputation for himself as the most active and enterprising visitor the Sarkese had ever known. It often happens, of course, that the newcomer to a place, whether an island or a city, will very soon outstrip the native in local knowledge. But it was more than this with Harold Pye. His thirst for learning was not confined to his daily expeditions to the many bays of Sark's indented coastline; to the famous coloured caverns of the Gouliot, the 'Dog' and the 'Pigeon': to the 'Convanche Chasm' below the Coupée on the Jersey side, and the Souffleur Cave in Little Sark, which, when the seas run high and the wind is from the north, spouts back the foam from its deep throat like an exhaling whale: it was not merely that he became intensely aware of the physical island – it was also that he began to sense the inherent nature of the place.

It was really this 'background' that he needed most, for Mr Pye was a wise as well as a virtuous man. He knew that his high mission might very well miscarry, if he failed to put first things first. And the *first* thing was the island itself, the strange, wasp-waisted ship of stone. He must understand her – the structure of her jaws and broken flanks, the rhythm of her alternating moods.

Until he had grasped the eternal permanence of the great ship he trod, it would surely be not only premature but dangerous to accost the crew aboard her with his love. He must fire them by degrees. He must be patient.

His first duty was to explore their home. His second to explore their hearts. His third to bring them joy. It did not occur to Mr Pye that he was taking upon himself a crusade of a kind well calculated to try the strength and patience of an archangel or a god with a soul as clear as the highest quality glass and the physical strength of the abominable snowman.

It did not occur to him: he was without a qualm in the world. His habit of concentration had schooled him so to fix his eye upon the target of his ambition, that he was hardly aware of the distances that lay between himself and the bright core of his dreams. As each problem arose he addressed himself to it with delight as though it were the last.

For Mr Pye all things were penultimate. He was always on the threshold, dealing with that minor technicality that had, of necessity, to be cleared up before the trumpets rang, and the heavens opened and the moon at last showed him her other side.

By the time Harold Pye had identified himself with every spur and shoulder, every perilous descent, every winding way among the idiosyncrasies of Sark's fantastic coastline from the Bec du Nez in the north to the Eperquerie with its wild cave in the extreme south – by the time he had gripped the island in the sharp, neat, shining vice of his brain – he was all but a legend.

When abroad and at large on the island he kept his silence – a silence of fantastic pregnancy more awesome than thunder. And particularly so as he was no slinker through the dusk, but a sharp, quick, daylight figure, an enigma of noon – now here, now there, ubiquitous and sprightly, for all the trim volume of his paunch – his brilliant and abstracted smile, un-nerving the great fishermen, and filling the island with outlandish rumour.

He was preparing his way: and at the same time he was preparing her – his island – for a revolution of the heart, for already he felt that she was his. A strange, proprietary instinct told him that he must offer back to the islanders, that which was *theirs*, but not before they were ready to receive it, for they must learn that it was to their ultimate good that he should hold a spiritual mandate over their wasp-waisted rock. That he had been treading its bony back for no longer than six weeks was of no significance. What mattered was that he had forced his way to the very core of what made the island into Sark, and Sark into the island. He had wormed his way into her dank, primordial caves; had stared his fill at her emblazoned flanks; had dived, a pear-drop in his mouth, into her cold April tide; had sat for an hour upon a fallen tree and drunk his fill of the sweet of Dixcart Valley where the primroses, the bluebells and the celandine, smothered the wooded slopes; and exposed himself like a sensitized plate to her every whim.

Now here, now there, silent as the sun as it skips in and out of the clouds, Mr Pye, his antennae flickering, was now ready to turn from the physical island and level the searchlight of his love upon the human heart – that ultimate quarry.

EIGHT

THE island sparkled from a night of rain. Every sound was distinct in the sweet April air. A dog-fight at the Colinette and the sound of a boy shouting near the prison could be heard by Miss George as she opened her front door and threw out some breadcrumbs; by Thorpe the painter as he began to pump up the rain-water from the underground cistern to his little tank in the rafters, and by Mr Pye over a mile away who was taking a lawn-mower to pieces as he squatted like a Chinese beneath the hairy palm tree, his cuffs rolled back neatly at the wrist.

So that when that clear, metallic voice broke free from the window of Miss Dredger's room, and was carried by a light breeze across the island, it was quite as much an event as for a plate full of pennies to be dropped in an echoing cathedral.

Clear and strong it came, muffled for a moment as Miss Dredger forced her vigorous head through the neck of her jumper, and then, free again, as though uncorked.

'Pull for the shore, sailor!
Pull for the shore!
Heed not the roll ... ing waves
But bend ... to ... the ... oar!
Safe in the lifeboat, sailor ...
Tumpty-tumpty-taw,
Tiddly-widly-pidly, sailor!
Pull ... for ... the ... shore!'

Miss Dredger's voice was more remarkable for its resonance than for its quality. She always had been fond of a jolly good tune, but until a month ago she would no more have thought of being heard singing in public (for in Sark everything is public) than of standing on her head on the harbour wall. For her nature had always been more sensitive than her voice.

But now everything was different, and Mr Pye stopped for a moment in his work upon the mower and turned a delighted face to the window.

'Pull on your clothes, sailor!' he sang out happily and to his joy, the resonant voice, taking up the tune, sang back:

'Pull on your clothes!
Let's have some breakfast, sailor!'

And then Miss Dredger again – quick as an adder:

'Porridge and loaves.'

Oh, this was too splendid. She had smacked the shuttle back. 'God bless you,' cried Mr Pye. 'And good morning to you, sailor!' Miss Dredger leaned out through the window and over the drive as precariously as a gargoyle on Nôtre Dame. There they stood staring at one another, drinking one another up until Miss Dredger, in a smaller, lighter voice that was this time all but in tune, continued the little verse as the blood mounted in her cheeks –

'Safe in the kitchen sailor!
There'll be toast galore!'

And then Mr Pye, as he stood on tiptoes, his sharp nose tingling with sentience:

'Not to speak of coffee, sailor!
Pull . . . for . . . the . . . shore!'

Oh, what a fine duet was made of that last line. They forgot they were singing to one another. For a moment they sang to the blue April sky above them, and the passing wisps of cloud and to whoever happened to be within a mile of Clôs de Joi, while the seagulls wheeled and the sunbeams blazed through their wings.

Suddenly, she was gone; and Mr Pye found himself gazing at her window-latch. Something had been added to their relationship. Whatever the quality of their voices by professional standards, a new note had been struck and it had rung true.

But it must not be imagined that Miss Dredger had been easy to tempt into the sexless orbit of Mr Pye's love. Patiently and day by day, his tact and sympathy had imperceptibly freed her from all sense of shame and had given her an inner confidence which she had almost forgotten. Memories of her last term at St Winifred's came flooding back.

The boundless loyalty which, as head girl, she had once poured into the pseudo-Gothic maw of her old granite school was now directed at the head of Mr Pye. Here was a man of mercurial energy – a practical-man – a wise-man – a good-man, and a sports-man. She only wished that he had seen her at centre forward – and she would sometimes ponder upon how fame can fade – and how the past can shed no glory in an island that had never heard of St Winifred's.

At first she dreaded to meet him at breakfast, for when, in the morning before she rose from her bed, she realized each morning with a start, how revolutionary had been the change in her life and habits since the arrival of Mr Pye, her heart would fail her and she would stiffen with resentment. But directly she was with him again her confidence returned, for life was all a-bubble and a-boil when he was near and she had no time for resentment or shame.

And so, gradually, she had come under his spell, and at last in the cannon-mouth, as it were, of platonic love, she surrendered with her hands thrust deep in her tweed pockets and a cigarette in her mouth and the white smoke coiling from her nostrils.

What a perfect day it was! Even the ghastly old desiccated palm tree seemed less on the verge of its vegetable death. The wisteria was budding bravely across the front of the house, and the twisted, storm-sloping trees at the rear of the long garden were a haze of leaf.

Through the gaps between distant houses and foliage, the surrounding sea was the softest and most melting of blues. Had Miss Dredger still been standing at her window she might have seen between the boughs of a sycamore something no larger than an ant upon the far cerulean water. It was the Jersey boat. Within an hour she would be in Sark harbour and disgorging the day trippers with their black sun-glasses, their mouth-organs, and their shorts rolled up to their crutches.

As Miss Dredger descended the stairs to prepare breakfast she felt a flutter of joy in her forthright heart, a sensation quite out of character. 'Oh, don't be feeble,' she said to herself, for she had little use for any form of flighty excitation – but she could not reason away the peculiar response, nor stop herself from trying to jump the last four steps of the stairs with a single bound.

Even as she jumped she was re-living those precious moments –

'Safe in the kitchen sailor!
There'll be toast galore....'

– and then the skid of her left heel, the quick twist of her ankle, and the angular flight through the air.

When she picked herself up from the floor of the hall, somewhat shaken and bruised but with no serious injury, she lit a cigarette and made her mouth into a rectangle as she inhaled. It was some consolation that Mr Pye had not seen her in mid-air – or spread-eagled in the hall. The sun was still shining, after all, and the birds were still singing, and there was a gentleman in the garden mending her mowing-machine, and altogether, apart from a bruised hip and a pain in her foot, nothing had changed.

So she strode to the kitchen leaving streamers of smoke behind her in the hall.

Mr Pye, entering the house for a moment to fetch a small piece of wire from a drawer, ducked his round head beneath the hanging wreaths, and wrinkled his sharp nose in a way that suggested that boys will be boys, or in this case, that Dredgers will be Dredgers.

From the moment that he first opened his eyes to this fair morning of liquid green and gold, he knew that the vital stage in his venture was about to begin. Up till now, save of course for his conversations with Miss Dredger and the few words he had spoken to Miss George and young Pépé on the day of his arrival, Mr Pye had hardly spoken to a living soul, although by now, as a result of his minute and brilliant description of all the characters he had passed in his wanderings, he knew by heart the names and occupations of pretty well every islander and resident, for Miss Dredger had acquired a great store of island knowledge during the last fifteen years, and she had an excellent memory.

And so it was that Mr Pye was at a great advantage, knowing as he did a hundred times more about those he passed on the stony lanes, than they knew about him.

There had been many attempts by various residents and islanders to elicit from Miss Dredger some information about her spruce and enigmatic guest, but Miss Dredger had a way of setting her face as though in plaster of Paris, and propelling the smoke from her lungs in such profusion, as to all but blind the vision of the questioner, who, by the time he, or she, could see clearly again, was left with nothing more concrete than a rear-view of Miss Dredger, receding with angular purpose through the middle distance.

But now it was time for this self-imposed silence of Mr Pye's to be broken, and Mr Pye rose from the mowing-machine which was now in better order than on the day when Miss Dredger bought it – and pattered smartly to his room, where he washed his small pink hand and filed his nails before turning down the cuffs of his jacket and descending to the kitchen.

There are certain days which seem to cry out to be filled – mornings that plead for action – the atmosphere vibrant with expectancy and high, heroic challenge, and this was such a morning.

As Mr Pye entered the kitchen, Miss Dredger was placing some toast on the table. He stood in the doorway watching her with his little hands clasped beneath his chin.

'Hullo there, sailor!' he cried.

Miss Dredger lifted her head. 'Sailor?' she queried – 'ah, but that is rather fun, Mr Pye.' Then she frowned a moment as she added, 'But we are really an army family, you know.'

'True, true, my dear ... but "Pull for the shore, soldier", would be rather odd, wouldn't it? After all, we had something of a sing-song, didn't we – you in the crow's nest: I on the deck!'

Miss Dredger folded her arms. 'It was a good show,' she said.

Mr Pye sat down at the scrubbed table – (he had turned it from anyone's kitchen table to a thing of beauty, its surface as smooth and white as ivory).

'But you were so quick,' he said. ' "Porridge and loaves" was masterly: although ...' he added, with a mischievous twinkle in his eyes, 'clothes and loaves don't altogether rhyme – now *do* they? Let us face it.'

'You face it for me, Mr Pye.'

'Now *that's* good *too*,' said the alert gentleman. 'You are unfolding, sailor!'

'*Unfurling*, Mr Pye.'

'Oh good, good, good, good, good! Oh *very* good.' Mr Pye had half risen from his chair, his face beaming.

'Oh, I don't know,' said Miss Dredger, whose heart was bouncing with the thought that perhaps she was a wit: 'It was rather feeble, really, but ...'

'No "*buts*". No "buts",' said Mr Pye. 'Now what's for breakfast?'

Beyond the kitchen windows the shadow of the house stretched to the north like a square of black water. The shadow of the gable and of a chimney broke the regularity of outline and the shadow of a restless seagull that appeared to be marking time on the chimney pot, gave agitation to the simple scene.

NINE

No sunbeams found their way into the kitchen but it was cheerful. Mr Pye had decided on lemon yellow walls and dove grey woodwork. As the two of them munched away happily, and as the iced tomato-juice and the cereals and the poached eggs and the curling toast as crisp as autumn leaves were devoured in turn, and as the exclusive China tea, dispatched regularly to Mr Pye from Swanage, was sipped with relish – Mr Pye, humming from time to time, appeared to be without a care in the world.

'The time has come for more than small decisions, my dear sailor,' said Mr Pye.

Miss Dredger glanced over her shoulder involuntarily, as though half-expecting to see a Jack Tar in the room, but then remembered her new nickname.

'Meaning?' she countered, in that quick, no-nonsense voice of hers. She was no chicken and her mannerisms of voice and gesture had congealed and were with her for life. That Mr Pye was ethically the senior partner was tacitly agreed – but there was nothing in Miss Dredger's manner that suggested this.

'You are aware, my dear, that I have been making a study of the island?'

'Aware! – who *isn't*,' said Miss Dredger, lighting a cigarette.

'The ancient feuds and the island squabbles are something that I will not allow to continue. I have, as you know, dwelt exclusively, during these first six weeks of mine, upon the rocks and the trees, yet all this was merely the preface – the physical preface – to my work – and you realize, my dear, that the time has come for me, with your help to turn this island into a living entity, a cosmos of healthy and far-reaching love.'

He turned to her, his nose as sharp as a beak, his eyebrows slightly raised, his face naked with integrity.

What could Miss Dredger say to this luminous creature? How could she answer him?

She wiped her mouth with her napkin.

'Mr Pye,' she said at last, 'much of what you say is lost on me, but you are a great scout.'

'You are very kind, sailor. A little more tea, please. Now, where were we? Ah, yes. Are you listening, my dear?'

'Very nearly, chief. I was admiring your cuff-links. You are always surprising me with something new. Sorry and all that.'

'I am glad you like them, sailor, but you must concentrate. Without concentration one is nowhere – one is afloat, but not attractively. One thing at a time, my dear! One thing at a time.' He beamed at her.

'Sorry, chief.' She glanced up to see how he was responding to this new appellation. Did he mind? He did not. 'Fire ahead,' she added, and took a long draw at her cigarette.

'I will indeed fire ahead, my dear – for I have a good deal to say. Our real work now lies before us. There will be many problems to solve, but I have just been having a nice long chat with God. It was most satisfactory.'

'With *who*?' said Miss Dredger, her cup had come to a stop half-way to her mouth.

'With God. You have heard of Him, I imagine, sailor? Come, come, come. Anyone would think I had said something exceptional.'

Miss Dredger had turned rather white.

'I was particularly pleased that He saw eye to eye with me in regard to the work that I intend to initiate today,' Mr Pye continued, transferring his fruit-drop from cheek to cheek.

'*Today*,' whispered Miss Dredger huskily. 'What's going to happen today?'

Mr Pye bent upon her a look of speculative purpose. Then he smiled gently. 'Be patient, sailor. Let me take my own time.'

He paused a moment to brush a crumb from his cuff.

'It is like this, my dear. The time has arrived for the most difficult, yet at the same time, the most enthralling stage of my adventure. From now onwards my target is no less than the very conscience of this island. I will not rest until it is inflamed with a new spirit. We are agreed upon that.'

'We?' queried Miss Dredger. 'But you have never mentioned all this to me before.'

'When I say "we", sailor, I am referring to God and to myself. He and I are on the best of terms. We understand one another. We have direct access to one another. Each one of us with, as it were, his walkie-talkie. I hear His voice in the tempest, yes, but I hear it also here at breakfast. He is, in fact, within this piece of toast. He was alive in the porridge. He is even now in your cigarette.'

Miss Dredger, glanced at her cigarette with a certain apprehension. If God was there or anywhere else in the room He was certainly unobtrusive. She directed a long and speculative stare at Mr Pye.

'You never told me you were religious, Mr Pye. I knew you were a good man, and a real sport, but I didn't know you were religious. I must say, it shocks me.'

'But, my dear sailor, surely I don't have to make statements about myself and my belief. Surely the way I behave is the lodestar of my faith. Perhaps you mean that I have never told you of our conversations.'

'What, you and ... and ...'

'Yes, yes, my dear; why are you frightened of that little word of three letters – G-O-D – after all, He is the very air we breathe.'

'I don't like it, chief. I prefer to be on my own. I prefer it if the toast is just toast, and my cigarette just a cigarette. Really, it's *too* spooky. As for you, I could not bear it if you were something else all the time.'

'Dear child,' said Mr Pye, leaning far over the table so that his chin almost touched the scrubbed ivory of the boards, while his eyes remained upon the face of his forward pupil. 'Dear . . . child . . . had you not these natural reservations, I would love you the less. To deny the universal and ubiquitous silence of my Friend, the Great Pal (for that is what I call Him, though He split Himself into a million fragments), is natural in the beginner, who asks for noise – something he can hear and touch and see and smell. I have never before spoken to you of the Pal, but surely I have *implied* Him. I had rather hoped that through me, you might have sensed the Force behind me. As with those oriental artists whose aim it is when peering at a tree, to draw that Tree that is behind the tree, so I had rather hoped to be the man behind whom stands the Man. But *what* a Man. Consider Him, sailor.'

Miss Dredger shifted herself in her chair and made a rectangle of her mouth, out of which a great deal of smoke poured forth. She stared at it fixedly.

'What an inspiration He is,' continued Mr Pye, 'this omnipresence, this adaptability, that we call God. It is through Him that we can best fulfil ourselves. I talk to Him in one form or another practically all day. Now He is the brook that sparkles in the Dixcart Valley. Next He is the Dixcart Valley in which the brook sparkles. Now He is the sea whereon the sailors toss and next He is the ship that's *being* tossed. Whoever one talks to is God, or the Great Pal, and although He is a million things at once, sailor, yet his language is articulate and intelligible, and I must tell you, my dear, that never once have we found ourselves chattering at cross-purposes. Oh yes, and we have our jokes, too, my Pal and I.'

'Jokes,' whispered Miss Dredger. 'With God. Oh no.'

'And why not, sailor? Is religion something mournful? Something dire?'

'I have never thought of it as something particularly funny,' replied Miss Dredger. 'Oh dear. . . . Oh, dash it all!'

Mr Pye leaned forward and tapped her in a light, friendly way on the wrist.

'But all this is of no avail, this transcendental splendour of belief – unless it is transmuted into action. Virtue is no armchair speculation. To know a thing, even to believe a thing, is not enough. It is merely the foundation. What is needed is the courage to take action. Virtue must be militant. Now *you* are naturally militant. And you have virtue. But your virtue up to now is a thwarted, inoperative thing. It is dried up for lack of air and the waters of that broad clear river that flows through to God. Your trickle is running away downhill, my dear, and between the wrong rocks. Ah, but you are such a natural evangelist! Such a grand creature. Will you join me? Will you double back until your little stream meets my river and join me in my skiff – and together, paddling happily to Zion, find with me, one glorious day, that we are particles, motes as it were, dancing in a haze of sunbeams. We also can be a part of the eternal love, but only if we work like blazes, my dear – and play like blazes too, for work is play and play is work, and a rare and full life can be yours – a life devoted to Salvation. A salvation of joy, and air, and brightness – a thing of the dawn.'

Mr Pye had risen to his feet as he spoke the last few words. His face was lit by a kind of light that seemed incongruous in Miss Dredger's kitchen.

Suddenly and all in a flash, Miss Dredger knew that something she had yearned for, all her life, was being offered her. Mr Pye had unlatched a window and flung it open, and there lay stretched before her a virgin country with forests and hills, to be cleared, to be climbed. And then, seeing the fantastic proportion, the outlandish scale of the vista, her heart failed her for a moment, but only for a moment, for as she stared, her imagination all but running amok, for it had not had an outing for thirty years or more, she saw the territory begin to shrink and dwindle – the great spaces contract, the forests melt into a tree or two that leant one way from the prevailing winds, and she saw the sea sparkling in the distance, and approach from every side, until below her there was something not much more than a great tree-scattered, cottage-scattered rock with a wasp-like waist.

And seeing how small it was and how seemingly vulnerable as it lay there on the vast blue and heaving carpet of the sea, she knew for the first time exactly what Mr Pye had meant when he had told her that Sark was just the right size.

And now she joined him in spirit, a missionary zeal filling her long tough frame, so that she rose from the table also and they faced one another.

'I don't know about your Great Pal who is all over the place, chief,' she said. 'I don't know about Him sitting in my cigarette, but I do know that goodness is goodness and evil is evil, and that if you want a fighting disciple, you could do worse than yours truly.'

'I never dreamed that you would fail me. As time goes on you will learn more about Our Pal. You will realize that to be true to Him takes courage as well as enthusiasm; and selflessness as well as sincerity. Are you prepared to give as well as to receive? Think of what you *will* receive, sailor! The ineffable joy of fighting sloth and evil, of having a belief: of working with and for the Pal.'

'I wish we could do without the Pal,' said Miss Dredger.

'Without God, my dear?' Mr Pye raised his eyebrows. Perhaps he was a fraction longer than usual before he replied. 'But He is of us and in us, and there is no escaping Him, my dear, even if we want to. Really, sailor, you *are* a one.'

They sat down again at the breakfast table.

'It was such good, clean fun, singing to each other this morning,' said Miss Dredger at last. 'I felt I could do anything, absolutely anything – but somehow, now that I know you are always talking to your Pal, I don't feel so healthy.'

'It will return, sailor. Have no fear. Your health will return. I do not expect you to believe, all at once, in something that has taken me many years to perfect.'

'I suppose not,' said Miss Dredger. 'But what do we do next?'

'I will tell you,' said Mr Pye. 'I will tell you and it will startle you. We will begin by cutting out of ourselves whatever growths there are – the foul growths of pride, jealousy, and hatred. We will have no enemies. What I am going to ask you to do will startle you, sailor. But I know your strength of heart; you have grit, my dear, so use it now. You will telephone Miss George.'

'Miss George! Why?'

'Because she hates you.'

'Because she hates me?'

'Because she hates you.'

'What a rotten reason – really!'

'Do you think so? Do you think that to draw the festering thorns from the flesh of her soul is a rotten reason? Let us wash her white, and find that little something in her heart that is not wholly squalid.'

'My God,' said Miss Dredger, and then after a long pause – 'My God,' she added.

'How would you feel, sailor, if while converting others to our Faith of Love and Laughter, you remembered Miss George? Scoop yourself clean, sailor. Drain away your bad blood. Go into the fight, impeccable, immaculate – your one-time enemies all but dazzled in the blaze of your charity. You will phone her, sailor, and invite her to a midnight picnic.'

'A picnic?'

'A picnic. This is your testing time.'

'Yes, that's all very well, but . . .'

' "But" is a word that revolts me, sailor. Come with me.'

He opened the door for her, and followed the smoke-trail to the sitting-room with its big bay window that gave upon the lawn and the dreadful palm.

'Pick up the receiver,' said Mr Pye, 'and twirl the handle.'

'I must have a drink first,' said Miss Dredger in a voice that seemed to come from the other side of the north wall. 'Holy smoke, but this is ghastly.'

She poured herself a gin and tonic. For a fleeting moment the last thin fibrous thread from the one-time solid root of her independence twitched in her, but died away for lack of support.

'Can't you phone her, chief?'

'I am not her enemy. It is not I who deny her the short cut across this garden, which would save her legs so many miles a week. To me she is a future crusader like everyone else on the island.'

'Did you say a picnic?'

'A picnic.'

'At this time of year?'

'Look out of the window – was there ever a lovelier day?'

'Where is it to be?'

'Derrible Bay.'

'Derrible Bay – good heavens, she couldn't get down there.'

'She must try. We will help her.'

'And what about getting back again?'

'She must try. We will help her.'

'The tide comes right up to the cliff-face, chief.'

'She must try.'

'Try what?'

'Try her number, dear! We are wasting time.'

Miss Dredger clutched at the handle and revolved it furiously like a wooden rattle.

At last there was a voice, faint but horribly distinct. 'Hullo,' it said.

Miss Dredger squared her shoulders. The room was vast with silence. 'Is that Miss George?'

'Naturally,' said the voice from the other side of the island. 'Who else could it be?'

'Quite,' said Miss Dredger. She could think of nothing better to say at the moment, but she barked it out like an order – so that meaningless as her reply had been, it was nevertheless militant.

'What do you mean by "quite"?' said the voice. 'Who are you, anyway?'

'The name is Dredger.'

There was a long and terrible pause – and then far away, but sharp and clear as a meat-axe – 'Well?'

'Yes, thank you,' said Miss Dredger, deliberately misinterpreting the question. 'Very well indeed. And you?'

By now Miss Dredger was beginning to climb from the invidious role which Mr Pye had invented for her, to something rather less humiliating. She had gained an infinitesimal amount of ground. She had trumped Miss George's 'Well?'. She bared her teeth in a kind of smile and turned her face to Mr Pye, but her self-satisfaction was smartly rendered null and void, for Mr Pye was shaking his head from side to side. 'No,' he murmured as though to himself – but within Miss Dredger's earshot – 'No . . . no . . . no. She is trying to be clever. That is not humility. *That* is not love.'

The voice from the Eperquerie seemed to rattle in the receiver.

'What is all this? I have a good mind to . . .'

'Miss George,' said Miss Dredger – 'be patient for a moment, if you please. Let me explain my reason for disturbing you.'

'I should think so,' said the voice. 'What *is* your reason? I told you several years ago that I had no wish to see your face again,' and then, as an afterthought, 'Or hear your voice,' she added.

'They are both in shocking condition,' said Miss Dredger.

She was almost enjoying herself again. She had never before leaned back and rested in the arms of her own wit. She realized that when one said rude things about oneself, it rather took the wind out of the sails of the foe.

'I will take your word for *that*,' said the voice, 'but I have no wish to speak to you and . . .'

'Are you free to join us, as a guest, of course, at Derrible, for a midnight picnic?'

The voice from the other side of the island sped along the wires.

'Are you drunk?' it said.

Miss Dredger glanced at Mr Pye. His eyes were closed, his hands were clasped on his lapels. He was standing on his toes.

He was a good man. Miss Dredger could see that at a glance. She turned her back to the telephone, a renewed woman.

'It is difficult to explain over the phone,' she said. 'I can understand how jolly difficult it is for you to understand my calling you – let alone inviting you to our picnic party – but I have great hopes of recovering your friendship. Dammit all, Miss George, the island's too small for such a long divorce from one another. After all, who else can talk about books as you can?'

'I don't get it,' said the voice. 'You know very well that . . .'

'Yes, yes, I certainly do, Miss George, but we are fixing that, my p.g. and I. We will cut a path for you across the northern corner of my garden to help you in your shopping.'

Another long silence ticked its life away. Miss Dredger could hear Miss George breathing heavily.

'Are you there, Miss George?'

'Of course I'm here.'

'You will come, won't you? It ought to be rattling good fun. Don't you think so? For the moment I'll say cheery-bye.'

'Just a moment, Dredger.'

'Yes – fire away.'

'Did you say Derrible?'

'That's it.'

'But my legs. . . ?'

'We are carrying you down, my dear.'

'Carrying me?'

'That's it.'

'How?'

'Ah! Wait and see! That is our surprise.'

'And when is all this happening?'

'Today week, at midnight, if the weather behaves. I won't tell you any more now, but it will be great fun, Georgy – *great* fun. . . .' and with the sound of her own voice ringing in her ears, Miss Dredger banged down the receiver, and turning to Mr Pye found that his arms were spread wide and his body taut, and his face alight with pleasure.

'He was with you, sailor – He was with you. Our Friend. Our God. Our Miscellaneous God. Our Prince of Everywhere. The

Great Pal. *Now* do you understand? He was in the wire itself that joined your voices. You have been blooded, sailor. Think of it. Miss George is changing now – because of you. Love has no master, Oh my smoking sailor! My Lady Nicotine! Your chief is very proud of you indeed!'

TEN

'Is that you, Tintagieu?' called out Thorpe the painter, through the thorn hedge. He had seen a whisk of crimson skirt – a violent colour and one which he would have diluted considerably had he been using it in a painting.

'Right in one,' sang out the rough and incredibly sexual voice of Tintagieu.

'Why have you been d-dodging me?' asked Thorpe in a somewhat far-away accent, as he tried to mount the bank and push the thorn boughs apart. This he eventually did, but not before he had received a very nasty scratch across his nose.

'I wouldn't dodge you, dear. I wouldn't dodge my little "box of paints",' said the husky voice. 'What's the matter with him? He's all sad and gloomy. Have they cut you off, dear? No more money from England? That's what comes of being a genius – I've told you that a hundred times – go in for some honest occupation.'

'Such as – what?' muttered Thorpe, scrambling down the bank on the other side. 'Burglary – or something like that, d-do you mean?'

'I supp-ose . . .' said Tintagieu.

'Do that again,' said Thorpe.

'Do what?'

'Turn your head over your shoulder, with that b-black chunk of hair across one eye, and your hand at your throat. D-do it again.'

'What for? Don't be daft.'

'I wish I could draw,' said Thorpe.

'That's the only thing I thought you *could* bloody well do,' said Tintagieu, taking a quite inappropriately high-heeled shoe off her little fat foot and shaking a stone from it.

'I am no draughtsman,' said Thorpe the Painter. 'I thought I w-was, once, but I'm not. Atmosphere. That's my c-corner. The Coupée at dawn! Melting distances and all that racket. And I know it's a racket, Tintagieu, I know it's easy and I know I'm a f-fake, and if that's illogical I don't care a damn, because I'm a failure – and I'm no ch-chicken either – and everything's been done – I t-tell you; everything's been DONE.'

'Don't let that upset you, dear,' said Tintagieu, 'it's still nice to do it.'

He stole a glance at the husky beauty. She was in some strange way both innocent and menacing.

Innocent in that she had no say in her own personality. She was merely the vehicle through which was poured the very juice of animal existence. She was and could be nothing else. Self-conscious as a monkey, and about as refined, she stood facing the painter like the incarnation of something questionable. Questionable – perhaps; but *complete* as an acorn.

Next to her the painter looked like something out of a book, something pale, shadowy, a man in search of a personality.

He took a step back, and shaded his eyes as he peered at her, while a black-backed gull swept overhead crying peevishly.

'My dear Tintagieu, you are as m-marvellous as ever.'

'I supp-ose . . .'

'Absolutely m-marvellous. You could make a fortune on the

films. They'd shoot you from below. Streamers of cloud behind your head and all that racket.'

'Shoot me from below? I'd like to see them,' said Tintagieu. 'Sounds bloody painful to me.'

'Oh excellent ignorance,' whispered Thorpe, edging forward a fraction, for Tintagieu was no magnet for nothing.

'Now, now,' said the deep, sexy voice, 'don't come too close, my little box of paints, there are people everywhere.'

'I can't see anyone,' said Thorpe.

'That's not necessary,' said Tintagieu. 'You don't need eyesight, you don't need ears. Sark is one big eye, and another big ear.'

'Perhaps,' said Thorpe, who had reason to know how right she was, for he remembered a certain enormous lover in sea-boots, who had once imagined Tintagieu to be his exclusive property, and how this misguided man had behaved when he was told of how his swarthy flame and a painter were to be found in a hayrick. How anyone could ever have seen them as they made those midnight journeys to the rick the painter could never guess. It always struck him as a very strange thing that Tintagieu had laughed herself into a state bordering on hysterics during the whole course of the unpleasantness. But the point was they had been *seen*.

'I'm a miserable type, aren't I, Tintagieu? Do *you* think so? Do you think I'm only h-h-half a man? Be honest.'

'Why keep on about yourself,' said Tintagieu, 'you're too serious for me, dear. You seem all stitched up. You have too many bloody buttons.'

'I'll pull the lot off here and now,' shouted the pale young man, tearing away at his clothes.

'Of course there's always an alternative to *tearing* them off,' said Tintagieu. 'But listen to me....'

'Oh, creeping hell!' shouted Thorpe, suddenly forgetting the big ear of Sark – 'Oh d-damn my upbringing! damn my family – damn my p-poverty, damn my paintings, and damn atmosphere! I love you, Tintagieu, I always have.'

'What, again! Come, come, come, come, come, my little paint-pot. We'll see what we can do for you – but for cork's sake don't look so pathetic – it puts me off. Come on, walk! walk!'

'Where are you going, Tintagieu?'

'Ormering.'

'Which bay?'

'Grève de la Ville.'

'I d-didn't know there was an ormer tide.'

'Well now you do, don't you. And you've still got your funny little beard. What's it for, dear? Do you ever paint with it?'

'I'll paint *you* with it. Oh, Tanty, I could eat you!'

'Very nice for me, I suppose,' said Tintagieu.

'I'm coming with you,' said the painter. 'Wait for me and I'll nip back to my place and bring a b-basket and a spike.'

'Don't forget the spike,' said Tintagieu, as she sat down to wait for him. She munched for a while at a stem of grass, her eyes half closed against the sun. Then she lay back and relaxed every limb and shut her eyes, and was motionless except for every once in a while when she swung her hand lazily across her face to brush away a persistent fly.

When Thorpe returned she got slowly to her feet and shook out the thick black flag of her hair, spat out the stalk of grass, and they walked in silence through the fields and lanes.

Occasionally Tintagieu would hum away at some popular jazzy tune, which she had heard over the wireless, or at the occasional Sark dances at the hall, or murmur in her subterranean voice:

> 'A-lolling on the shores of old Hawaii,
> Never tryee
> To understand.
> The moon is up above us in the sky-ee –
> As planned.'

Thorpe glanced at her with a faint hope that she might be drawing some parallel between Hawaii and Sark, with him, Thorpe, very much in the picture, but it was obvious that it had never occurred to her to think of the words.

Down the winding, zigzag path to the Grève de la Ville with

its acres of boulders, which now that the spring tide was away out, stretched far to sea. The Chapelle des Mauves, a curiously caverned rock, glimmered in the sun that was now dodging in and out of high cirrus clouds, so that shadows fled across the boulders of the sea-forsaken bay. And beneath these boulders could be found the delicious ormer, that after a severe thrashing is apt to taste like veal. They are tenacious creatures, and the toppling over of a boulder in order to see if there is an ormer on its wet under-surface has to be performed with the utmost rapidity, for if too much notice is given the creature will cling tenaciously. Hence the spike.

'An ormering we will go,' muttered Thorpe when they had turned the last bend in the path and were at last jumping from rock to rock in a seaward direction. There were a few who were already at work; bent double like gardeners as they moved from boulder to boulder.

'You s-see that smooth little upright rock with a s-sort of face at the top?' asked Thorpe, pointing rudely at an outcrop.

'What about it?'

'I made a sketch here once, of those cliffs and this rock in the f-foreground.'

'Not really, dear.'

'I never noticed it when I was painting it, but when I got home and looked at what I'd done, I saw that that rock was exactly the shape of a f-fat little man – face and all.'

'And what a beak he's got,' said Tintagieu.

'But don't you see – I n-never saw it when I was actually *painting* here,' the pale young man insisted. 'It was only when – Oh, by the way, what do you think of Mr What's-it at Clôs de Joi – Miss Dredger's place?'

'What, the Fruit-drop?'

'Is that what they call him?'

'That's what he is,' said Tintagieu.

'He's having a p-picnic tomorrow.'

'I know,' said Tintagieu – 'who doesn't?'

'At midnight. . . .'

'I know all about that, my love,' said Tintagieu – 'and I could tell you some very queer things too – if you want your hair curled. But what's on your mind, dear? What about him?'

'They've invited me,' said Thorpe.

'I know,' said Tintagieu.

He stared at her. He had only received his invitation a few hours previously.

They scrambled on together until they came to the rocks which in Tintagieu's opinion were the most likely to be hiding ormers 'over-leaf', and sure enough she was very wise, for between them they enjoyed a fruitful morning.

Returning to the cliff-face the painter noticed that they were alone in the Grève de la Ville and he suggested that they should rest in the mouth of a convenient cave where the shingle was warm with the sun. They sat down and almost at once Tintagieu stood up again. 'What's that?' she said, the thick, deep voice echoing in the cave.

Following the direction of her outstretched arm the painter noticed that far out to sea there was what at first appeared to be a long rock, but they both knew that there was no rock in that position. It was equally impossible that it could be a ship, unless it was upturned: even so it appeared to have no keel, but was more as though a long egg was all but submerged, its gradual upper arc breaking the surface of the sea.

The longer they stared the less they were able to agree as to what it could be, and after half an hour of abortive speculation they turned to each other with their natural appetites whetted by the delay. The golden sun beat down, and far, far away they could hear the murmur of the breathing sea, so utterly still and silent was the day.

An hour later they emerged from the cave.

'Tanty, Oh Tanty, for God's sake never l-leave the island.'

'Why should I?'

'I don't know,' said the young man, 'but *don't* anyway. I think I could change – if you don't desert me. I could change into something p-positively p-potent. To hell with atmosphere. I think I am really a cubist.'

'You be just what you like, dear,' said Tintagieu, 'but I'm famished.'

Hand-in-hand they started to climb the steep path.

'How are you, my little paint-box?' said Tintagieu.

'Transfigured,' said Thorpe. 'But somewhat w-weak in the legs.'

From a vantage point among the rocks someone whistled, and the note was echoed from the other side of the bay – a callow note, a saucy note, a knowledgeable note.

ELEVEN

MR PYE, his silence at an end, was now to be found in lively conversation with all and sundry, at the corners of lanes, on the beaches, in cottage doorways, down at the harbour, or sitting with a group of goggle-eyed listeners at the foot of the ruined Mill which stands at the highest point on Sark's bleak backbone. There was no place on the island too obscure. No place too public. There were his evenings at 'The Lobster', where he would hold forth on every imaginable topic with such delightful volubility and charm that the tavern would fill directly it was noised abroad that 'The Fruit-drop' was in his favourite seat near the window.

There were his afternoon outings when, with the ever growing circle of his proselytes about him, he could be seen taking his constitutional and flinging the gayest quips and sallies over his shoulder to the following horde.

Within a week of his breaking his verbal fast he had leapt from what was already a prominent, if enigmatic, position in the life of the island, to a yet loftier summit. The silent, spruce, mercurial little figure who had become almost legendary within his first fortnight 'ashore', was now twice the man. To his agility, his eager and intelligent face, and all that was visible about him, there was now added the Voice – and through the voice the outpourings of an athletic brain.

From the moment that he passed through the gates of Clôs de Joi an hour after Miss Dredger had hung up her receiver on Miss George (with a clang that reverberated in Miss George's middle-ear for the rest of the morning), Mr Pye lost no time in buttonholing the island and holding it, like the Ancient Mariner, with his glittering eye.

Mr Pye had no fear because it never occurred to him that there was anything *to* fear. His self-esteem and his self-confidence were almost palpable. His charm so devastating that there were few who could resist it for more than a few sentences.

Within the space of a few hours he had introduced himself, that day, to at least thirty islanders and a dozen residents.

Not all were prone to take it lying down. Not all were pleased to be accosted. Some were in a hurry, but their impatience was drained away as they eyed the almost transparent features which smiled back at them with such demonstrable love.

His pride was quite un-puncturable. He would listen carefully as the less tolerant and the rougher types insulted him. He was so obviously interested in what they had to say and he would gaze at them with rapt concentration, weighing carefully whatever oaths were being used, and when the abuse began to peter out, he would smile with such genuine friendliness that the rough and insular gentlemen who had never taken kindly to his presence on the island, knew not what to do.

'My, my, you are a strapping fellow,' he would cry out to some bibulous hulk. 'I am delighted to meet you.'

'Oh, you are, are you, eh, you fat little porker,' the hulk would reply. 'B— you.'

'Indeed?' said Mr Pye. 'But that's a very naughty thing to

say. How old are you? Now, now, now – don't tell me you're shy. A great big fisherman like you – Now I tell you what. I could make use of a strapping fellow.'

'Oh, you could, could you?'

'Oh, yes indeed, with that raw, that magnificent frame. You are quite, quite fundamental.'

'Oh, I am, am I?'

'I can see you at the oar, my friend, rowing into the sunrise, the dolphins leaping about you.'

'Oh, you can, can you?'

'Indeed I can – or with all your animal strength – I can see you harnessed to the chariot of our Great Pal. And yet, at the same time a humble fisher.'

'And who's your bloody pal, and does he think I'm a horse? Eh? Eh? I've got a ruddy good mind to pick you up, and to . . .'

'Oh, but I don't think so,' said Mr Pye. 'You've got more wisdom than to do a childish thing like that, haven't you now?'

'I ruddy well *will,*' says the huge man, 'and I'll . . .'

'Carry on,' Mr Pye might say. 'Pick me up and throw me over the cliff. I challenge you to do so.'

'Eh?'

'Here I am, waiting. But I know that your muscles were built for Love, not Cruelty.'

'B— me.'

'He would not like to hear foul language, my dear chap. Come with me, you big absurd child. . . .'

And Mr Pye, noticing that the huge hulk had suddenly capsized inside itself, would take the man to the edge of a cliff, and there they would stand in absolute silence. 'We must have our Quiet Times,' says Mr Pye. 'I will see you tomorrow at three o'clock and we will talk about ourselves, shall we, and you will tell me your troubles. You great, big fellow.'

And the huge, sour-visaged, red-necked, sea-booted mariner would mouth some unintelligible word, and proceed with trembling legs upon his way.

But such un-elevating incidents were the exception and for

the most part Mr Pye was, from the outset, on the happiest terms with those he accosted. Accosted? No, it was not quite that. There was no presumption in the way he approached his 'victims'. More than this, it was almost as though it was they who approached him. Something in Mr Pye's expressive presence – something magnetic – seemed to halt and to hold the islanders so that it seemed unthinkable to merely pass Mr Pye in the road without bathing in his radiance and dipping in the deep well of his wisdom.

Mr Pye was, by now, not only the most talked about person on the island, but had given such a shock to what had once been a comparatively normal community that he held the emotional life of the islanders in the palm of his hand.

All except Tintagieu. She didn't seem to be affected to the same extent. Interested – ah, yes – very much so – but affected – no. To those whose contact with Mr Pye had already resulted in a marked moral improvement, and who made solicitous enquiries as to the state of her soul, Tintagieu merely raised her thick eyebrows and blew a long and ruminative raspberry.

Yes, already within so short a while, he was master of a formidable band. And this without having actually launched the essence of his spiritual campaign. He had touched on ethics here and there as conversation demanded, but as yet his particular contribution to man's happiness – and his own belief in the true road to Love – was a closed book to the island.

For Mr Pye believed that it was best to do one thing at a time – and so he had kept his first stage to the purely *physical*, in the course of which it was established beyond doubt that he was a man of immense vitality – for all the curve of his paunch. In the second stage, the end of which was now approaching, it had been for him to impress the island with his *intellect* – and truly he was the most widely cultivated and knowledgeable gentleman who had ever set foot on Sark.

It was with this, his second stage, that he intended to not only impress, but to inspire confidence on such a scale that it became the natural thing for island problems to come direct to him, short-circuiting the famous Chief Pleas, the island Parliament.

It seemed impossible that the island could be turned upside down in so short a time. Age-old enmities, age-old feuds, were melting away in the warmth of his sunbeams. A new spirit was abroad in Sark – so much so that old friends of the island who were returning for Easter were amazed to receive as they disembarked at the stone jetty, so effusive a welcome. 'There's something different about Sark,' they would say, 'it's almost as though they like us.'

And all this was before the third and last stage – that veritable cataract – the stage where, his vitality and his intellect having been admitted, he could concentrate upon the Soul itself.

Mr Pye, an experienced crusader, knew the value of holding this trump card up his sleeve and playing it at that moment when the island was clay in his hand.

That moment was all but come – for Mr Pye had it in mind that all things being equal he would fire the first salvo on the night of the midnight picnic.

But meanwhile, much was happening at Clôs de Joi; for Mr Pye had no intention of marking time.

He had crossed the island on the day following the telephone call and had surprised Miss George by suddenly appearing round the corner of her kitchen, and by kissing her ring-encrusted hand, and then, still holding her fingers, by telling her with delightful rapidity the romantic story of the stones she wore, where they were mined, where they were, in all probability, cut and polished, and where they were first found in bygone times. He admired the settings; he admired her courage to wear so many rings not only on each hand, but on each finger – for above all the foibles of the individual were a kind of gift to God. It was the uniform, the grey, drab, unimaginative approach to life that was such an insult to the Great Pal whose very essence was variety.

Miss George sank back into a basket-work arm-chair, while Mr Pye walked smartly around the room, his hands behind his back as he pattered to the window and gazed delightedly across the sea to Guernsey.

'But, my dear Miss George,' he said, twirling around so suddenly and rapidly that he found himself facing Guernsey again instead of Miss George, and had to complete another half-circle before he could continue with what he was saying – 'much as I admire the view from your window, you must be very *lonely* here.'

Miss George lifted a huge, fat, freckled hand and smoothed her purple busby nervously. Whether she slept in it no one knew, but she was never seen outside it. Rumour had it that it was glued to her head and that she was really bald – and that the busby acted as a wig and a hat at the same time – but then rumour always had *something* horrid to say.

'And this room. It is a pretty little place, but very dirty, dear. Now, isn't it? Let's face it.'

Miss George opened her mouth, and rose heavily to her feet, only to find that she had brought the chair up with her, for the spread of her rear was formidable.

'Very dirty indeed,' said Mr Pye, smiling at her with his eyebrows raised, and he ran his immaculate handkerchief along a shelf and then showed her the black and shaming result. 'And do you know why you have become slovenly, my dear?'

Miss George shook her huge pastry-coloured head slowly from side to side, and the busby followed at a higher level. Her mouth was still open and the basket-chair was still at grips with her bottom.

'Shall I tell you why?'

The busby nodded.

'It is because you are a great big lonely woman. It is because you have nothing important to do. Would you like to have something important to do?'

The busby trembled.

'Something that made you proud to be alive? Would you like to feel a part of some great plan? Would you like to join me, and never be lonely again?'

The busby gave no sign. 'Come, come, don't be shy, Miss George. Would you not like to start a new life of love and endeavour?'

After a long while the busby nodded.

'And so you shall. I shall send a carriage to pick up your

belongings tomorrow. You are to have the west bedroom at Clôs de Joi and live with us. You are wasting yourself, you lonely old silly. Be ready with all your things by this time tomorrow. I will settle with your landlord. You have no more to fear.'

'But this is my house: I bought it,' said Miss George in a far away whisper.

'Then I shall sell it for you, my dear, and you will be free – free from earthly ties, free from squalor, free for action, free for love and laughter. Free to take your place in the ranks of my commandos. Your life is only just beginning, you lucky old thing!'

TWELVE

IT was one thing to forgive Miss George, and to let bygones be bygones, and even to have agreed to allow the woman across the corner of her garden without resentment, but it was quite another thing for Miss Dredger to have Miss George actually living in the house, and it was necessary for Mr Pye to call forth all his skill, and all his tact to deal with the situation. It was not enough that the Misses George and Dredger should be mollified. That would be altogether too negative a thing. It was for Mr Pye to prove to them that they were necessary to one another.

During the first few days the atmosphere was as tense as two spinsters could make it, but when Miss George realized that there was no excuse for laziness and that a number of her dirty habits were not appreciated in Miss Dredger's house she began to make an effort to settle down.

For Miss George, whether she wanted to or not, found far more interest in life, living with Mr Pye and Miss Dredger than she ever had upon her own. There were times when she saw no reason why she should have a bath, and resented being told there was one waiting for her, gently steaming, but such small pinpricks were, after a little practice, quite easy to ignore.

One afternoon, a day or two before the picnic, the three of

them were sitting in deck chairs beneath the ugly palm tree whose torn harsh leaves rubbed gently against each other in the slight breeze, with a husky sound. It was a warm day, but overcast with a hanging haze.

Between them was a garden table and the remains of their tea.

On the roof of the house four seagulls sat waiting for them to go indoors so that they could swoop on the crumbs.

'And is everything ready for tomorrow night, ladies?' said Mr Pye, wiping his mouth on a napkin. 'I have noticed how hard you have been working. It should be a memorable spread. The pair of you have done magnificently.'

'Oh, I don't know about that, chief,' said Miss Dredger, her head thrown back, her eyes closed, the cigarette smoke coiling round her. 'We have rather thrown ourselves into it, eh, Georgy?'

Miss George, who was forced to sit forward in her canvas chair in order that her busby should not be disturbed, scratched herself gently on her left knee.

'Agreed,' she said.

'There is nothing finer than sharing one's work and one's ambitions. There can be nothing more fulfilling, if the two concerned have learned how to *give*. That is the secret, to give, give, give and to forget all about *taking*. And equally there can be nothing more distressing than to have to work with another at close quarters, if there is a shade of bitterness, malice, selfishness, or envy. That is why I admire you two ladies. You have become integrate – magnificently integrate.'

'Of course Ka-Ka has helped us too – in her way,' said Miss Dredger. 'Credit where credit's due and all that.'

'Agreed,' said Miss George. 'Although it has been very much in *her* way, as you remark.'

'And not in yours?' queried Mr Pye, with a bright smile.

'Oh, she's been in our way *all* the time,' sang out Miss Dredger, opening her eyes and thrusting her head forward and eyeing her companions through a smoke ring. Oh, it was worth making jokes these days for Mr Pye was slapping his thighs and beaming at her, and Georgy was smirking affably.

At that precise moment the ancient Ka-Ka appeared at the front door and stared at them with an expression of such emptiness that it was a relief to the three beneath the palm to be able to feel the solid wood and stretched canvas of their chairs, which at least were of this world. Without these anchors they might well have been drawn away and into an extension of that ultimate vacancy that yawned from Ka-Ka's face.

However it lasted only for a moment and Ka-Ka turned about and returned to the kitchen.

On the whole Ka-Ka did more harm than good in the house, but in one particular way she was useful. She gave Miss Dredger and Miss George a sense of their own relative superiority. They were both younger than Ka-Ka: they were cleverer: their upbringing had been more delicate – in fact, by comparison with Ka-Ka they were all-but royalty.

This made for a kind of social ease in the house which helped Mr Pye not a little – for fundamentally, Miss George at least was not altogether happy as to what hypothetical position in society would be hers even if she ever entered it. This faint but persistent fear that the *crème de la crème* might easily fail to recognise her as one of themselves was the cause of her aggressiveness – or rather of what had once been her aggressiveness, for since she had come to Clôs de Joi she had been handled with such tact and forbearance that there had been, so far, no sign of an explosion.

'Will you never tell me how you expect me to get down that frightful cliff? I think it's a bit mean of you, chief. You know I'm not what I was, athletically, and my insteps have both collapsed.'

She dipped her thumb into some jam that had been left on the side of a plate, and sucked it. Then she looked up at Mr Pye again, with a rueful expression. 'Don't do that, dear,' said Mr Pye. 'It is not seemly.'

'What isn't, chief?'

'Using your thumb like that...' and then Mr Pye, noticing a blush begin to suffuse Miss George's huge pallid face, frowned at Miss Dredger until he caught her eye, and then lowered his right eyelid in the most meaningful of winks, having done which he cried out, 'And *you*, sailor! What are *you* doing? *I* saw you picking the currants out of that cake!'

Miss Dredger rose to the occasion in a way that might have been expected of her.

'Sorry, chief,' she said, 'sometimes I forget myself – Oh, dash it all, I wish you hadn't seen me.'

'Of course I saw you. Really! I don't know which of you is the worst.'

Mr Pye clucked with his tongue and pursed his lips, and Miss George smirked unpleasantly. The balance was again restored.

'So you want to know how we will get you down to Derrible?'

'I have asked you so many times, and you always say, "wait and see". You *are* a tease, you know. I wouldn't put up with it from anyone else.'

'She is rather champing at the bit, chief,' said Miss Dredger. 'And I must admit I'd like to know myself what you're going to do with her.'

'*Do* with me?' whispered Miss George, her eyes narrowing. 'I tell you one thing, I'm not climbing down that cliff, and I'm not climbing up again and why it was chosen I can't think when you know about my insteps.'

'You won't have to climb up *or* down,' said Mr Pye.

'Then how will I get there – that's if you *want* me to get there,' said Miss George, two tears beginning to gather at the corners of her small eyes.

'Now, now, now,' said Mr Pye. 'This is no time for self-pity. Of course you will get there. Not only will you get there, but you will do so in a way which will never be forgotten. You will make history – spiritual history. You will bring light into darkness. Have you no faith in me? Have you no faith in our Pal? Come, come, answer me.'

'Oh, I know all about that,' said Miss George somewhat testily, 'but our marvellous Pal can't think of everything at once. Does He *know* about the state of my feet?'

'Our Pal knows everything and He knows everything at the

same time. I have interceded for you. After all He is in all of us and all of us are in Him. What more could you want?'

At that moment the sound of hesitant footsteps approaching up the gravel drive caused the three of them to turn their heads. At first only the legs were visible, for a high, rough screen of prickly foliage flanked the drive, but a moment or two later the painter Thorpe sidled into view, and immediately Mr Pye was on his feet and was standing with his head thrown back, his eyes gleaming with pleasure, his lips parted, his nose shining in the sun, and his arms stretched forward in welcome.

'The artist!' he cried – 'it is the artist, ladies!' So vivid and ringing was his tone, that involuntarily the Misses George and Dredger began to clap.

'Sh ... sh ... ladies!' Mr Pye hissed at them gently, and frowned with one eyebrow up and one down.

'Come along, come along, my dearest fellow, and join us. Now *is* there any more tea, let me see, let me see,' and Mr Pye lifted the lid of the teapot and peered inside. 'No. Definitely no – but we can make some – can't we, ladies?'

The ladies nodded their heads.

'No, no – I wouldn't d-dream of it, thank you so much all the s-same,' muttered Thorpe, making his way across the lawn with a walk so hesitant as to look almost like a disease of the legs.

'No?' said Mr Pye. 'If there's one thing I like it's a direct answer. Come and sit down and tell us what we can do for you.'

'My dead brother-in-law used to paint. He was always at it.'

'We will keep that for later, shall we?' said Mr Pye, tapping Miss George on the knee with a teaspoon. He returned his expectant gaze to the visitor.

'It's about your party tonight,' said Thorpe.

'Yes? – but sit down, sit down –' and Mr Pye, hitching his trousers up and sitting neatly with his legs crossed, on the lawn, waved the painter into the seat he had vacated.

'Well, you know, you've invited m-me, don't you?'

'Well, of course I do, my dear chap – what a funny question,' said Mr Pye. 'I'm sure it's leading to something most mysterious.'

'I'm afraid n-not. It's very ordinary really. It's just to know whether if I take my sketch book down, you would mind if I do some sketches of it all – the moonlight and the f-firelight sort of m-mixed up, you know, and the different characters sitting in the groups and all the black and silver and red of it – the driftwood, and the openings of the caves – and the moonlight as I said before. And the chimney.'

'The chimney?' Mr Pye's ejaculation was quick as an echo.

'Yes, with its . . .'

'You know about the chimney?'

'Yes, of c-course I do – I used to p-paint it, looking up. T-terribly d-difficult, with that little circle of light at the t-top. Not that I've been down to Derrible for y-years.' He pulled at his little beard. 'Would you mind if I did some sketches, being your guest I thought it right to ask you.'

'Of course the chief won't mind,' said Miss Dredger, lighting a cigarette and making a rectangle of her tough lips so that she looked rather like an Aztec carving. 'It would be deuced interesting to see what he made of it – wouldn't it, chief? A kind of record and all that?'

'Why should I mind, my dear boy? What would it mean if I *did* mind? It would mean that I was ignorant of God's power. That I was dead to one of his more luminous manifestations. Art. What is art but the reflection of our Pal?'

Thorpe frowned. Was Mr Pye referring to him? Really that was a bit much to claim that art was his reflection.

'For you cannot tell me that you are not conscious of God in every brush-stroke . . .' continued Mr Pye.

'I was thinking of using pastels this time,' said Thorpe with a certain obliqueness.

'Of each chalk-stroke, then,' said Mr Pye with the faintest trace of irritation.

'You are the great Pal's vessel. He poured Himself through you. The moonlight on the ripples of the water, the . . .'

'Yes,' said Thorpe, 'but I'm not really interested in the r-r-r-ripples as such, reflected lights and all that racket. They may be nothing like ripples by the time I've finished with them. It's a kind of synthesis I'm after, and it s-seems to me that there'll be such a s-staggering lot of d-data down there tonight.'

'God – or as we prefer to call him, Our Pal, *is* the original synthesis Himself – my poor boy,' said Mr Pye.

'Is he?' said Thorpe.

'He is. Leave your sketches to Him.'

It sounded to the artist at first as though it were being suggested that he should leave his sketches to the Almighty in his will, until he realized that Mr Pye was exhorting him to leave the actual process of painting to the Deity.

'You mean, sort of, automatic painting.'

'Put it that way if you like,' said Mr Pye. 'Fall back into the arms of Our Pal, and let your pastels do the work for you. After all, you are only the medium – the glass pipe as it were.' He smiled up at the artist.

'That's all very well, Mr Pye, but has your Pal ever heard of expressionism?'

'He *is* expressionism.'

'And cubism?'

'He *is* cubism,' said Mr Pye.

'And what about atmosphere?'

'He *is* atmosphere.'

'A b-bit obsolete, isn't He?' queried the artist. 'It's a racket, you know – all those "isms".'

'Call things what you like, my dear æsthete, call things what you like. Words make no difference. What matters is that you reflect our Pal in everything you do. He will be standing at your shoulder.'

'Oh, I couldn't b-bear that,' said Thorpe. 'It would put me off f-frightfully.'

'There is something in your ignorance which touches me very deeply, my dear artist friend,' said Mr Pye – 'it is the ignorance of accident. There is nothing but good in you. You are on the wrong road – that is all.' He rose on his heels and put his hands on Thorpe's knees. With his head lifted he faced his guest and released into the humid air the electric current of his love.

The two women leaned forward, touched as it were by the intensity of the moment. He turned to them at last, and with a gesture of his head both confidential and authoritative he made it plain that it would be best for them to retire to the house.

Thorpe's eyes were shut, not only to keep out the blaze of benevolence, but because he just did not know which way to look.

'Would you be prepared to help me, and through me, our Pal?'

'In what way?'

'You have just seen Miss George.'

'Yes.'

'She is very heavy.'

'I suppose so.'

'She has flat feet.'

'Oh.'

'How then can she get down the path to Derrible, and up again?'

'Ah.'

'Have you any ideas?'

'I can think of h-how she could get d-down – but n-not how she could get up.'

'Really?'

'Yes ind-d-deed.'

'How would you get her down?'

'I would p-push her over . . .'

'My dear fellow! over what?'

'Over the p-p-precipice.'

Mr Pye got to his feet, and walked rapidly to the end of the garden and back.

'I have been praying for you,' he said. 'You are very naughty.'

'It was only a j-joke,' said the artist. 'I don't think of many: when I *do* it seems a pity to waste them.'

'You have charm,' said Mr Pye.

'I must go,' said Thorpe. 'I look forward to tonight. It was very kind of you t-to ask me. Is it going to be a very big party?'

'Yes and no,' said Mr Pye.

'C-can I bring Tintagieu?'

Mr Pye gazed at him silently.

'Regarding Miss George,' he said at last, 'regarding Miss George. What do you think of the idea of lowering her down the chimney on the end of a rope. I have the rope, two hundred feet of it, and I have hired the men – men of great strength, thew and spleen. I have also got the nightdress.'

'The nightdress!'

'Symbol of chastity,' said Mr Pye. 'You will understand it all later. But may I count on you, at beach level? There may be problems. Untying her, for instance. All things considered, it would be best for you to meet us here, and we can all go down together.'

'When shall I come?'

'At eleven-fifteen. The carriage for the ladies and the carriage for the provender will be here by then.'

'Can I bring T-Tintagieu?' said the painter.

As they turned from one another with a handshake, Mr Pye let loose his dazzling smile –

'I have so many surprises in store,' he said. 'It will be the greatest fun.'

THIRTEEN

THORPE, who had turned his back on atmosphere, made his way across the reflecting sands.

He had made his excuses to the picnic party which was still gathered about the blaze of the oven which Mr Pye had constructed so cunningly out of boulders, and with his sketch-book under his arm Thorpe had dwindled away into the luminous midnight air.

His mind was in a state of pleasurable confusion. The supper and the excellent wine, the best he had ever tasted, were, in a roundabout way affording him a degree of moral comfort which was quite new to him. But he was confused also, in a dreamy way, on account of Tintagieu, Mr Pye, and his art.

These three revolved through his brain from time to time, and posed their recurrent problems, but what menace they held was dulled by the drowsy aftermath of the repast.

Pausing in his tracks he turned to look back at the scene of the barbecue. He could see nothing but a point of vermilion, like a bead of blood, suspended in the night.

High above this hot and trembling point he saw in the midnight air the full moon hanging as big as a dinner plate. It ribbed the edges of the precipitous cliffs and was reflected in the sheen of the sands. Then he saw his footprints and was appalled. He had never known until this moment that he was pigeon-toed.

His first reaction was to wonder whether Tintagieu had ever noticed. His second to congratulate himself on the fact that it is only in wet sand, or when there is snow that such a thing could be seen. His third thought was to doubt whether his second thought was true, for after all footprints are not necessary for an onlooker to know whether one walks like a duck or an ant-eater.

His fourth thought was that he should try walking with his toes turned out a little, and this he put into operation. After he had gone a hundred yards he began to develop a pain in the knees.

'Rembrandt was no beauty,' he said to himself, 'and nor was Toulouse-Lautrec. I'm an artist, not a matinée idol.'

He skirted the fringe of the sea, and in a few minutes had reached the northern arm of the great bay. Far across the glimmering sands, its brother, as precipitous, but saddled with pale grass, rose to the moon like a thing of gauze.

He paused again and felt for his chalks. What a strange and beautiful bay! Honey-combed with caves, alive with flying buttresses of rock.

He knelt down on the wet sand and spread out his sketch-book. He must make marks, coloured marks, any marks, that might convey at least a fragment of the scene; the gloating light; the rhythm of the rocks.

But no. It was no use. It was the moon itself that baulked him. The moon, that fatuous circle. That overrated face that spawned the light; and it wasn't even her own light.

The whole thing stank of false romanticism. It reeked of a million postcards. It was a racket.

'Oh, God,' whispered Thorpe, 'why didn't I stick to life insurance! I don't want to paint anyway. Beauty's nothing but a bloody irritant.'

Suddenly he sat up on his heels and stared. Then he thrust out his bottom lip. Then he trembled. Then he spoke aloud.

'Five overlapping rectangles with holes in them. Three zigzags black and grey. A kind of leper whiteness – the paint all thick and crusty – I'll mix the stuff with sand. And no moon. No atmosphere. Just the core of it all. The heart of bone.'

A kind of exultation filled him, something he had not experienced for years, and he jumped to his feet and began to run. He had seen something in his mind's eye, a picture, dynamic, vital, savage, frozen into geometry, its surface hoary with dragged paint, a painting unlike any other painting – yet in the tremendous tradition of the masters. Who cared if his toes turned in?

He redoubled his speed, running with his arms stretched out stiffly behind him like wings or like a child pretending to be an aeroplane. His head thrust forward, his beard trembling with the speed of his progress, he ran on and on in the moonlight.

At the very moment when a stitch in his side screamed out for him to halt, he found himself soaring through the air, and the next moment he was lying on his face in a rock pool.

As he had galloped around the base of a high solitary rock he had tripped and with a suddenness that gave him no time for fear, he was all at once prostrated.

Badly shaken, but not seriously hurt, he got to his knees in the shallow salty water and pushed his dripping hair back from his eyes.

'Ah, my little paint-box – so you have gone *mad*,' the voice was like the slow crunching of soft gravel. Thorpe turned his head with a kind of happy snarl. After a long while he rose to his knees in the chilly water. 'I am an artist,' he said.

'Is that today's great thought?' said Tintagieu. 'What has bitten you, my sweet?'

'There are artists and artists,' said the artist.

'And which are you?' said Tintagieu, 'Get out of the water, love. I've seen some peculiar things on Sark, but to see my little paint-box haring across Derrible puts the bloody lid on it. What a cocksparrow! And after such a lovely supper, too – sitting there like mother's pride and eating for all he was worth, bless him, the greedy-guts.'

'How do you know?' said Thorpe, stepping out of the rock-pool, his clothes clinging to him like Hellenic draperies. 'What on earth are you doing down here? Were you invited?'

'What! Was I invited! What a sauce! Has Derrible been rented? Am I trespassing? That's rich, that is, you English monkey!'

'Well, what are you doing here? Didn't you know there was a picnic tonight?'

'Didn't I know there's a picnic! Hark at him. He hasn't cut his teeth yet, I shouldn't wonder, bless his little fat heart. The silly b——r!'

'What does it matter,' said Thorpe. 'It isn't my picnic. I couldn't care less. Let 'em all come.'

'They have,' said Tintagieu.

'What? Who else is down here?'

'We are being watched at this moment,' she said, 'by about a hundred eyes. If I hadn't thought you were dead I would have let you find your own way out of this pool.'

'Who else is here?'

'I'll tell you who isn't,' said Tintagieu.

'Well, who?'

'There's an old lady in Little Sark who's been in bed for seventeen years,' said Tintagieu. 'She isn't here. And there's the baby who's just been born down at La Porbat. He isn't here . . . and there's . . .'

'For God's sake stop pulling my leg,' said Thorpe. 'I'm cold. I must get back to the fire. Tomorrow I start painting. Come and see me, Tintagieu – about five.'

'Too busy,' said Tintagieu. 'I'll be putting my dolly to sleep at five.'

'You and your bloody dolly. I'm sick of that joke,' said Thorpe. 'But your breasts look superb in the moonlight, with those chasmic shadows. But to hell with volume. That's a racket if ever there was one! I must get back to that fire. I'm as cold as Old Harry.'

'He's here too,' said Tintagieu, 'and young Harry.'

'I know you're fooling me.'

'Come and see then.'

Against his will the artist followed her up the long slope of a rock on the other side of which was a tract of shingle.

All over it, as thick as limpets, and all over the rocks beyond, were the islanders, playing cards by the light of the moon, lolling on rocks, sitting in groups, lying on their backs and filling their glasses again and again from a great barrel which they had somehow or other managed to get down the precipitous cliffs.

'God in heaven!' cried Thorpe. 'What's the idea? What does it mean?'

'Should it *mean* something?' said Tintagieu. 'Can't a thing just be itself without its having to *mean* something?'

Since this was one of his own favourite phrases he knew that she must be pulling his leg. He smacked out at her in good humour, for the picture he had constructed in his mind, the re-creation of Derrible Bay, came back to him and he was at that moment a god – a sportive god with power up his sleeve. But she was too quick for him and evaded his friendly blow, and the next moment, with a 'So-long, my little paint-box,' she disappeared among the rocks, and he for his part, being glad of the opportunity, began to trot towards the fire beneath the cliffs.

FOURTEEN

'I SAY chief,' cried Miss Dredger, 'where's Georgy? She hasn't had anything to eat! It's a rotten shame. Has she hurt herself?'

Mr Pye, who was deep in conversation with a certain Major Havershot and was sitting on the other side of the fire, failed to hear the question, but Mr and Mrs Rice, who were on Miss Dredger's other side, turned their faces to her as though they were the twin parts of the same machine.

'Hurt herself? I hope not,' said Mrs Rice. 'Although I can't think how she could get down here. I don't know how I got down here – without a scratch.'

'*I* do,' said her husband with a note of bitterness in his voice. He had all but carried her down.

'It seems a silly place to have chosen,' said Mrs Rice.

'The chief does not make mistakes and nothing that he does is silly. You may not understand that at the moment, but, by Jove, you will find out later.'

'Indeed,' said Mrs Rice.

'In-deed,' said Miss Dredger – 'and not only in deed. In thought as well. *Thought* can be as powerful as action.'

Mr Rice gazed at her. He was a heavy lumbering man, with

so flat a face that it seemed to have been created by some sculptor who, experimenting in the art of low relief, was inquisitive to know quite how low a relief could go without disappearing altogether. Thousands of years of ice and blizzard, of scorching suns and withering sandstorms could not have reduced a marble face to anything like so featureless a thing as he had achieved by the simple means of being Mr Rice. His was the family face, and the rumour that he had had it trodden on by an elephant when young was quite untrue. All the Rices were the same. They had no profiles.

'I rather gather, Miss Dredger, and correct me if I am wrong, as we say in Sark, that you are a tremendous admirer, if not practically a disciple, of our host. Practically a disciple. No?'

'You gather jolly well right,' said Miss Dredger. 'He has lifted me up.'

'That's more than he could do to Miss George,' said Mrs Rice with a nasty titter.

'I resent that,' said Miss Dredger, taking her cigarette from her mouth and leaning sideways so that her tough, indomitable face was practically touching Mrs Rice's.

'She is my friend. If she is fat, then the Great Pal, for some good reason, made her so. We may not know why. But He knows why.'

'"The Great Pal", did you say?' said Mr Rice. '"Made her so", did you say? What can you mean? Do you understand, my dear?' (He turned to his wife.) 'Has she been to some plastic surgeon or something? Bless me, as we say in Sark, what *can* you mean?'

'Our Pal,' said Miss Dredger, 'has many names. Some may call Him the First Cause. Some may think He is the Sun. Some may simply call Him God. We call Him the Great Pal. Oh yes. I was once as startled as you, my friend. I call you "my friend", although I dislike you. We are allergic. But still, I call you "my friend" because I know that is as The Pal would wish it.'

'Very nice of Him,' said Mrs Rice.

'No bitterness, *please*,' said Miss Dredger. 'That is the very thing we are going to pluck out of this island, like a thorn from the flesh.'

'You are ambitious,' said Mr Rice. 'Very ambitious. No?' He passed his huge hand across the bas-relief of his face and came as usual across no obstacles. A gold tooth shone in the moonlight as he opened his mouth again.

'But you do not take me altogether by surprise,' he continued, 'not altogether. After all, we are not *visitors*. When things occur we are not the last to lay our ears to the ground – are we, dear?'

'We're not altogether backward, if that's what you mean, Arthur,' she replied.

'Not altogether,' Mr Rice agreed. 'After all there has been very little conversation on this island for the last few months that has not been about Mr Pye. It has been Mr Pye this, and Mr Pye that, morning, noon, and night – and I was quite put off by it all, it ruined my bridge; it ruined my temper, as we say in Sark, until – I *met* him. Ah: Ah; that was it.'

'I *loathed* him until the day I saw him,' said Mrs Rice – 'and heard his *voice*.'

'We're not religious, you know,' said Mr Rice, turning his big, bland face to Miss Dredger. It sounded as though he were anxious to clear himself of a stigma. 'But fair do's all round: that's something that's worth a thousand creeds.'

Miss Dredger thrust out her chin and inhaled deeply.

'You just haven't *begun*,' she said at last.

'What do you mean?' said Mrs Rice. '*What* hasn't Arthur begun? And what about me? I suppose I haven't begun either. Let me tell you that I began ten years before you were born. I never have been ashamed of my age, have I, Arthur?'

'Quiet!' said Miss Dredger. Something of Mr Pye's authoritative power had welled up in her. 'Quiet!' she said again, although no sound had followed her first peremptory order.

'Your ideas are too easy, and too glib, Mr Rice. You speak like an adolescent, my dear man. Your forty years on the South American pampas have been no guide to the treasures of life. Fair shares for all! – or whatever you called it! Really. It sounds like the bargain basement. And yet I used to be very like you once. Before I met the chief. I was also an extrovert.'

'Were you?'

'Indeed I was, but where, oh where is Georgy? I shall have to ask the chief again. He is really *so* naughty with his mysteries.'

She got up and smacked the sand from her skirt, but before she had taken a step, Mr Rice had risen and was holding her arm.

'I don't know that "the wife" would cotton on, but I seem to have an inkling of what you mean, Miss Dredger, and if I'm wrong you can call me *Beetlejuice*.'

'Eh?' said Miss Dredger. 'What's that, my dear man?'

'You can bally well call me Chimborazo if I don't see what you're driving at – you and Pye,' he said. 'Listen . . .'

But before Mr Rice could dilate his wife was beside him. Sitting on the ground the two of them had some kind of cohesion. There was no reason why they should not be man and wife; but now that they stood side by side the idea was grotesque.

Mrs Rice barely reached the height of his hip. She was almost square, with short thick legs supporting her at the lower corners. She wore a huge wide-brimmed straw hat held in place (quite unnecessarily, for there was no wind) by a long patterned scarf which was stretched over the crown and then down the sides of the head (bending the straw brim and forcing it to lie flat along her cheeks), and was then tied under her chin. The effect was pure Little Miss Muffet until one saw the face which was concentrated Spider.

'What is Arthur saying?' she said.

Miss Dredger exhaled and then, turning to Mr Rice instead of answering his wife, she said:

'Good man. We will talk about it later. Meanwhile, learn what you can, and draw her in.'

'Who?' said Mr Rice.

'Your wife,' said Miss Dredger. 'All are welcome to the Kingdom of Our Pal. There are no exceptions.'

Mr Rice turned his eyes to his wife and with his characteristic consideration for others he was glad that this was so.

'Chief,' said Miss Dredger, 'allow me to butt in. I've got the breeze up somewhat about Georgy.'

'Ah, sailor, my dear – now mind your feet – there's a good girl – you've covered that jelly with sand, and I *was* keeping it for your chum.'

'You're keeping something back for her – Oh good show!' said Miss Dredger. 'But where *is* she, chief? Where *is* she?'

'Sailor dear,' said Mr Pye, 'be patient – and trust your chief if you can.'

'Oh yes, of course I can, but . . .'

'I have been trying to explain to Major Havershot that, living in a two-dimensional world makes it necessarily more difficult for him to conceive of us living in the three dimensions. It is as though we both of us could *see*, and both of us could taste, but only one of us could *hear* as well. He cannot grasp what I mean by the fullness of life.'

Mr Pye patted Major Havershot on the knee and beamed at Miss Dredger at the same time. It was almost as though his face burst into light, so charged was he with the intensity of his universal love.

He had been strangely quiet during the picnic meal. Everything had gone so smoothly that there had been no need to talk. Not that Mr Pye ever needed an incentive. But tonight it was as though his faith had for the moment, by reason of its spiritual ebullience, left no room in him for speech.

Major Havershot began to fill his pipe with long bony fingers.

'According to you, Pye, I am missing by about one third. I do not for a moment admit this, but it is an amusing supposition. Surely, in that case, I would be unbalanced?'

'You *are* unbalanced, my dear friend. The whole world is unbalanced. There are a few of us, a very few, who fight to keep it upright. Let us pray that our numbers thrive and multiply and the seed of our seed for ever.'

'Hear, hear!' said Miss Dredger.

'There's no doubt about the world being unbalanced, Pye. No doubt at all. I give you that. I never have trusted it at the best of times. If you stamp on something *here*, it pops up *there*. If you leave it alone it goes bad. Now take Russia . . .'

'I am not interested in nationalities,' said Mr Pye. 'A negro and an Eskimo are the same thing to me.'

'Ah, but not to *them*, Pye. Not to *them*, my dear chap. Not by a long chalk! Take Russia.'

'The chief doesn't want to take her,' said Miss Dredger. 'What could he do with her?' (She smiled fiercely.)

'There is a lot I could do with her, sailor dear,' said Mr Pye. 'But not yet. There is a time to strike and a time to refrain from striking.'

'That's all very well, Pye,' said the major, 'but it is unlikely that the world will wait for the moment that *you* choose. Or isn't it?' he added, for Mr Pye's face was all but incandescent.

'Go on, my dear major,' whispered Mr Pye. 'Go on, my dear fellow.'

'Well, what I mean is – let us take it, Pye, that the Russians, if you follow me, are swarming over the horizon in their thousands, filling the sky with their bombers, Pye . . .'

Mr Pye popped a fruit-drop in his mouth. 'A murmuration of Stalins, as it were. . . .' he said. 'Now come, come, come, come – what would they want in Sark? If they came, supposing they had anywhere to land, and supposing there was anything in Sark for them to come for, I would tell them quite simply, to return to the land that gave them birth. To return quickly. It is only that they are naughty, just as we can sometimes be naughty. They have not found their Pal, that is all. One cannot condemn those who have never found their Pal. But one thing at a time . . . one thing at a time – it is Sark that we are healing now, isn't it? Not Russia. Russia can follow. Yes, dear. . . ?' He turned his face up to Miss Dredger. 'What is it?'

'Mrs Porter is trying to tell you how much she enjoyed her meal.'

'No! no! but how kind!' said Mr Pye. 'But where *is* the dear thing?'

'Darling Mr Pye,' cried out a voice from the other side of the bonfire.

Mr Pye raised his arms to shoulder level, an all-embracing gesture, and peered across the wavering firelit air for the face that belonged to the voice.

'Here I am, poppet,' it cried again, and Mr Pye fixed his eye on Mrs Porter, a faint frown disturbing his lambent brow. His nose, like a quill, seemed sharper than ever as though it were keeping pace with the penetrating speed of his thoughts.

To be called 'poppet' by Mrs Porter was not at all as it should be. The wine had obviously gone to the lady's head. Nevertheless he kept his arms in the air for a little longer, as though embracing all things, for Mr Pye was magnanimous to a fault.

'It's been the very duck of a picnic, you clever, clever little thing,' she cried, her voice in a higher register than usual, which meant that it was very high indeed. 'Picnics can be such a *bore* and the weather so *thoughtless*. In fact the more one knows of nature the more one realizes what a bloody-minded old thing she is. Oh, I could smack her sometimes. But tonight! Oh, I'll never forget it! The moon, the stars, the wine, the dusk, the whole cleverness of it – and all because of you, the sweetest cherub to have ever twinkled on his very own little feet!'

'Sit down,' said a very tired voice.

'Yes, dear,' said Mrs Porter, and she said no more for a very long time.

'That was kind of you, Mr Porter,' said Mr Pye.

'It was effective,' said Mr Porter. 'Drink is not good for her.'

'You are afraid of what she might say, is that it, my friend? What does it matter what she says? And I want you *all* to listen to this. Every one of you. The very dear Mrs Porter, who is withal *such* a friend, has been happy. What more could we wish?'

He ran his eye over the group before him in whose midst sat Mrs Porter, her lips trembling with her longing to talk. But there was no possibility of that. Mr Pye was warming to his subject.

Before him as he spoke, the great oven of cunningly arranged boulders was sending up its tongues of flame into the darkness overhead. The high stack of driftwood which had been collected together was getting low, but there was still enough for the next two or three hours. The boulders were vermilion with the heat, and the black tar bubbled and trickled sluggishly between them.

All about them lay the remnants of the meal. It had been a perfect affair as Mrs Porter had said. Nothing had been forgotten.

The duck and the pigeons had spun on the spit. The wines had circulated in wise and comely order – and the genius of Mr Pye was felt behind everything.

If it had a fault it was that Mr Pye's picnic set too high a standard. Any future banquet had little hope of being unequivocally appreciated – for there would always be a few to remember this classic spread, with Derrible aflame with fire and moonlight.

As Mr Pye spoke, the company, recognizing the authority in his voice, and warming to that note of rare sincerity, drew closer about him. There must have been two score of them who, finding by degrees that they were not so much a group as a congregation, began to fold their hands and think in whispers.

Certainly there was something in the way that the buttressed and precipitous walls rose up behind them that gave a cathedral atmosphere which, now that Mr Pye was touching upon subjects of fundamental importance, was most appropriate.

'My friends,' said Mr Pye, motioning Mrs Rice (with a happy frown and a wag of his forefinger) to be seated – 'my friends, I will not be hypocritical and ask you if you enjoyed your meal – because I *know* that you enjoyed it. I could see a happy light in your eyes and your eager expressions in the firelight. And I am delighted that this is so. But I want to ask you whether, having satisfied the body, it would be right for us to leave the mind to fend for itself? It it not just as possible for the mind to be as hungry as the body? And for the soul to be as hungry as the mind?

'Let us then have no reason to remember this night as something lopsided: but as something serene in its proportions – a thing in equipoise.

'Now I have been studying this island, as you all know. Some may have wondered at my curiosity. Some may not. For myself I can only say that my sense of wonder has grown. Here in this little island I have watched, in microcosm, the "world and his wife" go by – and sometimes I have seen, unless I am mistaken, the world go by with someone else's wife!

'But I have not come here to preach. I have nothing to sell. All I have, my friends, is something to *give*. For giving is as different a thing from selling as right is from wrong, as wickedness is from the ways of Our Pal – of whom I will speak in more detail later.

'I have something to give. To give with both hands. Then why am I waiting? I will tell you. Firstly because I have no power to give until that splendid moment when I see your hands stretched forward to receive. You can take a horse to the pond but you can't make it drink. My friends. You are the horses: but will you drink? Not yet, I say to myself; not yet. Although your throats are parched: although your lips are cracked: not yet: I say to myself: not yet.

'And what is my second reason for delaying the conversion...? Shall I tell you...?'

'Yes, yes, Pye, but take Russia,' said a voice. 'It seems to me that...' but the major's voice was drowned in an angry 'shushing'.

'We will have quite a talk about that some other time, shall we, major? Quite a talk,' said Mr Pye. The moonlight glinted from the lenses of his glasses and was reflected from the top of his head and from the waxen thorn of his nose.

'Where was I? Ah, quite so. I was giving you my second reason for delay. It will be a surprise to you. I hope a happy one. If you will all sit quietly here I will, I truly believe, return with an army.'

'How do you mean, chief?'

'You may come with me, sailor.'

Miss Dredger was at his side in an instant, her brogues churning the sand.

'Are you there, sir?' cried out Mr Pye.

'Very much so,' said Mr Rice. 'Absolutely here, and all agog, as we say in Sark.'

'Then I leave it to you to build up the fire, my dear chap. It is failing.'

As Mr Pye, with Miss Dredger at his side, began to move

smartly away across the sands they caught sight of Thorpe approaching.

'And how has the sketching gone?' cried Mr Pye.

'Altogether and for good,' was the nocturnal answer.

'Ah,' said Mr Pye, 'I think I follow – but . . .'

'Rectangles with holes in them – ha! ha! ha! ha!' was the only rejoinder, the last 'ha' scarcely audible, for the shivering painter was making rapidly for the fire.

Once or twice Miss Dredger threw out a word or two, questioning the reason for their departure from the fire: and for the direction that her chief was taking, which seemed to her to have no other purpose than to land them in a wilderness of pools and slippery rocks. But Mr Pye said nothing until they were all but in the wild, when he grasped her elbow between his thumb and forefinger.

'Sailor,' he said, 'I have chosen you to come with me because you are, in this evangelical adventure, no less than my right hand. My thoughts have been your thoughts and yours have been mine. We have held nothing back from one another. But tonight I have until now remained reserved. But only because there is certain strength in privacy, and I have needed that private strength until this moment.'

'That's fair enough, chief.'

'You see, my dear, I positively know that these rocks are alive.'

Miss Dredger, for the fraction of a moment, had reverted to her two-dimensional days, and shot a glance at Mr Pye – a glance of what amounted to suspicion. But it was only for an instant.

'It was not for nothing that I combed this island, dear – learning the ways of the place. I knew within a very short while that as a sounding board it took some beating. To trip over a stone at the harbour was to cause someone a mile away and on the other side of Sark to say: "How clumsy Mr Pye is." '

'True enough,' said Miss Dredger.

'Oh yes, I soon realized that to try and keep anything hidden in Sark is as futile as it is wrong – for what is there to hide, if you are selfless? And so I knew that to have a midnight picnic would be to draw the island down to the sea – to have it in Derrible would give them somewhere to hide among the rocks – and to have them here would be to have them in the hollow of my hand.'

'Good Lord, chief, do you mean that there ...'

'Exactly, sailor. Wait here for a moment – it will be a crucial one.'

He stood still for a moment and shut his eyes. Then without a glance to his left or right he walked smartly away from his lieutenant, his back as straight as a rod, his belly neat, compact and rounded, his nose pointing the way like a bird's beak. He began to climb the rocks until he came to a slanting ridge, and there he stood in the dazzling moonlight.

Miss Dredger clenched her hands together. In the profound hush of the night she could hear the sighing of the distant tide as it turned in its sleep, and then, as though to prevent itself from falling asleep again, heaved a slow breath, and the giant breast of the water shuddered and lay still once more, as though waiting.

And then, suddenly, Miss Dredger heard his voice. He had raised it a little so that it rang among the rocks with a strange, almost elfin quality – gay, authoritative, unique, a cadence and a tone never forgotten.

'I knew you would not fail me!'

Scores of heads looked up from the waste of shingle. Scores peered round the corners of rocks, from which vantage points, with the aid of binoculars, they had watched every mouthful of the picnic. The rocks, as Mr Pye had surmised, were alive.

'My friends! I am not here to make a proclamation, though it may look like it. I have not come to surprise you, though I may have done so. I have come because I had to come. You have drawn me to these rocks and it is my faith that I shall draw you from them. We have need of each other. You are many, I am few.'

Of the scores of moonstruck faces there were three who had their mouths shut.

'Why were you not called to my party? Why? Because it

was my wish to segregate you, to divide the residents from the islanders? Surely not. Was it because of the difficulty of providing enough for your healthy appetites? No. That would have been a challenge, no doubt. But I would have faced it.

'I will tell you why it was. It was because this is *your* island. To have invited you to Derrible would have been like inviting the Queen to sit on her throne, or a bishop to climb to his pulpit, or a kangaroo to make itself at home in Australia. It would have been grotesque. This is your ancient isle. I can invite you, at a stretch, to my house – but to invite you, all of you, to one of your own beaches, is unthinkable.'

He paused a moment, to extract a fruit-drop from his little box, and then flicked it into his mouth.

'My skipper, the Great Pal, who is here beside me, invisible though he may be to you, is conscious of all this. He is at my elbow, but He is at your elbow too. He is at everybody's elbow. He is in the joints of these high cliffs where they articulate. He is in that barrel of beer. He is worth meeting. He and I are full of hope. Of hope that you will follow me. Come, come, my silent friends: come out of the shadows. I have something very special to show you. Come – come . . . come.'

Acting in unison, as though they were all part of one enormous machine, the scores of Sarkese rose to their feet, and drifted like somnambulists in Mr Pye's direction, as with slow rhythmical movements of his arms he beckoned them towards him, while he retreated over the rocks, moving gradually backwards to the cliffs. Out of the crannies of the rocks they came, out of the caves, out of the shadows, and within a few minutes the great spaces of the gleaming tidal beach were susurrant with the sound of sea-boots sinking and lifting in the wet sand.

Miss Dredger had heard every word, but in spite of her faith in her chief, had never imagined such a scene as this. Awe-struck, she walked at his side, guiding him by little pushes or whispers of 'left a little' or 'more to the right', as, never turning his face from them he brought them forth from the rocks, while the fire beneath the cliffs grew momently nearer.

FIFTEEN

OUT to sea there was something that did not seem to be a part of the bay. The moonlight lingered on it, caressing its indolent length, but what it was Tintagieu could not make out. She was the only one left among the rock-pools. A breeze from the sea was sending its first few puffs across the rocks, and they lifted a hair or two from the black mass upon her head. She was eating a sandwich and drinking beer – apparently self-absorbed, and utterly careless of the fate of her uncles, and aunts and nieces and cousins and brothers-in-law and sisters out of law, and half-brothers once removed, and three-quarter sisters never to be removed, in all that horde, in fact, of interwoven humanity who were now like the famous rodents of Hamelin, following the Pied Piper across the lunar sands.

Born in Sark: bred in Sark: she was nevertheless more *on* than *of* the island. Something rebellious moved her to do the opposite: to always do the opposite. And yet, paradoxically, it was she, whenever anything derogatory was said of her home or her relations – (for her relations were everyone's relations, and everyone's relations were hers) – it was *she* who could be so particularly violent: she had left her tooth-marks in a tea-broker's wrist, and the weals had lasted him for his entire holiday: she had haunted a saleable house for five months, until it became finally so unsaleable that ivy filled the hall, and the island rats with their unique grey fur, made of the place a splendid G.H.Q.

A hundred tales were told of Tintagieu. She had slept with so many visitors, residents, and locals that she was no longer so much a whore as an institution. Something quite apart from normal laws: something to be proud of. There had been years when her timetable was so full that her inability to accept more than a fraction of the innumerable invitations that were tendered her in the name of bliss, had the paradoxical effect of giving her a reputation for a mad kind of chastity, a crazy, indecipherable coyness, among those who had but recently arrived.

'Oh, Mister So-and-So,' she would say, 'I know it is a lovely night indeed, with that same old fat-faced moon, but you do know, dearie, don't you, that I have no time at all: you *know* that my dolly needs me. I put her to sleep at five.'

'Your *dolly*?' the male would say. 'What dolly?'

'My china dolly.'

'You put her to *sleep*! Come off it.' Or: 'What can you mean?' or 'Fantastic,' or 'Good God. Damn your dolly,' or some such rejoinder would follow, according to the upbringing of the male.

'Yes,' said Tintagieu. 'My dolly wouldn't know what to do if I left her all alone, without her bath, and a gob-stopper.'

'Well, what about tomorrow night?'

'That would be lovely, dear,' Tintagieu might say. 'Tomorrow night. At the foot of the Bongo-Wongo cliff, at three in the morning. Remind me in a week's time, dear, to meet you tomorrow night – at the foot of Bongo-Wongo.'

She had a playful humour. Strong men would search the isle for Bongo-Wongo, which was a name of her own invention. She would stick to a few phrases. 'My dolly'. 'Bongo-Wongo'. 'I'm so expensive, darling' (which she would say with one hand on her hip, while the other played with her hair). She had a little repertoire of sentences and postures. They seemed to give her endless private pleasure. They seemed to make her utterly innocent. To talk with Tintagieu was to experience childhood all over again. She loved to make love as a child loves to play. But even a child can tire at times of its favourite game, and it was then, or when she had a previous engagement, that she resorted to her 'dolly', or to 'Bongo-Wongo'.

Her vitality was of a curious kind. Those who saw her for the first time would say she was lethargic. It is true that she was always going to sleep. She made no effort. People came to her. When she was alone she curled up like a cat, perfectly content with her own company. This had been quite maddening for her admirers, whose tossings and turnings had weakened the springs of many a strong bed.

One year she had been very careless and might well have found herself married, for she had been too lazy and vague to realize how deeply involved she had become with the Honourable Peter Cragg, a yachtsman of class. She had not even realized that the date of the wedding had been fixed and that she was to become his wife in the island church – for the Hon. Peter Cragg was a sentimentalist. He on his part had returned to England to get his old mother's house in order, and to find an apartment in the next road for his old mother. He had done innumerable things. When he returned to Sark with his best man a day before the wedding and overhauled the wedding details, temporal and spiritual – he made a vow that he would not see his bride until they met in the church. He was a romantic soul and was full of ideas like this. He was also very rich and full of lust. A fine fellow.

But Tintagieu, who had forgotten all about the Honourable Peter Cragg directly that gentleman had stepped off the island, failed to turn up for her wedding. Having forgotten all about her engagement, what could be more natural than for her to forget all about her wedding. After an hour of shuffling, the congregation eventually departed.

When the Hon. Peter Cragg learned that she had been found curled up in bed with her head beneath the blankets and that she had been woken only after great difficulty, for she had had an exhausting time on the previous night, he departed also, and has since then cared little for small islands or dark and sleeping women.

It was a warm night for the time of year, but it was not a warm time of year, so Tintagieu sat up at last and pulled on the duffle coat which one of her forgotten friends had left behind one bright and careless morning.

And then she gazed once more at that part of the shimmering sea that seemed to have congealed, and she found that the enigma had come closer – and then, all in an instant, she realized what it was. At that moment of recognition the slight sea breeze strengthened. She threw back her head so that her hair flapped like a pirate's flag, she arched her nostrils, she raised an eyebrow. And then she grinned like a child.

Hours ago, when the paraphernalia needed for the picnic was being carried down the zigzag path to the bay, Miss George had already begun to feel peculiar.

She had watched the proceedings with a sense of doom. Why had no one told her how *she* was to get down? The moonbeams had gloated on her purple busby but she had known nothing of this, nor would the knowledge have helped her.

Among the rugs, the ground-sheets, the sack of coals (to reinforce the driftwood), the cooking and roasting utensils, the barrel of fresh water, the quoits, the bell-tent, and a score of other things that were carried down the path, Miss George's arm-chair had not been included. It had come in the cart with the rest, but it was not carried to the bay.

Miss George had heard of the chimney, but she had never imagined and nor had anyone else until Mr Pye had come along, that it could solve the problem of her descent.

At the foot of the cliff in the northern elbow of the bay a natural archway led, not to a finite cave, but to a shaft that rose in gloomy darkness tinged with red, to where it drew breath, an irregular circle of breath, which from the base of the chimney, looking up, seemed no larger than a plate. To-night the plate was filled with stars.

When she and Mr Pye and the rest of the party had reached

a certain grassy knoll from which vantage point they could see the bay spreading below them in a luminous sheet of sand, Mr Pye ordered Miss Dredger, Thorpe, Mr Stitchwater, the Rices, the Porters, Major Havershot and the rest, including the carriers, to proceed to the zigzag path, keeping back only Miss George, to whom he gave his arm.

He had studied the lie of the land on several previous occasions and he knew the best way to reach the precipitous lip of the chimney. It was no easy affair, nevertheless, by moonlight when all the landmarks appeared strange and out of scale. The murderous hole was surrounded by thorn bushes, and irregular bracken-covered ground.

'Where are you taking me?' Miss George had muttered peevishly.

'Along a chosen path, my dear.'

'A chosen path?'

'A chosen path.'

'Who chose it?'

'Your chief chose it – with the aid of his Pal.'

'It's not a good way, to my mind,' Miss George had said. 'It is prickly.'

'How wise, how very wise. Prickles are more than they seem, my dear. They are symbolic. Through prickles to the land of milk and honey!'

'We never packed any honey,' said Miss George. 'Every other sort of sandwich. And my feet are hurting.'

'That's symbolic too. It may be that your arches are not the only things that have fallen.'

'But I still don't see . . .'

'There is no need to see. Vision needs no spectacles. Mind that branch, my dear, it is no good pushing through the scrub like that.'

Miss George was a difficult woman to steer through undergrowth, and it had been a relief to Mr Pye to negotiate her through the last belt of waist-high ferns. He told her with deep emotion to sit down.

'Sit down . . . where?'

'Sit down, my dear.' Mr Pye's eyes had been very bright as

though with tears. His legs had trembled, but he had stood as upright as a grenadier.

'You know I can't just sit down. I wish I could. Really!'

'Look to your left, my dear. And tell me what you see.'

Miss George, her eyes protruding unpleasantly, had found herself staring at her own favourite arm-chair. Her soft, freckled hand had risen to her face and she had tucked three finger-tips between her trembling bottom lip and her lower set.

'Good Lord!' she had whispered, in that wheezing voice of hers. 'How did it get here . . . and why are . . . what are . . . they doing, those men? Why . . . is that you, Mr le Neidre – and you, Mark Loupé? . . . Really!'

'It is me, Miss George, and no mistake about eet, and are you well for the time of year? I hope and pray so. . . .'

'Everything to hand?' Mr Pye had asked, his voice shaking a little for, strong as he was in his faith, it was not every day that he could claim to be putting into action what he believed in spirit – to be watching his belief bear fruit. The transport which he had begun to experience more vividly than ever before had had the effect of denuding his conversation of all its habitual sparkle. He had been left, this great moment, with nothing but the simplest and least provocative words at his command.

He had turned again to the two men.

'Everything to hand?'

'To hand?' Mr Loupé had frowned and bitten his lip.

'I have put it badly. Forgive me, my friend. You have the rope and hooks? You have fixed the screw-eyes into the lady's chair? You have rehearsed with an eighteen-stone boulder? You have no questions?'

'That's eet, Mr Pye.'

And then he turned his lambent face to Miss George. 'My dear,' he whispered, 'you are to be my first martyr – but with a difference. For you are to sustain no kind of wound. You will be frightened. Yes. What lady would not be frightened to go down this well in a chair, but . . .'

Miss George's face had gone green in the moonlight and she

had collapsed into her chair as though she had been struck behind the knees.

She had obviously been in no condition to take in anything that was said to her. For a moment Mr Pye had wondered whether his Pal were wise to have suggested so drastic a novitiate. So dire a tutelage. But who was he to question the supernal voice – the voice of his Pal? There had been no doubt about its authenticity. 'Lower the great weight,' it had said. 'Let her descend only to rise again. For Miss George is more than Miss George.'

'And a good deal more, at that,' he had thought, for in the Faith of the Pal there was no bar on levity unless it were malicious. A joke or two at solemn moments was sometimes salutary, for humour after all was a sweet and precious thing – not something to be ashamed of.

No. If it seemed cruel, yet it was the will of his Pal who was everywhere at once, and would no doubt go down the shaft with her, for He was in the wood and leather of her chair, in the ropes and the iron hooks, and even, who knows, in the screw-eyes.

Stretching himself he had turned to the men. 'It is going to be difficult for you, my dear fellows,' he said, 'and because this is so I propose to increase your wages by an additional bonus of two pounds to be divided equally between you. When you hear my first blast' (and Mr Pye had brought out the metal whistle to show them), 'you will prepare her for her descent, calming her all you can. At the second blast you will start to lower her over the verge ... very slowly; very slowly. An accident would spoil the whole effect – and my Pal' (he had said to himself as he turned sharply on his heel) 'would lose His trust in me.'

Of all that congregation on the beach, not a single figure had turned his eyes to the sea for over an hour. Rapt, motionless, their gaze focused upon the mercurial visitor whose hypnotic language, purring and dancing across the sands, involved them in a rhythm and a mood impossible to resist.

The Sarkese made no sound.

Among the islanders sat the residents and the visitors.

The bell-tent had been pitched and at its mouth stood Mr Pye, his back to the canvas and the towering cliffs. Beside him on his left sat Miss Dredger on an upturned hamper. On his right, where someone was needed if only to balance Miss Dredger, there was a significant emptiness.

Mr Pye had kept his eyes upon his congregation, picking out one character after another until, having made contact with the individual parts, he could concentrate upon them as a whole, and with an intimacy that would otherwise have been impossible. And so, keeping his eyes, as well as his voice, for ever on the move, yet always within the compass of the dappled pattern which his audience created, he was unable to see that as the tide was drawing closer every moment, it was at the same time bringing something with it. This something was, as yet, three or four hundred yards from the shore, but it had already caused Mrs Porter to wrinkle her little nose, which had once been the toast of Smarden. She had no idea that she had wrinkled it, but she had, for her membrane was of the rarest and most delicate order.

As Mr Pye debated upon the vision in his mind – the vision of a Sark, purified by its own recognition of the supernatural, purified by the ceaseless battle for self-improvement, purified and made happy by this common aim, so that it became the Mecca, the panacea, the envy, not only of other little islands, thwarted and eternally bruised with internecine warfare – but the envy of the whole world, who would come to know of this little paradise, not more than three miles long, and would set sail for its rugged coast, that they might learn the Faith.

But all this, Mr Pye explained, was a mere pipe dream were it for a moment forgotten that such a state could only come about as a result of individual sacrifice and much heart-searching. There was no easy way. Private grievances, jealousies, feuds and greed were sores upon the island's back – carbuncles of the worst kind.

But wait. It must be remembered that not a soul sitting there before him, at that moment, no single creature had any need to fight alone. There was no value or sense in loneliness for its own sake. Faith was not something that came easily. Mr Pye knew this from his own experience. How had *he* triumphed? He had triumphed not through his own abilities taken upon their own, but through the grace of the Great Pal, who was in everything.

Mr Pye had explained the nature of the Pal several minutes earlier and there was no need for him to go into all that again. What was important was that his congregation were in his power and so, taking a step forward he held up his arms, and at that very moment a gust from the sea brought with it something quite indescribably unpleasant. But the gust had gone its way and nothing followed and the members of the moonlit congregation, after glancing speculatively at one another, fixed their eyes on Mr Pye again.

'Courage!' said Mr Pye. 'Have courage! Courage to change your habits and to change them without groaning, to change them in a gay and happy way. Courage to test yourself. Courage to go where there is danger – spiritual and physical. It is best, my friends, to start with the physical and go on to the spiritual later. It's no good rushing it.' He clasped his hands before him and raised his voice and cried out with an intense and shattering happiness: 'Brothers! Sweet throng of brothers! Whatever your leanings – whether they have been, shall I say, "High Tide", or "Low Tide" – whether your imaginations can be stirred – dilated – so that you can comprehend at a single stroke the essence of my teaching, or whether your imaginations have atrophied so that you fly to me for purely emotional reasons – whatever the cause may be, I have news for you! News! my sweet throng, and news of high immediacy and pith. You shall be witnesses. "Witnessess?" I hear you murmur. "Witnesses of what?" I will tell you, ladies. I will tell you, gentlemen. Miss Agnes George is coming down the chimney.'

Simultaneously, and with a distinct crack like that of a whip, for there was no dearth of fibrositis on the island, every head turned to the northern elbow of the bay where the tunnelled entrance to the cave that was not a cave yawned from its jaws of stone.

The heads turned back again and the scores of faces shone vacantly in the moonlight.

'In talking to you tonight, in exhorting you to give the Pal a trial, I have left behind no trail of pious words – no phrases without substance – and to prove that this is so I am going to show how courage, high courage, can explode as it were with beauty and transfigure even the most simple of heart and mind, and the least heroic of frame and limb.'

Miss Dredger, who was beside herself with conjecture, lit a cigarette with a trembling hand and put the wrong end in her mouth, but she hardly felt the pain.

'Did you say she's coming down the chimney? – not Georgy surely – what can you mean, chief? What can you mean?'

'She is coming down the chimney. A lady, not in the best of health, is descending through the dark, not of her own will, but because it is right that she should do so, not only for herself but for us all. She is our exemplar, sailor. Our dear exemplar.'

Mr Pye took out his scout's whistle, and as he blew, the shrill note rang against the cliffs and rebounded to and fro, the echoes growing ever more distant and thin and plaintive until the absolute nocturnal silence was restored.

'If you would be good enough, my brothers, to stay where you are until I beckon to the foot of the chimney, it would help me to perfect my plans for her reception.'

No one moved; but all at once, after so long a while of silence, the flood-gates creaked, bulged and broke into fragments and a husky babble of conversation swept the beach, a babble that grew louder and louder and more and more excited.

Some were quite sure that they were in a dream and waited patiently for their wits to return, but for the most part the congregation accepted the fact that they had become the participants of an historic moment. They could converse, if the coherent ejaculations that poured forth could be called conversation – but they could not move without great difficulty, for cramp had settled on them like a plague of pins and needles.

'What Miss George can do, we all can do,' cried Mr Pye, and he blew his whistle again, and the echoes danced and died.

'It is through fear that she is being purged. Were she without fear she would be no better than a crocodile. Crocodiles are fearless through stupidity. We do not look to *them* for spiritual guidance. They cannot recognize fear any more than they can recognize evil. If they did recognize evil I doubt whether it would change their habits. But man is not like that, or in this case, woman, for Miss George is nothing if not a woman. Her fear is the forerunner of a bravery that we shall soon salute. Oh, my throng, my throng!' he cried, and his whole soul was in that cry. 'To your feet! Let us meet her.... She is even now descending with, can we doubt it, the Great Pal at her side.'

SIXTEEN

WHAT happened next was of a confusion so improbable, so unforeseen, that no one in recounting the tale ever kept to the same story more than once, or ever agreed with anyone else's version.

With no warning and cruel speed, Mr Pye realized that everything was slipping from his grasp. Something even more potent than the Great Pal had interposed its ugly self and plucked the prize from the palm of his hand. Until now he had had no cause for disappointment. On the contrary, his subconscious was congratulating itself on the progress he had made (his conscious self having, of course, no time to dwell on anything that was not on the highest level of humility and leadership).

But then, all at once, his approaching triumph was halted. His hope recoiled and collapsed, for the sea breeze had at last decided to puff steadily into the embayment and the stench of a small dead whale monopolised the scene.

Torn between extreme curiosity in regard to what kind of a descent Miss George could be making, and extreme nausea, for with every whiff the small whale reaffirmed its hold upon the bay, the islanders began to move hither and thither like lost souls. Some were pointing at the stranded thing, their eyes like saucers. Some were already vomiting. Some were actually running across the sands to the chimney and with their handkerchiefs to their noses, were peering up the great flue of rock – and indeed there *was* something happening in the gloom above them. Something was certainly coming down to the accompaniment of a thin wheezy scream. Others, of more delicate gorge, were already beginning to climb the zigzag path, to what they hoped would be an altitude less sickening.

The rest were moving about the beach like somnambulists. Those who had their handkerchiefs held them to their faces.

Had it not been for Mr Pye's faith, there is no knowing how this bewildering state of affairs would have ended. The shock for the congregation had been cruel. From the summit of metaphysics and the essence of love they had all of a sudden been woken to the beastliness of physical decay. The little dead whale must have been dead for a long, long time.

It was at moments such as this that Mr Pye rose to his full stature. Not for a moment did he despair. It would be too much to say that he felt no pangs. It would hardly have been human to have escaped them. But he turned his back upon self-pity and assumed, as he always did, undisputed command of the situation. His neat brain ticked away like a miracle of modern machinery.

Within a few moments he had organized the salvaging of all valuables left on the beach, which were to be deposited above high-water for the night.

Then, as the stink grew momently more revolting, he led Miss Dredger, Mr Porter, Major Havershot, the painter, the two Sarkese fishermen, to the foot of the chimney, where they found Miss George sitting in her arm-chair, the long ropes, slack and coiled upon the rocks. She was in a state of coma and stared unseeingly as they approached. When Mr Pye jerked on the rope as though it were a bell-pull, and received no response, he jerked again. This time there *was* a response, but of a very dangerous kind. The men above must have let her down and disappeared after the first whiff of updraught from the whale.

Not only this; they had failed to fasten the lines to anything at all, and so at Mr Pye's second pull, the four lengths of heavy rope skidded across the bracken-covered turf like four snakes and slipping over the lip of the chimney hurtled down to the cave two hundred feet below. It was a miracle that no one was so much as touched by this sudden and murderous descent. Such dereliction of duty was unforgivable, but Mr Pye forgave them instantly.

He was in no state to feel anything but compassion. His flock, his throng, as he loved to call them, had been cheated of fulfilment. They had sat so quietly. They had behaved so admirably. They had listened so hard. As the night had worn on he had begun to reach a state bordering on the ecstatic. It was as though he were so full of love and hope that he would not have found it strange to levitate or to walk an inch or two above the ground.

And then the small, dead whale and the disintegration that followed!

To some, the inevitable abandoning of his plan to present Miss George to the multitude as his first martyr might be judged as a failure – a let-down – even a tragedy. But from the point of view of the spirit, it was something more like triumph. For Mr Pye knew that love throve on adversity, that the whale had been sent to tease him, that it was all the work of that invisible power of darkness whom some called the Devil.

And so, at the very moment when most men would have broken down, Mr Pye exulted.

To Messrs Porter, Havershot, Thorpe, and Rice and the two Sarkese as they stood around the motionless Miss George, it seemed as though his spiritual being, shining as it did through his eyes, and in every little movement of his body, was going too far – as though there were something hectic about it. And yet it was not what he did, or even how he looked, it was that a kind of frantic emanation, a plethora of glory was being freed.

So identified was he in mind and spirit with the Great Pal that there was no such thing as failure. When everything has a purpose it would be plainly illogical to feel aggrieved about anything whatsoever. The whale had been sent. There had been a change of plan. That was all. He would have a chat with the Great Pal and proceed upon the next stage of his evangelical mission.

What he loved was to be tested. Oh, the splendour of the fight. Even as he gave the five astounded men the order to carry Miss George up the zigzag path, he began to sing to himself:

> 'From earth's wide bounds, from ocean's farthest coast,
> Through gates of pearl stream in the countless host ...'

The smell was by now terrible. Miss Dredger had not said a word. She had not a tittle of Mr Pye's resilience. She could not understand why her chief was so happy. She stared at Miss George, her hands clasped behind her. As she smoked fiercely, the wreaths were drawn up the chimney.

How they ever got Miss George up the interminable path, they never knew. They left her as she was, in her arm-chair, and took a leg each – a wooden one – and relieving one another in rotation, panted and sweated their way uphill, save for Mr Pye, who led the way, moving over the rocks like a spruce spirit. Miss Dredger took up the rear and coughed her way through cigarette after cigarette.

The whale was everywhere.

When within a few feet of the summit, Mr Porter, stumbling on an outcrop of sharp rock, broke his ankle and had to hop most of the way home supported on one side by Miss Dredger.

Thorpe was nearly dead with heart failure. The terrible ordeal completely wiped his vision clear of the great painting which he had in mind. He was quite dark and empty again like a sponged slate.

Out to sea where there was no smell at all, for the wind never veered and blew steadily from the south-east, Tintagieu floated upon her back, while the inhabitants of the island closed their doors and windows against the insistence of the little dead whale.

She turned over indolently in the phosphorescent water and

swam round the point and eventually waded ashore three beaches to the east. She had left her clothes on a high rock and would call for them the next day.

As she sauntered home, plump and dripping, with a bit of seaweed stuck on one shoulder-blade, she passed the Clôs de Joi. It was by now about four in the morning. But there was someone standing at the gate, his eyes raised to the stars. He was utterly lost in his own thoughts, but his little plump arms were twisted behind his back and his quick little fingers were scratching at his shoulder-blades.

Tintagieu knew that unless she waited in the shadows for him to return up the drive to Miss Dredger's house – and there seemed no likelihood of that – she must necessarily be seen; and so she called, as she passed, in that husky voice of hers: 'Well, I've never seen you do *that* before, Mr Pye.'

'My child . . .' said Mr Pye . . . 'my stitchless child. Do what?'

'Scratch, scratch, scratch at your shoulder-blade. Really, Mr Pye!'

'You are naked. . . .' said Mr Pye.

'No!' said Tintagieu. 'Is *that* what it is?'

'It is right,' said Mr Pye. 'Absolutely right.'

'What is, Mr Pye?'

'Your nakedness is absolutely right. You have come for guidance?'

'No, no,' said Tintagieu. 'I am simply going home.'

'We are all doing that, my dear, but what can I say to you?'

'Just say goodnight, Mr Pye.'

Mr Pye, filled with an inner light, bowed to the naked girl. It was a beautiful bow, subtle and courteous. Then he smiled at her with a charm that was all his own.

'Good-night, my dear,' he said, 'and good-morning. What a splendid thing is the human body – quite, quite splendid. But doesn't it feel cold?'

'It does, my dear, now that you mention it. It does indeed – the rebellious *thing*.'

'Ha, ha, ha!' laughed Mr Pye, but his gaiety petered out, as with a thoughtful frown he experienced a renewal of the inexplicable itching. It was only with great difficulty that he refrained from scratching his shoulder-blades again. Exerting his will, he gripped the top of the gate.

'Poor Tintagieu,' he said. 'Would you care to drink a jug of coffee with me? I would dearly like to have you grace my table. There would be something fantastic about it. Something superbly bizarre. Something primordial.'

Tintagieu stood quite still in the stony lane and gazed at Mr Pye. Behind her, hardly visible, three gnarled old trees leaned across the darkness. Her strong, plump, lazy body was half melted into the first of the dawn.

'What a stink!' she muttered. 'How can you *bear* it, dear?'

'I no longer notice it,' he said – and then in a rush and in a manner quite out of character with all she knew of his way, he leaned over the gate. 'Tintagieu.'

'Yes. What is it?'

'In your nakedness you will understand.'

'Will I? Understand what? I'm getting bloody cold, dear, and my granny told me to be careful of the cold.'

'I have reached a stage, Tintagieu – a crucial stage in my spiritual development. It is almost as though I am fused with the Great Pal and that He has found me His perfect resting place.'

'You will feel better soon, I expect,' said Tintagieu.

'*Feel* better?' queried Mr Pye. 'How could I feel better? I am so much at peace that I cannot imagine how such splendour can last. Nothing can harm me, dear. I am inviolable. Now let me make you some coffee – or perhaps a nip of brandy? It is a tremendous night. You, and the whale, and me.'

'The stink is terrible,' said Tintagieu, 'and my dolly needs me.'

She turned and moved away with a soft ease of movement, sweet, wet and salty from the sea, self-contained, childish, amoral, primitive, the mistress of many and the property of none.

SEVENTEEN

DURING what was left of the night, though Mr Pye had tried to sleep he could not do so. He counted little white whales jumping over a hedge: he counted purple busbies floating down Derrible chimney like parachutes: he thought of this and that, and of all the knots that would be his to untie – for the night at the bay had posed a number of problems: but all this did no good. He could not sleep.

Before he dressed to go downstairs he manoeuvred the two mirrors in his room until he could see the state of his back. What he saw disturbed him (in spite of his inner knowledge that nothing *could* disturb him). It was not so much that he was surprised, after such a night of pain, to be faced with the two concentrated patches of inflammation, one upon each shoulder-blade, for there would be nothing very unusual about his having been bitten at that time of year – it was not *this* that impressed him – it was that he should have been bitten so *symmetrically*.

Perhaps the dead whale had something to do with it. Perhaps

after a long while of drifting down the currents and the long tides of the sea, strange and poisonous insects and a variety of vermin had taken up residence along the length of the poor thing – multiplying and germinating even more fiercely as their huge host grew from bad to worse.

But this was mere conjecture and evaded the problem. The fact that the origin of his bites or rashes might have been connected with the little whale in no way touched on the strange perfection of their positioning – staking their twin claims as they did at the dead centre of his scapulae.

Mr Pye had never been ill. His was one of those enviable constitutions that really worked. His appendix had never grown too long, nor his wind too short. His glands had kept themselves to themselves, unless it were argued that Mr Pye was in fact the direct result of their influence. At times of epidemic he had always escaped whatever germs were going. He did not really believe in pain, but was full of compassion for those who imagined themselves to be suffering.

And so it was less easy for him to *accept* the itching than it would have been for the normal run of men.

Miss George was confined to her bed. She refused to speak to anyone. Mr Pye visited her innumerable times and told her about the Great Pal – but Miss George showed no enthusiasm for his Deity. He was as gentle and patient as a nun. He showed by not so much as the lift of an eyebrow any sign of surprise that Miss George should wear her busby in bed.

At his side was Miss Dredger – but not even to her would Miss George utter a sound. It is true that between the two of them they defeated Miss George's hunger strike – by the sheer beauty of their cooking – but this was the only concession allowed them.

The truth of the matter was that Miss George could see no reason why, Great Pal or no Great Pal, she should ever have had to be lowered down Derrible chimney. She had worked very, very hard to help Miss Dredger prepare the picnic, and to have been forced to put up with such ignominy was something she would never forgive. 'Damn the Great Pal,' she whispered to herself hour after hour. 'Damn the Great Pal and damn 'em all.'

Meanwhile, these days, while Miss George lay muttering to herself, with her windows closed against the whale, a new and strange relationship had matured between Mr Pye and Miss Dredger. She no longer merely looked up to him; she did more than this – she became his confidante, and as such she began to be fond of him.

She could not share his view that the anti-climax down at Derrible was an act of intervention on the part of the Great Pal and was all for the best. She rather felt that the Great Pal had let the chief down badly. In consequence she felt a certain proprietary concern – a wish to protect her buoyant exemplar.

He had shown her the inflammation at his shoulder-blades and like Mr Pye she was also much surprised at their symmetrical disposition.

Every day the pain increased, and yet Mr Pye would not go to the doctor.

'*You* are my doctor, sailor,' he would say.

'I know most of the answers, chief, but I must say these blemishes beat me.'

'Blemishes, dear?' said Mr Pye. 'Blemishes don't itch. They are merely unsightly – you must try and use the right word.'

'Sorry, chief,' said Miss Dredger, 'but what's important is not whether I use the right word, but how to get you well again.'

'It is all interwoven,' said Mr Pye. 'One cannot segregate things in that arbitrary way – words and illnesses, tadpoles and tears, volcanoes and dominoes are all interwoven. What affects one thing affects all the rest.'

'That's all very well, chief, but I have failed to *cure* you.'

'I'm not a ham, dear.'

'I insist on our fetching the doctor.'

'I refuse to see him,' said Mr Pye, but in a rather faraway voice. 'He could do nothing.'

Mr Pye smiled with a flash and a twinkle of teeth and spectacles.

'When my Pal is ready to free me from the discomfort He will act, sailor.'

He rose from the chair in which he had been sitting and, walking to the door, turned his back to it and worked his shoulder-blades to and fro against the panels.

'I do not in any case believe in doctors. Come, come, my dear, it is time for the poultice.'

'What good will the poultice do, if our Pal isn't ready. . . ?'

'There's no harm in jogging His memory,' said Mr Pye.

When Miss Dredger had finished applying the hot fomentations and was lighting a new cigarette from the stub of the old one, Mr Pye startled her by saying: 'She must come to us, sailor. She needs us. The west bedroom is not in use.'

'Who on earth are you talking about, chief?'

'A wild and primitive child,' he said. 'She needs Our Pal very badly.'

'But who?' insisted Miss Dredger. '*Who?*'

'Tintagieu,' said Mr Pye. 'What a force she could be for good.'

For a moment Miss Dredger sped back to the state of mind that was once hers, when alone, and splendid in her isolation, she scorned the world.

'No!' she cried.

Mr Pye turned the kindly searchlight of his gaze upon her. It seemed as though the room were lit with his love.

'My dear,' he said, 'You must not speak like that. What are we here for but to bring salvation. We are not here for our own pleasure, but to gather the outcasts to our heart. What have you to say?'

Miss Dredger bit her stern and uncoloured lips, flung away a freshly lit cigarette and drove her hands deep into the pockets of the corduroy skirt.

'Sometimes I get sick of the Great Pal,' she said.

'We have all of us had our moments of rebellion,' said Mr Pye. 'I understand. There is no compromise in our work. We either believe or we do not believe. We either sit on the fence or we don't. It was only after I had burned that fence for good that I found myself and became free. When there is nowhere to sit one either lies down or stands. I chose to stand for standing gives stature; and stature, pride; and pride poise; and poise, power – what does power bring, dear? – it brings with it that immense decision – that terrible choice – is one's power to be directed to the good or otherwise of our brothers – if we say for the *good*, then let us be unequivocal or we will be back again where we started – in the land of half-measures, of indecision, and there we would be, on that dreadful fence again – that fence risen anew from the ashes, and us atop of it, one leg on either side. What do you say?'

Miss Dredger swung her head and slapped an invisible cloud of imaginary dust from her thighs. Then she pocketed her strong, capable hands in a way that must have been a great strain on the fabric.

'I say "yes",' she said at last, half closing her eyes against the smoke which drifted from her nostrils. 'I will do what you say, chief.'

'What Our Pal says, dear.'

Miss Dredger inhaled deeply. 'That's it,' she said.

'And now,' said Mr Pye, 'a little supper, and then, if you would be so kind, dear – another poultice.'

That night Mr Pye suffered cruelly. He reminded himself of Job, but received little solace from that gentleman's boils. But towards morning he fell into a deep sleep and when Miss Dredger knocked at his door with a glass of tomato juice she received no response. It was possible that he had risen early and was out on one of his famous walks. Certainly she had never known him sleep as late as this.

She opened the door quietly, and there he was, curled up like a child, his thumb in his mouth and his sharp nose lying along the pillow, and a smile, not of resignation but of positive relief on his face, that luminous face that but for the sharpness of the nose might have been described as cherubic.

'Good for you,' she muttered to herself. 'Sleep on, chief; sleep on. You jolly well deserve it,' and Miss Dredger tiptoed out, with a creak of leather.

The whale was now lying off Peter Port, Guernsey, much to

the chagrin of that island, for if she was high in Sark, she was now upon the very crest of self-expression.

After much argument and many attempts to put their plan into effect, the Sarkese had at last managed at high tide, with the help of hooks and grappling irons, to tow her out to sea, and let her go. The idea was for her to take advantage of the Great Russel, a redoubtable current which should logically have set her on a course for Spain.

But she had other ideas, and ignoring the laws of tide and current, she made for Guernsey like a possessed thing, rolling as she went, with a swarm of screaming seagulls wheeling above her like a royal escort.

The wind blew into Guernsey from the sea, and as that angry island which had so lately been convulsed at the plight of the Sarkese, closed its doors and windows against the little white whale, the Sarkese opened theirs and breathed again; and grinned.

It seemed that they had already forgotten all that Mr Pye had taught them about love.

Mr Pye slept on and on and it was not until eleven o'clock in the morning that he opened his eyes. He was immediately aware of his relief from pain and he sat up in bed, positively beaming.

'So you've decided that I've had about enough of it, eh, eh, you positive old scourge, you....' he cried out to the Great Pal. 'Well, here I am, absolved from whatever my sin was – for I don't know, old chap, I positively don't, so I may commit it *again* – and then – oh dear, down you'll come on me, with what next, I wonder? – there's no knowing with a Turk like you.'

Mr Pye chortled to himself, glanced at his watch, raised his eyebrows, tapped himself on the chest with both sets of knuckles and sang softly but with a happy vibrance:

> 'Who would true valour see
> Let him come hither,
> One here will constant be,
> Come wind, come weather....'

He swung his plump legs over the side of the bed and stood on his toes with his arms out to his sides and breathed deeply. Then, lifting his spectacles from the bedside table, he wiped them carefully with a silk handkerchief and perched them on his nose.

Undoing the buttons of his pyjama jacket he pursed his mouth and was about to whistle that gay little four-note call, which was always the sign by which Miss Dredger knew that he would soon be down for breakfast, when he unpursed them again, and crossed the room for his hand-mirror. It occurred to him that he would like to be the first to see to what extent the inflammation had subsided.

Sitting down before the large mirror at the window, but turning his back to it, he manoeuvred the hand-mirror into position and at once an icy sweat began to pour down his high forehead and into his eyes. His face had assumed the ghastly and semi-transparent nature of a wax candle. His knees went weak as though dissolving and the hand-mirror shook in his grasp.

For a little while, with his eyes closed, he leaned forward and the perspiration fell from his bowed head to the floor.

Clutching at the one hope that his imagination had played a trick upon him, he raised his glass again. But there was no gainsaying what he saw – it was no chimera, but a palpable fact, bizarre and terrible.

From the centre of either shoulder-blade there had begun to sprout the tips of tender, milk-white feathers.

Mr Pye rose to his feet. For the first time in his life he felt ill, but he moved rapidly across the room and locked the door. Then he took a fresh towel from a drawer and wiped his face and hands.

The shock was such as would have unhinged many and it was now that the great well of his spiritual resources so sedulously garnered over the years were there, to be drawn upon.

At last he spoke – and his voice was tense and hardly above a whisper.

'What is it, Pal?' he said. 'What is it? Why have you done

this to me? What is it you expect of me? It is too much, you know, this prank of yours. What can I do with wings, for pity's sake?'

There was no reply. The room was quite silent save for a moth at the window, which fluttered up and down the glass.

Beyond the rain-spotted panes the long fields gleamed in the racing light. From far away came the immoderate cry of the Seignorie bull. Then the silence settled again and even the moth rested, and leaned its head against the hard grey putty at the foot of the window-pane.

While Mr Pye stood perfectly still his face was as white as clay, but his brain moved rapidly to and fro across the terrain of this strange new country in which he suddenly found himself. Had he gone mad? No! No. Certainly he was not mad, for there was no difference now in the way his mind worked from the way it behaved before he had discovered that he was growing wings. If he was mad then he must always have been mad. And he had not always been mad, unless to be an evangelist is to be mad. If that were so then he was proud of his insanity – proud to belong to the tiny company of zealots who were prepared to stake their faith in the spiritual values and to have the courage to voice their belief to the world.

Was he asleep? Was he dreaming? No. He knew that he was not dreaming. If he were dreaming then it was a dream of a kind that he had never experienced before. To make trebly sure, he brought the mirrors into alignment and stared once more at the phenomena.

They were crisp, forceful little feathers, obviously full of life and purpose. It seemed to Mr Pye that they had grown the merest fraction since he last saw them, but this must have been due to the shock he had sustained. In themselves they seemed so innocent, so healthy. There was nothing ethereal or wispish. It seemed almost natural for them to be there, thrusting their downless tufts quite painlessly through his skin.

Mr Pye quite suddenly pulled himself together both in soul and body, and putting on his pyjama jacket again he marched to the bathroom with his towel and sponge-bag.

Ten minutes later, when he emerged, pink and shining, from

his ablutions, he took a step or two to the top of the stairs and whistled the four sharp little notes, and these were repeated by Miss Dredger in the kitchen.

At breakfast Miss Dredger said: 'Golden slumbers weren't in it, chief.'

'That is true, sailor.'

'Never knew you sleep so long.'

'True, my dear ... true.'

'Another cup of coffee, chief?'

'More often than not, sailor.'

'Now what on earth does that mean?'

'Forgive me, my dear, my mind was far away. What did you ask me?'

Miss Dredger made her mouth into a rectangle. It was full of coiling smoke like the fumes from a witches' brew.

'I suggested some more coffee.'

'Yes indeed, dear. I think not....'

'In that case I will boil a kettle for your poultice. You have hardly eaten anything.'

'No poultice,' said Mr Pye.

'Chief! What is it? You have always relied on me. You said I was yoûr doctor.'

'So I did, sailor. But I have recovered.'

'Let me be the judge of that.'

'Sailor,' said Mr Pye. 'Say no more. Let me be proud of you. Show me that you can drop a subject. You do not want to be like our dear friend upstairs, do you, who cannot let a thing alone – cannot let bygones be bygones. Just as she wears only one hat, she thinks only one thought.'

'That is true, chief. Yesterday I heard her shout out something utterly beastly.'

'Poor thing,' said Mr Pye. 'She means well.'

'That's just what she doesn't,' said Miss Dredger; 'you should have heard what she said.'

'No tales, if you please,' said Mr Pye. 'I am going for a walk.'

'Chief,' said Miss Dredger, getting to her feet, 'I have never heard you talk so sharply before. Have I done anything wrong? Where are you going? Where are you going?'

Mr Pye removed his glasses and wiped them with his silk handkerchief. He took out his little box and helped himself to a fruit-drop. He stood up. He took a step towards her and then he smiled at Miss Dredger with a sweetness hardly credible in a man. Then he moved reflectively to the door, pausing as he passed through it in order to execute with an old-world charm that was quite inimitable, a little bow to his faithful lieutenant, and then with a tilt of the head he was suddenly gone without a word.

EIGHTEEN

A COUPLE of hundred feet below him the bottle-green water washed the shores of the old Eperquerie harbour. The rain had stopped and a pale sun shone across the sea, and the red and black seaweeds swaying to and fro in the shallows seemed to shine unnaturally.

Mr Pye sat upon the old weather-pitted barrel of a cannon, which at the cliff's edge pointed its rusty nozzle at the sea. Reputed to have once given Napoleon food for thought, the old thing now lay half-buried in the short, rabbit-nibbled turf.

Across the sea a faint thickening of the horizon implied France, and piled above this tenuous implication there were great domes of cloud.

Mr Pye, upon the cannon, sat very straight indeed, his hands in his lap, his knees drawn up, his feet together, his head turned to the sea, but his eyes out of focus.

Mechanically his hand stole into a waistcoat pocket and withdrew a fruit-drop, but he forgot to put the bright green thing into his mouth. Again he was motionless, his hand raised and the sweet between his finger and thumb.

The world that he knew, the rational world, the world whose natural and physical laws he had always taken for granted, was suddenly exploded. He would have been, of course, among the first to challenge any suggestion that the world was fundamentally rational or that everything in life could be explained

– for the Great Pal was not rational, nor was beauty rational – and self-sacrifice and religious inspiration were certainly not rational, but nevertheless he knew that if great tracts and areas of life (which he among the rest of mankind had always relied on to be consistent) were suddenly to behave illogically or defy the laws of nature, then it would be of little use for him to follow his evangelical star, for chaos would yawn at him at every turning and his star might itself fall suddenly down the sky and become (why not?) a catfish, as it fell.

What other explanation could there be than that he had reached so elevated a condition that the body had no option but to try and follow where the soul was leading, and for all he knew he was now not so much a little lower than the angels, but on a par.

But Mr Pye was not so sure that he wanted to be an angel or to find himself upon equal footing with the heavenly host. It was one thing to be an angel in Paradise, but quite another to be an angel in Sark.

If it was the work of the Great Pal then he felt he should have been warned. After all, the responsibility was a heavy one for even the purest soul to carry. There was, of course, something very flattering about it all, but the complications that loomed ahead were legion.

Was he to divulge what had happened and appear to the Sarkese, and indeed to the world, in his plumage, and by means of this sign, start a spiritual revival? – or was he not to do any such thing? Was it not possible that in their ignorance he would be considered as a *freak*, for after all wings are not the monopoly of the seraphim but are equally to be found upon the backs of ducks.

Could he not do more good, and would it not be less vulgar, to keep his feathers a close secret, and to carry on his evangelical work, with at his back the palpable plumage as evidence of his vocation? Surely this would avoid ostentation and at the same time give him an authority denied to the wingless. But would his wings be hideable? How large would they grow? Was there any chance of them staying as they were? And more important still, was there any hope of their *withdrawal*?

Directly he posed this last question to himself and realized that, rightly or wrongly, it was his overpowering wish to be free again of these all-too-corporeal symbols of his worthiness, he suffered his first doubt as to his spiritual integrity.

He lifted his hand automatically and transferred the fruit-drop from his fingers to his listless tongue. How strange it was that, unfledged, he had been at the height of his messianic powers, but that now, in the early glory of his plumage, he should hesitate and question the very roots of his faith.

What on earth, or in heaven, was He up to – that Great Pal of his? Surely he must have known that it was a psychological mistake of the first water to saddle a mortal with such a hyper-physical burden. Perhaps he felt that Mr Pye could walk happily into the fisherman's bar at the Ormer Tavern and stand the good folks a round of 'schooners', without turning a feather, or go for a bathe in Dixcart Bay with a couple of wings flapping at his back. Perhaps the Great Pal was confident that Mr Pye was on so elevated a level that he could frisk along the sea-walk at the harbour and meet the Guernsey boat in that condition. The Great Pal was sanguine. For the first time in his life Mr Pye blasphemed.

'To hell with this,' he muttered. 'I'm not a peep-show.'

And then it occurred to Mr Pye that perhaps his feathers had nothing to do with the unimpeachable life he had led. Perhaps there had been some cosmic error, some incongruity of substance, time and space – but this seemed to him, on consideration, less likely than the ironic probability that in his zeal and love for rectitude, he had really *gone too far*.

Mr Pye stood up and straightened his back, and as he did so he felt the first faint brush of the feathers against his shirt.

He turned from the cannon and began to climb the winding path that led to the Seignorie road. Then for a moment a somewhat wry expression altered his face. 'These little wings are sent to try us,' he murmured, and then gripping his hands together behind his back he set out smartly across the island.

Ten days later he crossed to Guernsey and so to England, which island, though she knew it not, was the weirder for his presence.

NINETEEN

As Mr Pye walked briskly along Welbeck Street, his umbrella impeccably rolled, his bowler hat perched firmly upon his round head, he carried with him, for all the apparent crispness of his progress, a sense of acute melancholy. The figures who passed him seemed to be like creatures of another world. A great gulf now lay between him and his kind. His kind? Perhaps he could no longer claim to belong to the world he saw about him, now that his shoulders yearned for air less thick than that which sagged over London; less raw than that which raced through Sark's torn trees.

He was intensely lonely. Lonely as a gull among rooks. Lonely as a child among old men. Lonely as an old man among children. Lonely as a new boy in a great school. Lonely as the soul that has lost the body that gave it shelter. Lonely as the body when the soul has fled.

But as he walked he twirled his umbrella, for the gay habits of a lifetime go on, just as, after death, there are movements in the limbs, and the body goes on struggling out of habit.

A lady approached him, walking slowly, and contentedly, and as she came abreast of Mr Pye she trod upon the side of her shoe, so that she staggered and gave way at one knee, and instantly Mr Pye had thrown out a gloved hand and supported her elbow. She turned to him and thanked him with a grateful smile, and Mr Pye removed his hat with such courtesy that, as she was about to leave him, she turned again. But there was nothing she could think of saying to the strange, plump little stranger, so spruce, so gallant – save, 'It is these high heels. I am always doing it. Thank you for saving me,' and then she turned and moved slowly away and Mr Pye could hardly sustain the tumult that filled him for she had reminded him of his isolation. He ached for normality as he remembered those days when he was last in London, pacing the pavements of the great, grey city, bloodshot with buses, while he formulated his far-reaching plans.

But now it was so different. It was not simply the acuteness of his isolation, for he had always been alone in one sense or another; nor was it entirely that he was forced to go about the streets with the insufferable secret at his shoulders; it was that he felt to the very core of his being the bitter irony of his predicament. He had striven to save an island from itself. He had poured out his love. He had worked hand in glove with the Great Pal, who knew, if anyone knew, that he had not spared himself. And for it to be he, Harold Pye, who should be singled out to suffer, gave him not only a sense of injustice, but a twinge of doubt. And it was this that was so disturbing, for if he found that he distrusted the Great Pal, who else was there left with whom he could commune? Who else could speed him on his way?

Where was the justice in it? But perhaps there *was* no justice. He knew that it was for saints to suffer – in fact how could they be saints unless they *had* suffered – but martyrdom of this *sprouting* kind was too much, and perhaps there weren't any saints anyway, and perhaps he wasn't one himself. Perhaps he was simply a freak.

And still he twirled his umbrella, and still he lifted his face to the world; and still there was that little automatic smile on his lips; but just as there was something less clean-cut, less virile, about his faith and something blurred about its form, so there was, as he crossed the road to the corner of Harley Street, something less clean-cut about his spine, and something blurred about the outline of his shoulders.

He had had to acquire a new wardrobe, and the loose jackets that he had been forced to buy off the peg did much to hide the wings which, luckily for him, could be folded over one another with no pain, and kept in place by loops of elastic.

A few yards up Harley Street he stopped and consulted his watch. Then he drew from another waistcoat pocket a little notebook. It had been no easy thing for him to organize his appointments, but eventually he had been able to fix them at hourly intervals throughout the day. There was now only three minutes left before his first appointment with Sir Daniel Thrust.

Although he had little faith in the idea that his trouble might have been brought about through some obscure physical condition, yet (in spite of this and in spite of his disbelief in medicine, let alone surgery), he was determined to leave no possible stone unturned, and so when he stopped at a tall door about a hundred yards from the corner, he presssed the bell firmly like a man who knows what he wants. The door opened almost at once and he was led to a large waiting-room, where he sat for no more than a minute before he was conducted to the consulting-room.

Sir Daniel Thrust rose to greet him. He was a gaunt, cadaverous man and it was impossible to see him without being reminded of the bone formations that underline the flesh. He was tall, very tall, compared to Mr Pye, and his shoulders were angular and hunched forward, which exaggerated his look of emaciation and suggested to every patient who ever came to him for advice that a death's-head of a doctor is not the best thing to inspire immediate confidence. But this was only before they heard his voice. Once he spoke it was quite different. His voice was slow and deep and cultured and suggested that were it ever necessary he could deliver 'On the Road to Mandalay' with great effect.

'Mr Pye, I believe: do sit down.' His voice was like a confidential bassoon.

'Thank you,' said Mr Pye, 'thank you, indeed.' Mr Pye sat very upright and took off his spectacles to wipe them.

'Now let me see ... Mr Pye, I have your letter here ... yes ... exactly ... mm ... aha .. you have been living in Sark ...

I once spent a holiday there, fishing ... very, very satisfactory as I remember it, for a *very* short holiday, but rather small for an *island* ... hm ... I used to think ... now let me see ... ah yes, you were not explicit as to what your trouble was ... but would come to me if you could feel quite confident as to professional secrecy being scrupulously observed to its last iota ... I like that phrase, Mr Pye ... but of *course* it will, my dear sir, it is in our blood to keep things hidden.'

'It is certainly in mine,' said Mr Pye.

'Is that so?' said Sir Daniel Thrust.

'That is unhappily so,' said Mr Pye, returning his glasses to his nose.

'Unhappily? You have something you wish to hide?' came the modulated boom.

'Exactly.'

'Something physical? ... come ... come ... we seem to be playing the game of twenty questions – or animal, vegetable, and mineral, as we used to call it ... ha ha! ... but come, come, my dear sir, and tell me what the matter is. Do you smoke?'

'Never,' said Mr Pye, 'never,' and he brought out his little box and took out a fruit-drop.

'May I?'

'But, of course: what are they?'

'Fruit-drops.'

'I see,' said Sir Daniel.

Mr Pye looked up and placed his finger-tips together.

'Twelve days ago, in Sark ...' He paused.

'Yes,' said the specialist – and then because the silence throbbed – 'In Sark, twelve days ago,' he echoed inaccurately, hoping a repetition of the words would help his patient who was sitting perfectly still with his eyes closed, to come to the point. As Mr Pye continued to sit quietly, Sir Daniel got up and took a turn around his desk – he was used to embarrassed patients who for one reason or another imagined that their dreary symptoms would shock him. He had learned not to hurry them.

'Yes, I remember Sark very well,' he said at last. 'As I recall it has a peculiar geological formation, its strata all the wrong way up, or in the wrong order or something of that kind. And you were there the day before yesterday? Just think of it – while I sat here at my prosaic desk you were probably fishing. How did you travel over? I expect you crossed to Guernsey and then flew.'

Mr Pye opened his eyes. His face had coloured to a luminous tint of old-rose. Sir Daniel sat down in his chair and pretended to be making a note on his blotting pad, but he was mechanically at work on his favourite doodle. Why was the man blushing? What on earth had he said?

Mr Pye had risen to his feet. He now walked to the desk and facing Sir Daniel, with his hands grasping his lapels he whispered, 'Did you say *flew?*'

'I believe I did, Mr Pye.'

'You have come, at a bound – at a single unpremeditated bound, very close to my trouble, Sir Daniel. I did *not* fly but unless you can help me it looks as though I shall soon be able to. That is why I have come to you.'

'I do not understand,' said Sir Daniel, after a long time during which he had been doodling on his blotter at extraordinary speed. 'I cannot see any difficulty about flying, provided you have bought your ticket.'

'I will need no ticket,' said Mr Pye, and as though the consulting-room were his rather than Sir Daniel's, he began to walk to and fro across it with his hands folded together under his chin.

'Ah, you have a private plane,' said Sir Daniel.

'I have no private plane,' said Mr Pye, 'but I have private wings, and I wish them to remain private. Better still, I hope you will be able to give me medical advice as to how to get rid of them.'

Sir Daniel tilted his cadaverous head on one side. Then he stroked his jawbone with the long and unblemished fingers of his right hand. Under his desk he had a bell which he sometimes had to use, and the equally unblemished fingers of his other hand played listlessly with it, stroking the knob and revolving it gently for it was a little loose. At last he smiled.

'Did you say wings?' he asked.

'I said wings,' said Mr Pye. 'I am growing them. They are now a foot long.'

'They ... are ... now ... a ... foot ... long,' echoed the specialist. 'You . . are ... grŏwing ... them.'

He brought the words out very slowly and as he did so he pressed the bell. Then he excused himself with a cough that seemed to come from under the floor boards, and left the room with long strides like a mantis. A moment later two young ladies in white came in and escorted Mr Pye downstairs and out into the light breeze that blew down Harley Street.

Mr Pye had made no effort to remain. He knew that the atmosphere had been wrong and the man had been wrong, and his broaching of the subject had been wrong. He had learned what not to do, and half an hour later when at his second appointment he sat facing an even larger desk forty feet farther down Harley Street, he was careful to show the second specialist his plumage without wasting a moment in preliminaries. This second doctor was short, dark, and fierce, and looked as strong as a bulldog, but was forced to go to a cupboard and pour himself out and gulp down a tumbler-full of naked whisky before he returned to Mr Pye for a second look.

It was a gruelling day Mr Pye kept his fifteen appointments. He extracted from every one of them a solemn and super-professional oath of secrecy, but this is all he *did* extract for none of them were able to collect their wits. They had never, they all insisted, had such a case before – but this information was not much use to Mr Pye. Some of them were anxious to take photographs or to X-ray his scapulae, but Mr Pye was adamant. He had by now spent over two hundred guineas for their advice. It seemed he had done nothing save squander time and money, and of these two the more serious was time.

No one could help him. No one could pluck a solution from the insoluble. Why should they? How could they? He and he alone must find an answer.

Even more lonely than ever, he returned to his hotel, took the lift to his room, locked his door, removed his jacket, shirt, and vest, un-looped the elastic, and lay upon his bed with his face to the pillow, his thumb in his mouth like a child, while his wings, free for the first time for many hours, unfolded gradually of their own volition, and as they unfolded, Mr Pye, exhausted in spirit, fell into a deep sleep.

When he woke it was three in the morning. For some time he could not think where he was. The room was in profound darkness. He rose to his knees on the bed and felt for the switch of the reading lamp, turned it on, and remained there for a few moments facing the wall. During those few moments his memory returned in a clear surge. The rest had refreshed him.

Every incident of the day was crystal clear. But this was not all. It seemed that suddenly the whole history of his misfortune presented itself to him in a stronger light, from the moment when he first felt the irritation at his shoulder blades until the perilous edge of this sliding life on which he was now balanced. Not only this. It was not simply that his memory presented him with a sequence of interlocking facts, clearly stated, but that he was on the edge of a discovery. What was it that sent a shot of painful excitement through him? Why was he walking up and down the hotel bedroom as though possessed? What was this discovery which he felt but could not as yet entirely formulate?

He marched into the private bathroom of his suite and turned on the hot tap. He would luxuriate among soap-suds until the vision turned itself into something less vague. He was almost there. It was so simple that he could not grasp it. It was too obvious for his delicate and complex brain. But it would come. He knew it would come. The water roared into the bath and the steam rose.

That it was three in the morning, that London was asleep, and that he was as fresh as a daisy, gave him a power of concentration impossible in the daytime.

He lay for a while in his bath with his eyes shut, allowing the pregnant chaos in his mind to settle and distil. His wings lay comfortably immersed along his sides. His sharp nose pointed at the ceiling. The fruit-drop which he had placed on the side of the bath began to melt and a thin green trickle ran down the steaming marble to the water. And then in all its simplicity the truth came to him.

He had grown wings because he was too good for this world. What then should he do to cause them to withdraw themselves or to shrivel away? Plainly, to change his nature. To no longer be too good for this world. He must be positively the reverse. He must be bad for it. Perhaps it would not take more than a little wickedness for the balance to be adjusted. Possibly there was no need for him to travel as far *down* as he had travelled *up* – and that the merest whisk of wickedness would be all that was needed to send the pinions packing. This was guesswork; but surely there was nothing speculative about this logic. The degree of his reversal was a technical thing – but the principle was solid as a rock.

Mr Pye sat up in his bath, awestruck by the vastness of the concept and appalled by all that it involved – but his predominant sensation was not awe but hope.

At about four in the morning he got out of his bath and wearing a blue towel like a sarong, returned to the bedroom and sat with his back to the electric fire, allowing his feathers to dry gradually, for they were difficult to reach.

Longing above all for them to disappear, yet he could not help admiring their resilience and their snow-white beauty. He could not, now that he saw for the first time a chance of getting rid of them, help feeling that if he succeeded, and if no eyes but his (and Harley Street with its sealed lips) were ever to see them, that something would die with him that might have *proved* not only *his* moral pre-eminence, but the existence of the world beyond.

But such thoughts were mere chaff in the wind. Something altogether more real had to be faced. There was no need at this stage to plunge into the whole business of the supernatural. He was a mortal, and he wished so to remain. There was time enough for immortality later. He could not have it both ways. Glory and normality make restless bedfellows.

And what about the Great Pal? Why when for years he had

taken his smallest problems to Him, had he now failed to take advantage of His omniscience? Was it his human vanity; his fear of ridicule? Was it because he knew that he could never live up to his pinions? Whatever it was he was now in no condition to hob-nob with a spirit, as in the past, when in an ecstasy of intimate understanding he would feel the all but palpable presence of His Pal at his side. But now he was withdrawn almost resentfully from the only possible cause of the trouble, his former Ally.

When he was quite dry he rose to his feet and pulled the strong elastic loop over his head and pinioned the callow wings against his back.

Then he dressed rapidly, as though he were trying to keep pace with his thoughts. The idea of going to bed never crossed his mind. He darted here and there collecting his belongings and packing them swiftly and expertly into his suitcase as though the prodigious, the monstrous concept that had bared itself before him in the bath had injected him with radium. He was, as far as his vitality was concerned, the Mr Pye again who had first landed in Sark, who subjugated Miss George, who held the crowds at Derrible in the palm of his soft, little hand. Was he happy? Of course he was not happy in the way a sinless child can be happy. He was all but walking in the slime of the pit. He was gambling with his soul. He was suffering a revolution of his entire being, a churning up of brain and heart so that his body might be free again. For all he knew he was blaspheming through the keyhole of Heaven. How could he be happy?

But he was alive again, as he always had been until the wings grew out of him and sucked the juice of his morality from him and left him like a copy of himself – his reflexes at work – but his breast as empty as a Sarkese cave when the wild seas withdraw.

He was alive again and in that life was hope.

Whether or not it was evil for him to try and free himself from the feathered incubus in so appalling a way he could not tell, but that he had formed a plan was all-in-all and it was this that restored to him a zeal comparable to his zeal as a missionary.

He tiptoed down the stairs of the beautiful hotel, his suitcase in his hand. A few dim lights were left burning all night long and they helped him, when he reached the ground floor, to find his way to the front entrance and the night porter's lodge.

The night porter was asleep. He was a thick-set, aggressive looking man, even in sleep, with waxed moustaches. His false teeth were on a shelf at his elbow. His head was thrown back and he was hissing like a goose in his sleep.

Mr Pye crept to the door, placed his suitcase on the ground and after one or two failures he found the two knobs which, when turned simultaneously, freed the latch, and the door opened quietly. Before he let himself out he stopped and returned to the centre of the hall where a tall vase of flowers stood on an expensive table. It had occurred to him that there was no time like the present in which to start to put his plan into operation. He could feel that the loose jacket which he wore was stretched more tightly across his back and was far less comfortable than it had been yesterday. The wings were growing at the rate of about an inch a day and there was now a definite swelling at a level just below the shoulder. Neither time nor opportunity must be lost. He must do something wicked. Something he had never done before. 'I must *not* do good,' he whispered to himself. 'I must *not* do good ... I must do *bad*.'

He was, of course, not going to pay his bill. That was quite simple. But surely he could do something less negative than that, before stepping out into the darkness. Looking around the hall the flowers caught his eye. He gathered them up in his fist, lifted them dripping from the vase, and then with his head turned away and his eyes shut, and a sick sensation in his stomach, he broke off all the heads.

After a little time, when he felt less dizzy, he opened his eyes and placed the murdered gladioli on the table and wiped his hands with his handkerchief.

The table was an oval shape, possibly walnut – the hall was too dimly lit for him to see the grain, but its surface could be felt and it was a sheet of impeccable smoothness. Mr Pye took out a pair of folding nail-scissors, opened them to an angle of about thirty degrees, and scored two thin mutilating lines across its satin surface. He turned his head sharply over his shoulder, but the night porter was still hissing like a goose. By now Mr Pye was feeling very ill indeed, but pulling himself together he approached the irritable looking watchman in his braided uniform, and cut off his waxed moustaches. They fell upon the sleeper's shirt where they lay against the lurid linen like small black claws.

That was certainly enough for Mr Pye and he made his way to the door, picked up his suitcase and, closing the door behind him, moved out into the night.

Later that day he bought a cape, some books, and sent a telegram to Miss Dredger warning her of his return; and that same evening he took the Weymouth train from Paddington. He crossed to Guernsey by the mail boat. At six the next morning he left his cabin and with his new cape billowing about him in the watery wind, he stood at the port rail and gazed, not at Guernsey, through whose harbour mouth the *St Helier* was about to be coaxed, but eastwards, beyond Herm and Jethou, to Sark, that other island.

The *Ormer* got away at close on eleven, and an hour later Mr Pye was climbing the slippery steps at Creux Harbour and there, yet again, were the coloured cliffs towering above him. There was the tunnel through the rock. There, was young Pépé. There, was the rusty old crane. There was Thorpe dangling his legs over the sea-wall. There were the champing horses and Mr Pye could hear, in the ancient silence, the creaking of their harness, and the wash of the tide against the long sea-wall. And there, her arms folded and her feet astride, was Miss Dredger. This time they knew one another – or thought they did.

TWENTY

'I HAVE a surprise for you, chief,' said Miss Dredger.

They had climbed the hill and were passing through the dogs at the Colinette. Miss Dredger had not spoken much on the way up the harbour hill, not because she had not got plenty to talk about, but because it seemed to her as though something had altered, very subtly, in their relationship. What it was she could not quite say. His replies to the questions she had plied him with at the harbour had been inaudible or delivered with an elusive facetiousness, which she would never have associated with her chief. It was not that he was positively discourteous – how could he be *that*, but there seemed to be a *potential* rudeness in his every gesture, his every intonation. The charm was still there, but it was now more like the charm of something vaguely dangerous, like a baby with a razor in its hand.

Oh yes, he had been sweet. He had doffed his bowler as though to a queen. But this new element returned and perplexed her. Not only this, she was worried for another reason also. Why, when she had admired his cape, had he whispered in a new and peculiar voice:

'It is my cape of good hope, and if it isn't I will probably bite your nose off.'

Now that was an odd thing to say. She was used to his drollery – but why had it sounded so sinister? And what was it that seemed to have changed about his deportment – his physical presence? He was as crisp and alive upon his feet, as perky in the turn of his heel, and the way he cocked his head – but was there not something heavier about him? Was he, in a word, quite as upright? That spine of his that had been the envy of all, for by contrast all the rest of the world was round-shouldered, had *that* not altered too? Was it not slightly less so?

He had not answered her last remark, and as they had now passed the school and the loaf-shaped prison and were rounding the bend by the Manoir, she repeated it.

'Look here, chief,' she said, '*do* answer me, or at least give me a clue whether you've heard me or not.'

'I am all ears, sailor. Cough it up.'

'I said I had a surprise for you.'

'In the form of?' said Mr Pye.

'In the form of Tintagieu.'

'Tintagieu?'

'You remember you said that she could be a Power for Good?'

'Did I? How surprising.'

'What do you mean, chief?'

'What do *you* mean, sailor?'

'I mean I've done it. It went hard with me, but women are like that.'

'Like what?'

'They find it hard to share their homes with other women.'

'Do they now? And you've installed her. Is that it?'

'It was difficult. She would not come at first. But I told her how you needed her.'

'Needed her! Good gracious!'

'You said you did.'

'How very ingenuous I must have been and how *communicative*.'

'I don't understand, chief – you told me that the Great Pal . . .'

'Oh, that old thing.'

She gazed at him aghast. Mr Pye was shuddering slightly, but he twirled his umbrella and, removing his bowler hat, replaced it at a jaunty angle, quite out of keeping with his round face and pointed nose.

A field mouse ran across the road ahead of them. For a moment all that was good about Mr Pye, his avid interest in all natural phenomena, his love for all forms of animal life, not excluding the rodents, his championship of the meek and lowly – all this was with him for a moment – but steeling himself he raised his brolly like an assegai and loosed it at the little scampering field mouse. His slender spear from Bond Street missed, of course. He was no Zulu.

But the umbrella, tightly swaddled in its own midnight, looked impressive enough impaled and shuddering in the grassy bank.

'No mouse for lunch today,' he said. 'I could have done with a grilled ear. Quite delicious – with lemon. Have you ever tried it, sailor dear?'

This time it was for Miss Dredger to make no answer.

Indoors sat Tintagieu, ready for anything. She had listened in amazement when on the previous day Miss Dredger had bearded her in her den and after a great deal of inhaling and exhaling, and stubbing out of cigarette ends, had put it to her that Mr Pye, odd as it might sound, had need of her, of Tintagieu herself; that Mr Pye considered that with a nature as uninhibited as hers he could, with her upon his left hand, and with Miss Dredger herself upon his right, deliver the final blow that would bring Sark to its knees, a posture long overdue.

Miss Dredger had pointed out that Mr Pye was a man of means and that Tintagieu need pay no rent. She would be with them as a working rather than a paying guest. What was more, Mr Pye was nothing if not generous, and had every respect for the dictum that a workman is worthy of his hire.

It would not be easy work, but it would be thrilling work. The back of it was broken already, and it needed only the three of them to deliver the *coup de grâce*. 'It is not that your morals are bad,' Miss Dredger had argued, 'it is because you simply haven't any. That is what appeals to the chief. He sees farther than most men – in fact he sees farther than any man. In his opinion you are absolutely innocent like a piece of clay, or like a bird of prey that has no choice. It can only be itself. That is what he says. But your innocence has been bent all one way. With the help of the Great Pal, he can bend you all the other. What about giving him a surprise? What about being installed (I've got a jolly little room ready for you) when he returns tomorrow?'

Of course Tintagieu had been astounded, convulsed, fascinated, insulted, flattered, and then convulsed again. It was the strangest proposition ever put to her – and one so much less simple than she was accustomed to. For a long while she could not be convinced that Miss Dredger was serious. She believed she was having her leg pulled – though who could be less likely to cross the island in order to pull her leg than Miss Dredger?

Tintagieu argued that it seemed to her rather daft to assume that people had to live in the same house in order to forward the work of the Great Pal. Why, supposing she was holy enough and she 'bloody well wasn't and didn't want to be', couldn't Mr Pye's disciples operate from different parts of the island? But Miss Dredger pointed out that to be consistently near Mr Pye was to be constantly refreshed and invigorated. People lapsed so soon, she said, when they strayed from Mr Pye.

'But you've got Miss George already,' Tintagieu had said, her voice seeming to make its way through soft gravel. 'How many more do you want at your headquarters? Besides, how could I make love with Miss George crashing all over the house, and Mr Pye popping up here and popping up there? What's more you probably lock the front door at night. You won't want them shinning up the drain-pipes, will you, like steeplejacks?'

'Who?' said Miss Dredger.

'How do I know?' said Tintagieu. 'I'm not Moses, am I, or some other old prophet with a beard.'

Miss Dredger gave Tintagieu to understand that she was

quite correct in assuming that a jaundiced view would be taken of anyone clinging to the drain-pipes at night, whatever their intentions, not only because it was crude and anthropoidal, but because the pipes would not stand the strain, and the expense of re-erection would be considerable.

She also gave Tintagieu to understand that after a day or two under the same roof with Mr Pye she would probably be far more interested in cracking her nocturnal lovers on the head, directly they had reached the level of her window-sill, than of welcoming them in, for when the spirit of the Great Pal had suffused her she would aim at something higher.

'What!' Tintagieu had said, for she had rather lost the gist. 'Do you mean in the attic?'

No, Miss Dredger did *not* mean the attic. She would like to raise another point. Tintagieu was not to call Mr Pye the Fruit-drop.

'Doesn't he like it?' Tintagieu had asked.

'He doesn't know about it,' said Miss Dredger. 'Thank Heaven!'

'Then why worry?' said Tintagieu.

'Because it jolly well shocks me!'

'Oh, I see,' Tintagieu had said. 'You want to protect him, kind of, eh? The dear little fellow.'

'How *dare* you!' Miss Dredger had risen from the old couch whose springs no longer sprang.

'You love him!' Tintagieu said hoarsely. Then, after a long pause: 'Like I used to love my little woolly bear.'

'Rot! Ridiculous parallel!'

'And you're a ridiculous couple of converging lines,' Tintagieu had muttered happily. She did not understand what Miss Dredger's remark had meant, but she had done a little geometry in the Sark schoolroom.

But while all this had been going on, another part of Tintagieu's brain had been gradually seduced by the idea of what good fun it would be to take this never-to-be-repeated opportunity. To take Miss Dredger at her word, and to occupy the bedroom she had been offered: to pretend as the days went by that she was succumbing more and more to the evangelical influence of the odd little man. Surely to pretend to discipleship would bring with it the very plums of amusement. She would out-rival the Dredger and the George in naked zeal. She would have the whale of a time.

'Miss Dredger,' she had said, 'I will come tonight. If Mr Pye needs me – as you say he does – then he can bloody well have me.'

'You are coarse,' Miss Dredger had replied. 'But you are virile. Have your supper here, and bring some flowers for the vases. You can lock your door, can't you, while you're away?'

'Without a key, Miss Dredger, I would be a lost woman. I have to protect my dolly.'

And now she was sitting on the couch in the living-room, a room not unduly large but into which the whole ground floor of Tintagieu's cottage could easily have been fitted. She heard the latch of the garden gate and the faint squeak as it opened.

She had dressed herself in a way which she imagined would be appropriate in a missionary. Instead of her slacks and jersey she wore a narrow black skirt. Several years ago she had been able to pull it on fairly easily, but now, owing to the voluptuous increase in her hip and nether girth it was a thing which she had to work her way into by degrees to the accompaniment of a straining and a bursting of seams and a flow of startling language. Sheathing her as tightly as a chrysalis, it reached to half-way down her shins and forced her to walk with ridiculous little paces. The idea was to be *formal*. It seemed to Tintagieu that for an evangelist to be free and easy in her clothes would be a kind of contradiction, like turning cartwheels at a funeral. Above the skirt she wore a black blouse, also on the small side. She had added buttons so that it was done up tightly at the neck where a small white collar like the frills which butchers put round mutton chops relieved the general blackness. The whole effect, which was intended to strike a sober note, struck something very different.

Mr Pye, when he saw her, stood transfixed. There was not a sound or a movement until Tintagieu, rising to her feet, spread wide her plump arms and with a look of amazing piety: 'Welcome,' she whispered.

'Is this your surprise?' he said to Miss Dredger, who was staring over his shoulder. Mr Pye suddenly began to spin his umbrella through his fingers. Miss Dredger did not answer. Then she raised her voice angrily: 'Why are you wearing that extraordinary outfit? Damnably inappropriate, damnably!'

'Come, come, my dear. You are too harsh. After all she is the shape God made her, isn't she?'

'I doubt it,' said Miss Dredger.

'Will you please stop vexing our chief,' said Tintagieu, in a voice husky enough to dissolve any man's knee-caps. 'I have put on black because the Great Pal can't bear bright and vulgar colours or any kind of pride. He wants me to be demure – that's what He wants me to be, doesn't He, chief?'

Miss Dredger, caught on the wrong foot, blew clouds out of her nose like a mustang on a frosty morning.

'Do you know what you look like?' said Miss Dredger at last. 'You look like a . . . a . . . a . . .'

'Indeed she does *not*,' cried Mr Pye, turning with a swish of his cape. 'She looks nothing of the kind.'

'I wasn't going to say that, chief,' said Miss Dredger.

'No?'

'No, I was going to say she looks like a loose woman.'

'Well, if she does, all I can say, my dear, is that no loose woman has ever been found in such a tight squeeze. However that may be, my dear Tintagieu,' said Mr Pye, flinging away his bowler so that it skimmed through the air and landed neatly on a cushion at the far end of the room – 'however that may be, you raise an interesting philosophical point.' (He took a few neat paces into the room and then as he whipped his cape off his shoulders in order to fling it away – for he was in a mood for flourish – he changed his mind with the cape in mid-air, and instead of breaking into the rhythmic progress of the capacious cape, he allowed it to flow on through the tense air and complete its billowing circle by finding itself once again upon Mr Pye's affected shoulders.)

The two females stared at him in amazement. Something had

happened in London to change him. Miss Dredger had noticed the facetiousness that was mixed with his charm, but this spearing of mice, this flinging about of hats and flourishing of capes, all this was rather hard to reconcile with the radiant evangelist who had never before displayed so keen a sense of the flamboyant. They now stared at him in tense expectancy, trying to combine in one image the luminous disciple of the Great Pal, and a toreador of plump and feckless charm.

'I was saying,' said Mr Pye, adjusting his cape at the shoulders, 'that you have touched on a philosophical point of no little interest. But what it was I can't remember, and I can't say that I want to. That the Great Pal expects us to go around like mourners is, of course, poppycock.'

Tintagieu stared.

'You are tremendous, Tintagieu. You are all but fabulous. You look like five-foot-three inches of sex, lagged like a boiler-pipe in mourning. Why you should ever have feared frost with such a heating system, only the Great Pal could possibly know and He, my sweet, unlike you, has no intention of splitting.'

'You have never spoken in this crude and blasphemous way before. I cannot understand you. Has anything happened to you? What is it?' cried Miss Dredger.

'What do you mean – "what is it"? What is what? I'll tell you what is what. . . .'

As Mr Pye was speaking a twinge – a pulsing sense of movement or growth – had made itself felt at the roots of his wings, a sensation that suggested that they had reached a stage in their development, and that from now on they would be able to thrust with renewed vigour.

Mr Pye sat down suddenly on the arm of a chair. He had turned very white and perspiration had gathered upon his brow as thick as dew. Miss Dredger was beside him in a moment and kneeling before him in consternation. 'Chief . . . chief . . .' she muttered, '. . . what is it?'

Tintagieu, who had been as quick off the mark as Miss Dredger, and who had tottered forward in the claustrophobic skirt (her legs were screaming for freedom), on trying to bend down found that she could not do so without her skirt disintegrating about her feet in a storm-cloud of ruptured seams and a sound like the rending of a sinner's soul.

And so she had tried to straighten herself and had lost her balance and fallen in a voluptuous heap at the foot of the missionary. When Mr Pye opened his eyes and saw her there he was instantly reminded of the crying necessity for evil. He must do evil and be sharp about it. Nothing mattered compared with his need to send these damned wings back to wherever they came from.

But it is no easy matter to just do evil because you have decided, rationally, that that is the thing to do. Mr Pye had no experience in that direction. No devilish habits had been formed. His whole bias was towards the good.

He had been trying very hard. He had broken off the heads of the gladioli. He had ruined the beautiful surface of a table. He had not paid his bill. He had been 'difficult' with Miss Dredger. He had made a number of remarks in the worst taste he could think of. He had done a few odd things on the boat over, including nudging a lady's handbag over the rails and into the sea, and making faces at a child in a carry-cot so that it howled and woke at least three other babies – but all this was small and petty. These kind of things made no difference to the length of his pinions. The sense of movement on his back had jogged him violently and he was very much afraid.

Tintagieu was trying to rise from the carpet and was repeating to herself the curious phrase: 'Pluck me, Charlie.' When she was on her hands and knees Mr Pye bent forward and delivered a shameless, vicious blow upon her rear with the palm of his hand. Pushing Miss Dredger to one side, he reached the door and, turning as he did so, he saw nothing as he put his little pink tongue out at the ladies, except four eyes that were perfectly round and two mouths that were wide open.

TWENTY-ONE

By the time that Mr Pye reached his room the noise that was to go on for at least twenty minutes had commenced. It was a noise as uninhibited as the howling of a wolf-pack, but there was nothing hungry or vicious in the noise. It was simply uncontrolled to such a degree that it seemed to belong more to the animal than the human kingdom. It was Tintagieu laughing: laughing helplessly, her diaphragm shuddering like a plucked wire, her body sprawled out like something that she had no longer any control over or any wish to control, as it rolled this way and that in an agony of mirth, the tears streaming down her cheeks, her hands limp on the carpet, her blouse and skirt long since burst apart, so that Miss Dredger looked down upon a kind of heaving wreckage.

'Pull yourself together,' she whispered fiercely. Tintagieu, her sides bruised and sore with laughing, turned her head slowly, her breath shuddering at her throat, and her eyes blurred with tears. She sought out the face of Miss Dredger from the hazy mists above her and directly she saw the stern look upon Miss Dredger's face, Tintagieu began to howl again, slapping the floor feebly at her side, raising her knees, shooting out her feet and letting them fall like deadweights to the floor, while her back arched with the gale of her laughter so that for moments on end she was touching the carpet only with her heels and the back of her head. Her body had become the playground for some elemental gang. She yelled, she moaned: and when at last she climbed to her knees and hoisted herself up by the arm of a chair, and saw her skirt lying on the floor and her black lace blouse hanging in strips over her shoulders, she was suffering from so acute a pain at her waist that she was forced to clutch her sides with her hands.

Miss Dredger had been waiting for the opportunity to give this irreverent girl a straight talking to – but when at last Tintagieu regained control Miss Dredger could not think of what to say, for the whole pattern of behaviour in the house had changed so fundamentally. Miss Dredger felt no certainty as to where or why she was. She hardly knew *who* she was. Was she the lady who used to look after a gentleman – Mr Harold Pye? If so, then it must have been another Mr Pye and not the figure who had turned at the door and thrust out his tongue at them like a pernicious monkey.

Miss Dredger was intelligent enough to begin to feel increasingly scared. Not only was she scared because it is frightening to find someone you thought you knew return to the island, after only a few days away, and behave like a stranger – behave in contradiction to all that he was previously, so that he could now strike a woman, put out his tongue, and make meaningless sweeps through the air with a brand new cape; but she was scared more particularly because it seemed to her that something sacred was being defiled – some high purpose of the spirit, some apprehension of love and beauty.

'Oh, that old thing,' Mr Pye had said, referring to the Great Pal. Was that not a terrible and cynical thing to say?

A voice cried down the stair: 'Sailor! Where are you?'

Miss Dredger strode to the foot of the staircase. 'Yes, chief.'

'How's Miss George? – I'd forgotten her.'

'She's much the same, chief.'

'I'll see her for a minute.'

'Very well, chief.'

'I don't want any lunch. I will remain in my room – I must not be disturbed.'

'You'll be hungry with no lunch.'

'I need hunger.'

'Very well, chief.'

'What about Tintagieu?'

'What about her, chief?'

'Was that her laughing just now?'

'It certainly was.' Tintagieu had wandered into the hall. 'It certainly was,' she repeated with a voice of gravel.

'You will begin to make preparations for an orgy, the two of you.'

'An orgy!' cried Miss Dredger. 'What has come over you, chief? Are you ill?'

'Yes and no,' said Mr Pye.

Tintagieu sat on the bottom step of the stairs and rested her elbow a few treads higher, with her cheek on her fist, and her huge black eyes were turned to the top of the stairs. But Mr Pye was not visible, only his shadow on the wall at the top of the landing.

Miss Dredger was smoking with a ferocity and a concentration that suggested that she was feeling nervy and tired – Mr Pye was becoming *too* much. It is one thing to be the disciple of a true visionary and another to find yourself with an inconsequent and feckless eccentric, let alone the silent, marmoreal Miss George, brooding through the long hours of the day and night – and Tintagieu who had the morals of a monkey.

Miss Dredger's head was also turned to the top of the stairs. She also was watching the shadow: the shadow of Mr Pye's head that was quite motionless and in profile. It was as round as the shadow of a plate and the nose as sharp as a bill. The only things that moved were the shadow-lips and they opened and shut with a horrid precision, while the voice that kept pace with them came from another part of the landing. Then the shadow of the head turned and the nose was gone and the whole thing from crown to belly began to slide across the wall, and the cause of the shadow raised its knuckles of flesh and blood and tapped on Miss George's door.

There was no reply except a sound like heavy water moving among weeds in the throat of a cave.

Mr Pye, remembering that he was now free to break all the conventions in the cause of sin, opened the door quietly and put his head into the room. It was in half darkness, but Mr Pye could see her eyes fixed upon his face. She was sitting bolt upright, the purple busby towering into the gloom. Her domeing shoulders seemed to fill the room. Her flesh shone dimly like a snail's.

'Well?' said Miss George. 'And what do you want?'

'My dear,' said Mr Pye, 'you *know* what I want. I want our Georgy back in health again, laughing and playing as she used to do among her loved ones.'

Miss George stared at him with inexpressible hatred.

'*Loved ones*,' she whispered, as though her words had been previously dipped in vinegar. 'That's *very* good, that is. *Loved ones*, ha-ha-ha ... why, you horrible fat little man, I *hate* you.'

'And why not?' said Mr Pye. 'Hatred is very close to love.'

'Mine isn't,' said Miss George. 'It's very close to itself, and that's the way it's going to stay because I will never forgive you. Never! you beast! I want you to die. Oh, then how I would laugh! Ha-ha-ha-ha-ha. Oh, then how I would laugh! Cruel rotter!'

The sweet round face of Mr Pye showed little interest in what Miss George was saying. He was wondering quite what would be the best way of lengthening his sin-list. Obviously here was an opportunity of doing something really rather unkind. But while he was thinking he went on talking mechanically.

'And why do you hate me so much, my Georgy-Porgy? What is it irks you, dear? Out with it! Was it because I had you lowered down the chimney? Was that it? You were to have been my first martyr, dear. But you have not lived up to any such title, have you?'

'I pray for your death every night,' said Miss George.

'And your prayers remain unanswered, dear? You are evidently on the wrong wavelength.'

Mr Pye had decided what he would do. It would be his biggest sin up to date. It might begin, if not to shorten his wings, at least to halt them in their growth and give him breathing space.

He moved gradually closer to Miss George and, when he was within reach of her, snatched at her busby. It was his idea to uncover whatever there was to be uncovered, for surely Miss George was either bald or had some terrible disease, for why else was she never to be seen without the horrible hirsute thing? But all that happened was that when he tugged at the monstrosity, instead of it coming away in his hands and disclosing the ghastly secret of Miss George's scalp, what happened was that the whole thing, head and hat together, were jerked towards him as though the busby were her hair. Of course this was not so, for many reasons, and one was that, although the jerk forward had shocked, terrified, and jolted her yet she had suffered no active pain in the sense of having had her hair pulled.

Whatever it was that held her busby in place, it was a very powerful substance and Mr Pye, after a moment of shocked silence on both sides, turned suddenly from the bed for a great cloudy and venomous figure was beginning to rise out of the sheets, its murderous little eyes burning like red currants.

It was lucky for Mr Pye that he was nimble, for a moment later he would have been asphyxiated by the sheer collapsing weight of eighteen stone.

But he had ducked and side-stepped into the corridor, neat as a bird, and walking smartly down the passage to his bedroom at the top of the stairs, he had locked himself in and flung off his cloak.

He could hear Miss George wheezing her way along the passage, but he had turned the key, and was anxious for nothing so much as to untie his wings which were beginning to strain against their bonds. Oh, to free them for a while so that they could unfold along his back and stretch their feathers group by group as one stretches the numbed fingers of a wounded hand, when the bandages have been removed.

So eager was he that by the time Miss George was hammering at his door he was sitting on his bed stripped to the waist, while his wings spread out their plumage like white fans.

But Mr Pye was the only one at peace.

'What is it? What is it?' cried the voices from the hall below, for they could hear the thundering of a clenched fist on the panels of Mr Pye's door and the sound of panting.

Miss Dredger and Tintagieu had reached the foot of the stairs when the thudding suddenly stopped. Miss George had crouched down and was applying her eye to the keyhole. What she saw brought on a heart attack that might in itself have been fatal even if she had not reared herself up again and staggered backwards the three paces to the head of the stairs, where she lost her footing and fell head over heels in prodigious and shattering cycles, the uprights of the banisters being mown down like ninepins as she bounded to her death.

TWENTY-TWO

TINTAGIEU and Miss Dredger had narrowly escaped annihilation. Not only would Miss George have crushed them to the ground had they not leapt back from the foot of the stairs, but the pieces of the banisters had crashed about their feet and hurtled through the air. But they had not received a single scratch.

For a moment they stared horrified at the huge dead thing in the hall with the busby crushed in like a concertina, but still on her head. Then, as Miss Dredger opened her mouth to shout for Mr Pye, there was a knock at the front door.

Tintagieu, who had been feeling chilly, for her clothes had finally disintegrated when Mr Pye had left them to go upstairs, now wore a black oilskin slicker. Her hair that had been done up in a puritanical knot, now hung loose across her shoulders. Miss Dredger's shout lost itself in her throat at the sound of the knocking at the front door, but it was Tintagieu who opened the door to reveal the artist.

He saw the corpse at once.

'Is she dead?' he asked.

'Must be,' said Tintagieu.

'Why?'

'It was the father and mother of a crash. She hasn't moved since.'

'Good morning, Miss Dredger.'

Miss Dredger nodded.

'What a thing to paint! Have you phoned the doctor? Where's Mr Pye? How did it happen? She is pure Goya. Personally I feel quite sick and dizzy. Do you mind if I sit down? Is the doctor coming? Where's Pye – oh Lord, I *am* going to be sick – excuse me. . . .' and he made a dash for the lavatory.

Miss Dredger started up the stairs and when some way from the top began to shout.

'Chief! Chief! Come quickly, chief! There has been a terrible accident.'

'I told you I was not to be disturbed,' said a clipped voice.

'Chief, you don't understand. Georgy has killed herself.'

Behind the door Mr Pye was trembling, but his voice was as cold as before:

> 'And if one green bottle
> Should accidentally fall
> There'll be two green bottles
> Standing on the wall.'

Tintagieu was now at Miss Dredger's side. 'That's no way to talk,' she shouted. 'Come out and give a hand, Mr Pye. The Paint-box is here. We'll get her on a couch.'

'Ring the doctor,' said Mr Pye. 'There's nothing I can do. She was a silly old trout anyway. There'll be more room in the house at last.

> 'Just "Tanty" and me-ee-ee
> And Dredger makes three . . . ee . . . ee
> We're happy in our . . .
> Blue . . . heav . . . en. . . .'

Now this levity was so appalling a thing to hear coming through the door that Miss Dredger and Tintagieu moved together for mutual support. This was not just rudeness or bravado, it was something altogether more sinister. Tintagieu, who had entered in upon the whole thing rather in the spirit of a private joke, now felt herself involved in something more satanic. The neat little missionary had another side.

Young Thorpe phoned the doctor and then joined the two women at the top of the stairs.

'What's keeping you, sir?' he shouted to Mr Pye, through the door. 'There's a dead w-w-woman downstairs: Miss George. Aren't you interested?'

'Not very,' said the voice.

A hush then hung in the air outside Mr Pye's bedroom. They could hear their own hearts beating and the ticking of Mr Pye's alarm clock on the other side of the door.

Then they crept down the stairs, skirted the spread-eagled lady, and by common consent walked shakily through the front door and on to the lawn, where they sat on the grass at the foot of the tired palm without a word until the doctor arrived.

He verified their opinion. She was stone dead. When he had gone Tintagieu turned to Miss Dredger.

'I wouldn't spend another night at the place for a thousand bloody pounds.'

Miss Dredger lit a cigarette. Her hand was trembling.

'The dead don't frighten me,' she said at last. 'The real Georgy has flown.'

'But not the real Pye,' said Tintagieu. 'He is still in the house.'

'Tanty,' she said, and it was the first time she had used the diminutive. 'I'll be honest with you. I don't think I'm usually a funk, but I don't mind telling you I'm scared.'

'Of the Fruit-drop?' asked the artist.

'Of Mr Pye!' said Miss Dredger. 'I have never let him down before, but it doesn't seem as though it's really him in that bedroom now. It's as though it's someone else. Ever since he stepped ashore this morning I've noticed it. He used to be so thoughtful, so kind, so gentle, and so happy. Dash it all, Tanty, he's not like that any more. I don't understand him.'

'You must never try to,' said a voice and at once their three heads turned to the house. Mr Pye was standing on the upstairs veranda with his hands on the railing.

'To try to understand is to never understand. Either everything is understood at once, by the heart, or it is never understood at all. At this moment I happen to understand something. Something very small but, in so far as I understand it at all, I understand it perfectly. You must all leave me. I need a little time alone. Georgy will be dealt with shortly. You must leave me. You must go at once. Tintagieu to her small and tolerant cottage, my artist friend to his studio. As for you, sailor, you must go to the Lagnommiare where they will board you at my expense.'

His hands began to shake upon the railing. The three had long since risen to their feet. Their dissimilar faces were turned to his.

'Go!' he suddenly cried. 'Go, my friends, before it is too late. I cannot explain to you, but something cosmic is at work in me. I stand upon hell's border. Go! Go! Go!'

They went.

The island began immediately to buzz with a hundred variations on the theme that Miss Dredger had been flung from her own house by her own guest and that Tintagieu and Thorpe had been secretly married by Mr Pye in his fraudulent capacity as a priest – Great Palist Order – and that Miss George had been murdered with a skewer. Later in the day there was a certain amount of coming and going at the Clôs de Joi. The vicar, the doctor, and the undertaker came at various times; Miss George was carried upstairs by four powerful fishermen and laid upon her bed. The blinds were drawn and candles were lit in her room.

At last Mr Pye was alone in the house. He locked every door and drew every bolt and curtained every window.

Then he lit a couple of lamps and leaving one in the empty living-room, took the other to his own bedroom. He still walked swiftly. He still cocked his head, and popped fruit-drops into his mouth, but in the depth of his weak eyes there was fear.

He placed the lamp on the chest of drawers and tried to pray, standing on his toes, his face turned to the ceiling, his hands clenched beneath his chin. But the Great Pal seemed out of range and all that Mr Pye could hear was the sound of his own voice.

The evening changed to night and the moon dodged in and out of the low clouds.

Outside the house, but in the grounds of Clôs de Joi, young Pépé and his friends crept to and fro in the undergrowth, or doubled up and made dangerous runs across the moonlit spaces that divided one black ambush from another. Later on they pretended to be owls and whooped and whooped until they thought of throwing stones. When they had broken two windows they became nervous and melted from Miss Dredger's garden.

All that night Mr Pye could not sleep. He paced from room to room, circumambulating each in turn, leaving out only Miss George's bedroom. Yet time passed so slowly that it hardly seemed to have the power to push the hands of the clock from one minute to the next.

He had made vents in his vest and shirt through which he had passed his wings so that, at least, he moved in comfort. But these wings were no shorter. No, not by an inch. It was for him to do some heinous thing – but what? ... what? ... what? Ghastly and unmentionable visions passed through his mind and sickened him. Pacing from room to room, his brain dilated with ghoulish thoughts, he turned into the sitting-room for the hundredth time and pumped up the lamp again until its friendly hissing filled the silence.

Moving to the bookshelf he chose a book at random, more for the colour of its spine than anything else, and returning to the lamp he was about to sit down when his eye fell on one of Miss Dredger's ubiquitous packets of 'Three Star'. He had never smoked before but tonight he drew out one of the four cigarettes that were left in the packet, and placing its printed end between his lips he bent over the lamp, as he had so often seen

Miss Dredger do, and with his cigarette tip immediately over the white-hot mantle he inhaled gingerly. Apart from the fact that both his eyebrows were singed off in the updraught, he managed very well, but after the third draw he inhaled too deeply and choked unhappily. In raising his arm in order to crush the cigarette out in a glass dish on the mantelpiece, he felt the distinct sensation of a never-before-used and never-before-even-dreamed-of muscle coming into play for the first time. Mr Pye shrugged his shoulder again, and again there was a sense of fresh forces at work in the region of his scapulae. Each time he tried it seemed for a moment that there was the danger of severe cramp, but the plucking of the muscles at his back was merely the preliminary to something more creative. Turning his head as he shrugged again, he saw out of the corner of his eye a section of his white wing rise to the level of his shoulder. For the next hour he was able to lift his wings simultaneously. As yet they had little strength, but he could now flap them gently up and down.

Yet what was the point of his doing all this if his over-riding desire was to rid himself of the unwanted things? There was no point – but even in the direst circumstances, man is curious and prone to irrelevance.

He was now getting cold. The time of night that strikes the shrewdest chill into the bones was upon him. There were two hours to go before dawn.

He picked up the book which he had selected and flicked over a page or two but the humour of the writing was so remote from the mood of his terrible predicament that he replaced it on the shelf. It was as though someone about to be devoured of a crocodile were being asked to smile by a photographer on the bank. Mr Pye retraced his steps to the table, lifted the lamp, and carried it into the hall and up the stairs. As he passed a window on the stairs, and was holding the lamp well away from his body, he did not realize that for a moment he cast the sharp black pattern of his silhouette on the curtain, so that Old Ka-Ka's nephew, famous for the peculiar state of his mind, on rising to his feet in the field adjoining Miss Dredger's (where he had lain in an alcoholic stupor since midnight) and on gazing stupefied at the glow of light in a window of the house (for there is nothing else to look at in the darkness before dawn), saw to his confused amazement the strange black shape of an angel moving across the lamplit curtains.

Ka-Ka's nephew had always had a healthy fear of death and angels, and in spite of the all but inactive condition of his brain, now saw in the pinioned apparition the sign of his own demise. In a state of terror he staggered to his congested home with the witches' seat on the chimney-stack, and waking his father, mother, six brothers and seven sisters, he created such pandemonium that the doctor was called and Ka-Ka's nephew was taken the next day to Guernsey asylum.

But Mr Pye knew nothing of all this. He had merely passed a window with a lamp in his hand. Before going to his room at the top of the stairs he opened Miss George's door and raised his lamp.

The hideous thought of striking the corpse with his umbrella burst like an abscess in his brain. To strike and so load the scales against his natural goodness that by this single act he might set in motion the strange power of his shoulders. The power that, surely, if it could conjure feathers from the fabric of goodness, could equally withdraw them at the hint of such a sin. But to have even thought of such a monstrous idea was as much as Mr Pye could manage – and the room began to move before his eyes and it was all he could do to close the door and find his way through a dizzy haze of nausea to his room where he collapsed upon his bed. There he lay until the dawn broke over the island.

When Mr Pye woke at last the morning was well advanced. He heard his name being called and there was the sound of footsteps in the hall.

Getting to his feet and reaching out for his glasses only to find that he still had them on his nose, he could not at first collect his thoughts, nor remember why he was partly dressed, but as the moments passed, the interminable hours of the previous night swam back into his memory. He called out to those below that he would soon be down. It took him some time to bandage his wings and adjust his cape, which he noticed with a shock was now incapable of hiding what was developing into a hump at his back.

That day was very full. There were all kinds of arrangements to be made in regard to the late Miss George. She was taken away that same afternoon to a cottage near the undertakers. With some difficulty the addresses of at least three other Georges were found among her letters and telegrams were sent to England.

Not only was the day particularly full but the week that followed it. Mr Pye's time was, according to his diary, filled up as usual with reminders of the various gatherings he had promised to attend. The clubs he had started on the island were all flourishing and he was deeply committed. He had never for instance failed to attend the meetings of 'Faith's Fishermen' (a society he had formed and which he addressed every Friday). There was also the monthly whist drive at the Pal Club. He was down to give prizes at the Cattle Show and to speak in favour of a closer union between the residents and the visitors. Next year, if all went well there was to be an effort to go even further and forge a link between the visitors and the day-trippers, but this, even Mr Pye could see, would be uphill work.

What a week it was to be. Mr Pye, now no longer interested in doing good, saw that in between club attendances and the funeral of Miss George, his diary was filled with other appointments. He had no less than three ancient and bedridden women to visit in their little dark houses; seven children to speak to about their increasingly unpleasant habits; four visitors to conduct on geological explorations of the caves, and a number of other engagements. What was he to do? He was in no mood and in no condition to fulfil all these obligations. What is more, he realized that if he did fulfil them he would be, by reason of his devotion to duty, doing all he could to cancel out whatever small successes he had gained in the cause of iniquity.

No. He must cut the lot. He would let them down. He would disappoint them. The old women: the bedridden: the sick and afflicted: the loyal members of the Pal

Club and Faith's Fishers: the eager tourists who were so looking forward to the caves. They must all have their days ruined.

Mr Pye knew that this would cause an unparalleled stir. It would turn the island into a seething cauldron of conjecture – but 'I must have the courage to be evil,' he whispered to himself as he polished his glasses at the front door of Clôs de Joi. 'I must have the courage to offend.'

And so he had, for the only engagement – if it could so be called – which he *did* attend, was Miss George's funeral, and he was late for that, arrriving only for the actual burial, and in an outfit of such blasphemous immoderacy that Sark has never since ceased to speak of it, nor has anyone who witnessed the exhibition been able to walk by the churchyard from that day to this without that picture of Mr Pye pattering his jaunty way to the grave-side, and twirling his cane as he went; Mr Pye with his cape turned inside out so that the pale green lining floated about him in impious folds: Mr Pye threading his way through the mourners; the islanders, all draped in darkness, black as tinkers' pots. Mr Pye in his tropical suit, a lavender scarf of sensuous silk at his throat, a pair of pointed yellow shoes upon his feet, and, shading his round and famous face, and at a profane angle, a panama hat upon his head – a hat which he had no intention, so it appeared, of removing in the presence of the dead.

The vicar's words fell from his mouth one by one like stones falling upon soft turf and then suddenly stopped falling. The black rookery of mourners congealed into a single lump of malignant stupor. A hideous hush filled the graveyard as with gooseflesh. And in this hush, Mr Pye, taking a turn up and down the length of the grave, stopped for a moment, and in the silence dug the point of his cane into freshly dug earth, and lifting a wodge of it on his ferrule to the level of his eyes, he stared at it with his head cocked on one side.

'Just the stuff for tomatoes,' he said, and then as he turned and stepped briskly away and through the graveyard gate, twirling his cane as he went – 'Just the very—' they heard him repeat, 'Just the very.'

Nearing his house he felt a spasm at the shoulders, and he began to trot. As he trotted his hope grew – but he was deadly tired from the strain of the last few minutes. For profanity and desecration were the anathema of his soul. As he trotted he heard someone running behind him, and turning his head he saw that Miss Dredger was at his heels.

'Chief! Chief!'

Mr Pye stopped, and regained his breath.

'Yes, sailor?'

'You are sick. You are mortally sick.'

Mr Pye gazed at her. He saw the fear in her eyes and he saw also the indomitable loyalty that had once been his to enjoy.

'Sailor,' he said, 'you are the only soul I can trust. Come with me.'

'Of course, chief.'

'You are afraid of me, sailor?'

'I am,' said Miss Dredger, 'and I am afraid for you.'

'If I told you of my deep trouble, could I trust you to the last drop of blood in your body, that you would keep its nature darker than death itself?'

'You could,' said Miss Dredger, 'and you *know* you could. It is when you are secretive and rude that I am afraid.'

'Sailor.'

'Yes?'

'Are you prepared for *anything*?'

'Yes, chief, anything.'

'I have grown wings.'

A gull banked and circled as it passed overhead. A leaf fluttered from the trees above. Miss Dredger's lower jaw had fallen open like a trap and she had become deathly pale. She turned from him and began to kick at a tuft of grass, and then with her back still to him she straightened herself, and standing absolutely upright she drew her shoulders back, hollowed her back, and with her arms rigid she clasped her hands together behind her. Thus she stood for a few long seconds before she turned about.

'Come on, chief,' she said, 'let's get indoors. We can't do anything out here. Well, well, well, of all the people who have ever stayed with me, you take the cake,' and whistling a reminiscent tune, she began to stride along, Mr Pye at her side, until, as they reached the drive, he joined her in her nostalgic music – and then, involuntarily and simultaneously they broke out into quiet song:

'Pull for the shore, sailor,
Pull for the shore
Heed not the rolling waves,
But bend to the oar ...'

TWENTY-THREE

THAT the cause of Mr Pye's unnatural secret was, in the first place, his unnatural piety was enough for Miss Dredger. She had a highly practical outlook on life and saw at once how impossible it would be if her chief were discovered to be some kind of hybrid. However awed the Sarkese might be to have something on the island that was half man, half angel, yet by the very limitations of human nature, Mr Pye could never be other than primarily a freak. And so Miss Dredger, out of her solid horse-sense, was forced to admit that Mr Pye had no alternative but to counteract his good with forms of evil every whit as potent – until the crisis had passed.

'I will understand, chief,' she said, 'if you talk it out with me, I will certainly understand. I'm not so darned daft that I don't see that at times you must *catch up*, and to shout at me and be beastly may help you.'

'There's enough I can do without making you even more unhappy than I have already made you, my dear. What is necessary is wickedness on the grand scale. It is so difficult, my dear. You see I have lost touch with the Great Pal somehow. I have no flair for real evil. The only way I can do it is by acting, but I suppose if I really hurt my fellow mortals often enough, it may do some good in the end. The trouble is I haven't much time left. People are already staring at my shoulders.'

It was true. There had been much speculation on the island as to why Mr Pye, who had once been so upright, was now strangely uneven along the spine. But this was merely part of the seething turmoil of conjecture and counter-conjecture, of rumour wild and moonstruck, of rumours of all kinds, of stories fantastic but not one, though they were stretched to breaking point, was as strange as the reality.

Committees were getting together at the island hall; groups gathered to discuss what should be done, for obviously a man who could so blaspheme in a graveyard should be sent off the island. He had been seen doing a hundred detestable things. He had been seen skipping up to children's sand-castles, and kicking them gaily into the air, so that the bays echoed with the angry shouts of parents and the howling of their progeny. He had been seen pinching children in prams. One man claimed to have seen him setting fire to an old man's beard, but as the old man in question denied that this had taken place, and what is more still had his beard unsinged for living proof, this particular story was grudgingly relinquished.

But what, as the next days and nights went by, were the wary islanders *unable* to observe? They were unable to see Mr Pye drinking a steaming cup of cocoa at two in the morning. They were unable to see Miss Dredger standing at his side, her chin thrust forward, her eyes full of dogged courage. They were unable to see her tighten his belt for him, push a box full of sandwiches into the light haversack he carried over his shoulder, nor hear her say – 'Good hunting, chief,' as she opened the front door for him and watched his plump little purposeful figure disappear into the night. And they were unable to see which way he went, and could never know that as the hours went by he was moving indefatigably to and fro from house to house, starting at one end of the island and not only ending at the other, but moving silent as a ghost down all the tangential lanes, leaving not a cottage free from his right hand, which, by the end of his strenuous expedition was very sore indeed. For it is worse than shaking hands with a hundred people one after another, to turn on tap after tap after tap. How many taps he turned at the base of those great metal tanks that stand against the wall of every house of the island, he could not tell, for Mr Pye soon lost interest in counting them.

It was a case of tap after tap, tap after tap, some loose, some stiff, but none of them holding out against his forceful little fingers for long. At first he shut his eyes rather than see, faintly in the darkness, the precious rainwater gushing into the darkness down whatever slopes surrounded him, gushing and spreading so that wide areas of ground about each house, became like shallow lakes, or where the ground was less even, flooding its way down the nocturnal lanes; forcing a sluggish way through grass and weeds; or pouring freely over some cliff edge and down the dark walls to the saline sea.

As Mr Pye returned home weary and sore of hand, but hardened in spirit, for it is impossible not to become impervious to the sting of guilt after the first seventy taps, he could hear in the silence of the night an ubiquitous hissing – a sound that came from every part of the island, the sound of water as it leaps for freedom : the sound of water finding its own level.

Only Miss Dredger knew of this. She agreed that it was worth doing but held that it was an extremely *naughty* rather than an *evil* thing to do. But it would help.

The trouble that this caused the island switched the searchlight of notoriety from Mr Pye, for a day or two, for there was no kind of way to tell who had perpetrated such a mean and senseless act.

Of what else was the island unaware? They were unaware that Mr Pye was studying book after book on witchcraft. That it was he who had burned down three hayricks in Little Sark, but more important than a score of these minor misdeeds at which he was becoming a past-master – they were unaware also that he crept almost nightly through the darkness to Dixcart Valley where the bearded thing was tethered, nor could they know that when he left the valley an hour after his face was as white as tallow and his eyes glittered with a peculiar light.

What had he said to it in that dark place, where the rivulet slid over the stones? What had he heard it say? What was he doing to his perjured soul?

It was not only the islanders who were unaware of these nocturnal expeditions into the unknown. Miss Dredger was herself quite ignorant of them. She had no secrets from him. She worked like a Trojan for her chief. It was he, Mr Pye, who by this new secret of his own was leaving her yet again out of his confidence.

It was a week later when measuring Mr Pye's wing-span (as she always did just before breakfast every morning), when, hardly daring to believe her eyes, she took a sharp breath which caused her chief to ask what the matter was.

'The *matter*?' she whispered – 'Hold your horses, chief, hold your bally horses.' Again she stretched out her tape-measure and consulted her list of previous findings which was beside her on the table.

'It's true!' she cried. 'It's true! The tide has turned, by Jupiter! Oh, chief, it's going out!'

'Out!'

Mr Pye sprang around, like something made of india-rubber.

'Out! Out!' cried Miss Dredger. 'The tide!'

'Damn the tide, sailor! What about my wings?'

'That's what I mean, dear! The wings are going *in*!'

Mr Pye trembled. 'What do you make me?' he whispered.

'Four foot two and a quarter from tip to tip.'

'And yesterday?'

'Four foot three, chief. Four foot three – Oh gloriana!'

'And for how long had we been stuck at four foot three? How long, sailor – over a week, wasn't it?'

'Six days.'

Mr Pye stood on his toes and beat his wings, and the draught they caused sent a napkin scurrying across the kitchen table.

'We've got it on the run, sailor.' Mr Pye turned his face to her and smiled so tenderly and strangely that Miss Dredger, who was reminded of his gallantry in earlier days, could hardly keep the tears from her eyes.

'I must redouble my efforts. This is no moment to rest upon

my pinions. Ah, sailor – what would I have done without you?'

'Nonsense, chief.'

That night, when Mr Pye let himself out of his window on a rope, for one of the stairs creaked, and made his guilty way to the Dixcart Valley, he realized something very terrible. It was no longer difficult for him to sin. It had become natural. And worse than this. He had developed a taste for it.

Within a quarter of an hour he had reached the wooded tip of the valley and followed the ferny track downhill to where a fallen tree lay across the stream. Turning to his left in the darkness he found a large grey goat tied to a stump of alder. The white beard of this odoriferous beast gleamed balefully in the starlight.

'Oh, thou,' said Mr Pye in a faraway and most peculiar voice, after which he added 'hail'.

The goat nodded its head and its chain clinked in the night. Its face was long enough for wisdom in all conscience. As for its eyes, Solomon sat in one of them, and Confucius in the other. They were pure eloquence. The satanic horns were less elevating and so was the mouth – a thoroughly unpleasant line, where Satan had obviously been at work.

Mr Pye marked out a fresh circle on the ground and hopped inside it. The previous ones had been worn away by the goat's neat little scrabbling hoofs. As he began to scratch further signs inside the circle and light a short black stub of candle, he thought of the Great Pal, but instead of being afraid, as he had been for the last week, he now rejoiced in his insurrection.

TWENTY-FOUR

IGNORANT that a fabulous drama was unfolding itself chapter by chapter on the little stony island that from the sea looked as barren as an old fossil, the day trippers swarmed ashore at the Creux Harbour at eleven in the morning every day of the week. Now that the summer was advanced there were boats from Guernsey twice a day, and from Jersey every Tuesday. These day trippers, in the unanimous opinion of all islanders, were the lowest type of animal life. Tintagieu and Thorpe, sitting on the sea wall, watched them as though they were witnessing the disembarkation of thrice murrained cattle.

Certainly there was an awful lot of meat coming ashore.

'I wonder why I come down here practically every m-morning,' said Thorpe. 'I seem to get some dreadful pleasure out of looking at the D.T.s. Perhaps they make me think I'm some g-good after all.'

'Did you ever paint that picture, dear?' asked Tintagieu with that voice, half purr, half growl.

'Which one?' said Thorpe. 'I've p-painted a thousand pictures in my head. What was it?'

'When we were down at Derrible, my love. When the Fruit-drop had his picnic and you fell into the pool because you had such a good idea.'

'No, I never painted it,' said the artist.

'Ah,' said Tintagieu, after a pause. 'Naughty little paint-box. I'll break up all your brushes and squeeze out all your tubes.'

'Please c-come for tea today,' said Thorpe.

'Not today, dear. Not today – much too busy, and your bed is so uncomfortable.'

'Darling Tanty, my old fat b-beauty – my "love-in-idleness",' said Thorpe at last. They had been dreaming away with their eyes shut. 'Tanty – my plump adorable, let's drop in on the Dredger. I'm sorry for the Dredger. The Fruit-drop m-must be tearing her nerves apart.'

'He's torn the island apart,' said Tintagieu. 'He's the only man who's ever frightened me.'

'Come on,' said Thorpe. 'Come on, "edible".'

They slid down from the sea-wall and strolled down the little quayside, where the water was so motionless that the French yacht from St Malo that was moored at the southern end was no more incisive than her reflection. As they paused to look down at her, for she lay a few feet below them on a three-quarter tide, a handsome Frenchman put his head out of the hatch and stared about him with a dreamy smile until he caught sight of Tintagieu. He rolled his eyes, and Tintagieu, at Thorpe's side, appeared to offer herself as it were on a plate, although she hardly moved, and her tongue was barely visible as it slid between her lips.

At that moment the head of the Frenchman's wife appeared alongside his. She had tawny golden hair and a dark blue tooth, a disgrace to her upper jaw. Directly she saw Tintagieu she disappeared from view, taking her husband with her, and as far as Tintagieu and Thorpe were concerned, they were swallowed for ever not only into the darkness below board, but the capricious shadowlands of memory.

Thorpe and Tintagieu walked slowly through the tunnel in the rock where their voices sounded hollow and prodigious like the voices of Wagnerian gods.

'What do you make of it, Tanty? What's going on at Clôs de Joi? Something bloody queer or I'm a c-cod. Old Georgie's death, for instance! was that just an accident?' He pulled his thin beard and raised his eyebrows at his plump companion.

'Oh yes, *that* was all right,' she said.

'Yes, but when you were there, didn't you *f-feel* anything?'

'What kind of... ?'

'The Fruit-drop.'

'Well, I told you, my little scatterbrain. I *told* you. I *said* he scared my bloomers off me, dear. Didn't I? Why don't you artists ever wash your ears?'

'What's come over him, Tanty? Mr Porter stopped me this morning in the avenue and told me he'd s-seen the Fruit-drop go up to one of the de Fliebas children, lift it up and bite its ear.'

'There's a doctor coming over from Jersey, they say,' said Tintagieu. 'He's come to make a study of the brain.'

'What, the Fruit-drop's?'

'Of course. Who else has got a brain worth studying?'

'How can he study it, unless he takes it out?' said the painter.

'What an ass you are,' said Tintagieu. 'They'll *talk* together.'

'Ha, ha, ha, ha!' laughed Thorpe. 'He'll get more than he b-bargained for. Eh?'

'He will if he's like me,' said Tintagieu. 'I got something I never bargained for all right.'

'That swipe on your b-bum?' said Thorpe.

'The very same,' said Tintagieu. 'There was I all ready for a frolic – done up to kill like purity, my love ... and then *whang*. I can still feel it.'

By now they were a quarter way of the hill and were on the tail of the D.T.s and twenty minutes later they pushed open the garden gate of Clôs de Joi. Even as they started up the drive they heard a familiar voice, followed by the gay, intelligent laughter of the little man who had given Sark so much food for thought that it was no wonder that it suffered from flatulence.

'Come in! come in! come in! come in!' he cried. 'Deck-chairs, sailor! Chairs for our visitors!' and 'Sailor,' he cried after her as she was about to disappear into the house, 'coffee! and some of those drop scones – what? Well, well, well, well, if it isn't Tintagieu! The one and only inimitable Tintagieu, whose locks are like the raven and whose bonny brows are something or other in Scotch, but nothing at all in English, and *who* wants to learn Scotch?' he practically shouted, as he slid between them and took them each by the elbow, and led them rapidly to and fro all over the lawn as he talked. His face was as round and rosy as it had been, when in time long past, as it now seemed, though it was in reality only a few months ago, he had first come to the island and brought with him such a fountain of love and hope, and also such a future. A future that had affected not only Mr Pye, but in one way or another the entire population. A future that was now the present and through which they were even at that very moment floating, as though on time's black current, for beneath the gay patter and the iridescent surface and the bubble of immediacy, was the inexorable movement of primal darkness.

'And *you*, sir, *you*, the artist, the beauty-maker, how are you, sir? What are *your* thoughts? What are *your* ambitions? What are you painting these days? Ah, I would dearly have loved to be a painter had I not received that call to other fields – and what a wheezy call it was, and how wet the fields were – ha! ha! ha! ha! ha! – but I am beyond you, no? No? And *you*, Tintagieu, have *you* never longed to paint, to draw, to wield a full brush and slap the colours on, one! two! three! and away we go, plunging into the golden ochre, whisking the crimson from the palette, flicking on the viridian and they presto! there you are, a thing of beauty, a radiance, an act, an utterance!'

'That's not my idea of painting,' said Thorpe.

'Of course it isn't, my friend. Why should it be? You are altogether more tentative. But that would be *my* way of painting. We can only speak for ourselves in these matters.'

Thorpe, who had rather screwed up his courage to interrupt Mr Pye, for he did not want Tintagieu to suppose that he was unable to stand up to such a spate of words, now wished he had kept his mouth shut. Rather resentfully he added, 'I don't know about "tentative".'

'But I do,' said Mr Pye, 'I know all about it. It is nothing to be ashamed of. It is merely that you are a man on the defensive more than a man who attacks. I would not say you are timid – that is not the word. I would say you are *careful*.'

'Are you talking about me or my painting?'

'They are the same thing,' said Mr Pye. 'How can anything come out of you that is not you?'

'You told me once that I was a channel,' said Thorpe, rather irritably, 'and that what p-passed through me was not me, but God. I was just a k-kind of pipe, you said. It was absolute rubbish, of course, but it hardly tallies with what you are saying now, does it? Oh, these *theories*,' he added in a voice of scorn and with a flourish of his free arm (for Mr Pye still held the elbow of the other) – 'these theories about Art, they are all absolute n-nonsense.' (He was winding himself up, for Tintagieu was listening – he hoped.) 'Can't you see the whole thing is an organized racket? The p-painter digs his heart up and tries to sell it. The heart specialists become interested, for the thing is still b-beating. The hangers-on begin to suck the blood. They lick each other like c-cats. They bare their fangs like d-dogs. The whole thing is pitiful. Art is in the hands of the amateurs, the Philistines, the racketeers, the Jews, the snarling women and the raging queers to whom Soutine is "ever so pretty" and Rembrandt "ever s-so sweet".

'What do the galleries know? They are merely m-merchants. They sell pictures instead of lamp-shades and that's the only difference. And the critics – Lord, what *clever* b-boys they are! They know about everything except painting. That's why I came out here to get away from it all. The jungle of London with its millions of apes. I came out here to find myself, but have I done so? No, Mr Pye. Of c-course I haven't. For artists need competition and the stimulus of other b-brains whether they like it or not. They must talk painting, b-breathe painting, and be c-covered with paint. That is the kind of man I would talk to. A man c-covered with paint. And with paint in his hair and paint in the brain and *on* the b-brain – but where are they, these men? – they're in the great cities, among the m-monkeys where they can see each other work and fight it out, while as f-far as the public is concerned they might as well be knitting, or blowing b-bubbles, for even you, Mr Pye, if you don't mind my saying so, haven't got a c-clue to what it's all about, as your ridiculous "slap it on", "whisk it off", and "hey presto" attitude shows all t-too clearly. Your idea about colours is "the m-more the b-better", and "bright as p-possible", like a herbaceous b-border. Colour, Mr Pye, is a process of elimination. It is the d-distillation of an attitude. It is a credo.'

The painter, breathless, turned his head to Tintagieu. He had not let himself go like this for years. He had forgotten that he cared so much – and when he turned to her his eyes were shining. But hers were shut. What was she thinking? He turned to Mr Pye. They had come to a halt by the ugly palm.

Mr Pye's face was pink with admiration. He ran his eyes over the painter as though he had never seen him before. He turned his head quickly to Tintagieu as though for corroboration and then he ran his eyes again all over Thorpe. 'That was superb,' he whispered, as though to himself. 'What an argument this young man could put up if he only had the time. What do you think, Tintagieu? – but here comes our sailor with the coffee.'

His outburst over, the painter felt rather foolish. Tintagieu had a far-away look in her big black eyes – but when Mr Pye turned to her suddenly and cried: 'A penny for them! A penny for them!' she muttered: 'I must go.' She turned to Miss Dredger. 'Come and see me,' she said, 'any evening, dear, but *not* after nine.'

'Damn it, Tanty, you can't go s-suddenly like this, just when ...'

'Must go, dear: must go, my paint-box-darling. Dolly needs her bottle – you should know *that* by now.'

TWENTY-FIVE

As the days passed and the wings showed no sign of slowing the pace of their withdrawal, Mr Pye and Miss Dredger, with their bond of secrecy between them, became almost hectically excited. The tape-measure told them that, over the total wing-span, Mr Pye was losing a steady two inches a day. By simple computation he should be free of them within forty hours.

But the dark and clandestine journeys to Dixcart Valley in the small hours of the morning were still a dreadful secret that Mr Pye was unable to share with his loyal lieutenant. The terrible thing was that his abundant virtues, his joy, his friendliness, were now no more his real self than was the other side, that darker side, which had grown and grown until it was now *as natural* for him to hurt as to heal, to sink as to rise.

Of course the habits of a lifetime made it seem that he was in a great measure the same Mr Pye, for to turn up the corners of that piquant little mouth was more involuntarily easy than not to do so – but these automatic reflexes could not alter the fact that in order to rid himself of the wings he had gone too far in the other direction.

One mild evening, as the last hours of his plumage grew nearer, Mr Pye and Miss Dredger sat side by side. They had gone for a long walk and had turned down the path that led from the Seigneurie Road to the Port de Moulin bay. They did not, however, turn down the wet secretive path of ferns which descended to the rocky beach, but keeping above it came to that flat bluff from the precipitous edge of which it was possible to obtain a bird's-eye view of the bay, with the severed Moi-de-Morton on the left, and to the right, isolated from the main cliffs and knee-deep in water, that natural effort at cubism, the Grand Autelet.

They stared down, breathing the salty air, and watching the shadows of the clouds as they slid across the pale green water.

A cormorant sped across the bay, an inch or two above the surface, and then rose to join a hundred others on the huge square rock.

'Always reminds me of a chopped-off skyscraper,' said Miss Dredger, having noticed that Mr Pye had also been following the flight of the bird.

'The Autelet?'

'Yes, chief.'

'Certainly very abstract.'

'Yes, most unnatural.'

'Like me,' said Mr Pye.

'Oh, chief.'

Mr Pye raised his hand to his brow and, shading his eyes watched the progress of a couple of children jumping from rock to rock, far below, no larger than sunflower seeds. Before he dropped his hand he scratched himself across the brow.

'Must have been bitten.'

'It's the time of year for it, chief.'

'Well, I've lost my chance, dear.'

'Chance of what, chief?'

'Of sailing away through the sweet, translucent air. Of stepping out over the edge of this precipitous headland and, like that gull, of being borne across the bay and the sea, and up into the sun, and down and up again, and away and away and then, perhaps, to return and to perch at last, who knows, on the back of the old Abstract.'

'Ha ha ha! I would love to see you there. You would suit the Autelet.'

'And it would suit me, sailor. Perhaps I should have been a gull.'

'I can just see you landing, chief! And what would you do then?'

'Oh,' (said Mr Pye with a twinkle) 'I'd sit down, sailor, and have a fruit-drop.'

'Ha, ha, ha, ha, ha! you are a one, chief, you darned well *are*, you know. But oh, chief, this is a great day. Your chance to fly may have gone, but your chance to live in that full and generous way that was once yours, has come again. Tomorrow you will be free.' She frowned. 'You have certainly been bitten, chief. Twice.'

'Free?' murmured Mr Pye. 'Free . . . ?' he repeated even more softly, and to himself. 'Free for what . . . ?' He traced a circle on the ground with his cane and his hand trembled.

To their right there was a narrow spine of cliff which blocked away a section of what would have been a wider panorama, and in this cliff a square window had, many years ago, been drilled through the solid rock-face. Before they returned home they trod gingerly over the sharp debris that had never been cleared away from the landward mouth of this window and they stood a few moments at its seaward lip, from where they gazed down a sheer wall of sickening rock. They both had excellent heads for heights, but when Mr Pye said, 'What a place to take off from,' Miss Dredger shut her eyes.

'Oh, stop it, chief,' she said; 'we've had enough of that.'

TWENTY-SIX

THAT evening Mr Pye and Miss Dredger sat facing one another on the upstairs veranda. They had dined well and now they relaxed. A bottle of old wine stood between them. They had drunk to each other's health several times.

'I have another toast,' said Miss Dredger, her eyes sprarkling.

'Yes, sailor?'

'I drink to the utter destruction of all wings.'

'Did you say wings or things?'

'We could start with wings,' said Miss Dredger.

Mr Pye raised his glass. 'To the destruction of all – oh, but one cannot drink to *that*,' he said. 'Think of all the butterflies, the robins, the magnificent eagles – surely we can't drink to . . .'

'Well then, we'll cut out the birds,' cried Miss Dredger. 'Except for vultures, they aren't very . . .'

'But they all add variety to life,' said Mr Pye.

'Well, so did you, for that matter, chief, but it was the wrong variety, wasn't it? Eh?'

'I am not sure that you are not being a little pert, my dear.'

'Pert, chief? – oh, no!'

'Then we will let it pass, sailor!' He switched on the radiance of his smile and Miss Dredger basked for a while in its penetrating warmth. She was unreservedly forgiven and they were closer than they had been for a long while. Were it not for Mr Pye's nocturnal expeditions to the Dixcart Valley they would have been intensely happy; happy, for instance, in planning how they could restore Mr Pye to his former position of spiritual supremacy on the island – a supremacy that had been undermined by a number of unpalatable incidents. Contented as they were, sitting on the veranda, yet the air between them was not charged with the mutual confidence which, when it exists, can never be mistaken.

For a long time past, in fact ever since Mr Pye's first misdeed, when he kicked over the elaborate sand-castle of a small bandy-legged child, the island had been gathering its indescribable forces together (for the shock had been considerable) in order to take action of some kind against the mountebank.

The inhabitants were not at the best of times much given to acting in unison, and it took a long time for them to agree as to what could be done to formulate even the most tentative plan. But the residents, in spite of their distrust of one another, had been able by reason of their comparative scarcity, to mobilize themselves and discuss the whole question of Mr Pye. They had had four meetings and all of them had been held in Mr Porter's large house that overlooked Port-à-la-Jument. Mr and Mrs Porter had the largest sitting-room, or lounge, as they preferred to call it, in Sark. What could be seen of its walls were spinach green and were covered with the stuffed heads of big and little game from Tanganyika. The meetings were watched remorselessly from every wall by the glazed eyes of antelope, giraffe and hippo, buck and lion, zebra and leopard.

With this glass-eyed audience about them they argued for hours on end, while Mrs Porter brought in periodical pots of tea, and Mr Porter watched out of the corner of his eye the gin and sherry in the Bristol bottles finding their lowest level.

He could not have it both ways. Either he enjoyed the fact that he had the best house in Sark, and insisted that the meetings should take place in his 'lounge', or he submitted that Stitchwater's house would do equally well, and so economized on his gin and sherry.

Torn between the two he decided upon the former, but not, unfortunately, with the best grace.

As Miss Dredger and Mr Pye sat in quiet contentment on the veranda of Clôs de Joi they could not know that a posse of residents was approaching them from the direction of the derelict windmill. A vote had been taken at the Porters' and they had chosen that particular evening.

The residents bore down upon Clôs de Joi in close formation – so close in fact that it might have been supposed that Major Havershot had given the order for his platoon to break step – as though it were crossing a particularly attenuated bridge. There were some in the group, notably Mrs Porter, who could not have felt more out of place had they been actually proceeding in column of route – three abreast, and with a brass band blaring.

She had tried to detach herself from the body of the martial group, but it felt even worse to be an isolated straggler, and she quickened her pace again and worked her way to the comparatively obscure centre of the contingent.

Mr Rice and his wife were well to the fore, the latter's perfectly square body moving forward with dire purpose upon small curved legs like the legs of Edwardian armchairs. Her husband, twice as tall as his spouse, stalked vaguely at her side, taking one step to every four of hers, so that it seemed almost as though she were running.

When they reached the gates of Clôs de Joi they came to a halt while Mr Porter struggled with the latch. He was somewhat out of temper anyway, and to be held up by the obduracy of the gate and his memory of how much of his gin Mr Rice had put away during the last two hours brought out the worst in him.

'Can't you do it, dear?' cried Mrs Porter in a quick bright tone, for she felt better now that the youth-march was over. Her voice, proceeding from the centre of the halted squad was like a sparrow's. 'You used to be so good at machinery,' and then, turning to a Mrs Tallboy on her left, she added, 'It's *true*; sewing-machines, fire-places, and those big tin balls in lavatories – *anything*, in fact, he used to do for me.' She raised her voice again and chirruped: 'Can't you do it, dear – you used to be so *clever*!'

'Shut up,' said Mr Porter under his breath. His forehead was damp with sweat.

'Can I help you, old chap?' said Mr Rice. 'It's no good forcing anything, as we say in Sark – eh? eh? Let me have a go at it.'

'Keep away,' said Mr Porter irritably. He had begun to climb over the gate, apparently thinking that he could manage the latch better from the other side. His jaw was thrust out aggressively as he swung his leg over the top bar and at that moment, quietly and with no warning, as he sat astride like a rider on a white horse, the gate swung open beneath him and he was carried silently through an arc of forty-five degrees, with a smoothness that was quite maddening.

At once the group moved forward up the drive, leaving Mr Porter to climb down by himself. Only his wife remained behind for a moment. 'You do look silly sitting up there,' she said.

'I'll wring your neck when we get home,' came the fierce reply and Mrs Porter, turning upon her thin, high heel, lost no time in joining the others on the lawn.

It was one thing to go into committee and to make decisions as to what to say and what not to say, and to be very wise and indignant in Mr Porter's big lounge overlooking Port-à-la-Jument, but it was another thing to know just how to launch the attack, when on arriving at the house of the culprit that gentleman is to be found smiling gently down from a balcony.

It is difficult, even when standing upon the same level, to broach the subject of another man's misdeeds. Even as the spokesman of a delegation, it is no easy thing to essay, smacking as it does of smugness – and taxing, as it does, the courage. But to be forced to look *up* from a lawn at evening and meet the gentle and compassionate gaze of a mercurial genius, that indeed is something to test the wit and the integrity of the best of men.

There it stood, the delegation, waiting. A light breeze whispered through the near-by trees and stirred the bamboo clump. The dry and uncared-for fingers of the tired palm tree rubbed themselves together with a sound like sandpaper.

And still Mr Pye smiled down at his friends, and Miss Dredger, who sat more or less hidden behind the veranda railings, stared at the group below with her chin thrust forward – the very picture of grit. It was not for nothing that she sprang from English loins.

It was Major Havershot who let go the first salvo.

'Good evening, Mr Pye, my good man, sir.'

Mr Pye was all attention. He leaned far forward over the railings, his whole attention focused upon the major. His head was slightly upon one side as though to assist his hearing. Nothing could be more flattering to Major Havershot than to find himself commanding such complete attention. But his satisfaction on this score was short-lived.

'My friend,' said Mr Pye in a voice hardly louder than the sound of the breeze in the desiccated fronds of the palm, yet audible to everyone present, 'what a shocking opening was yours. What a redundancy. What a profligate waste of words. Let me see. What did you actually say? "Good evening, Mr Pye, my good man, sir." Surely "Good evening," or "Good evening, Mr Pye," would have covered the ground. As for "good evening, sir," that would put you in a socially inferior position, unless you have in you, at this moment, a jocular strain – which I somewhat doubt. "Good evening, my good man," would have been equally invidious. I am not your good, I am not even your bad, man. I am not yours at all. Your whole sentence was an abortion, major. You tried to convey too much and you conveyed nothing. You came a cropper, major. You have wasted your opening round – and you know what *that* means in battle. "Good evening" would have been quite enough. Simple. Direct, honest, and customary. But enough of this – you have failed, and we can start again. What do you want – you and your friends? Why am I so honoured?

What have you come for? Come, come, come, let us have no back-sliding. And – just a moment, before you start – spread out, if you please – spread out in a semi-circle – let us see one another. You with your little problems, and I with mine, but all of us *visible* – that is the great thing; let us all be visible. If there is anyone here who is afraid to look me in the eyes – let him be gone. I would not wish to embarrass him, or her. Let them turn from us now and wend their way in whatever direction they wish to wend it. There is no room for cowards on my lawn – No! Nor in the shade of my palm.'

'It isn't your palm!'

It was a horrid voice: high-pitched and ignorant.

For a moment Mr Pye, although he did not show it, was at a loss – but before he had time to open his mouth, Miss Dredger leapt to her feet.

'Stupid ass!' she cried. 'How could you know what belongs to whom? Do you think I broadcast my private affairs? Do you think I need a confidant apart from my chief? As it happens that palm tree does *not* belong to me. As it happens it belongs to Mr Pye. As it happens I gave it him last night. It was his birthday. So!'

An absolute silence not only reigned but appeared to extend its empire. Even the breeze had dropped.

At last Mr Pye coughed gently. 'Thank you, sailor,' he said, turning to her. 'I think that little matter has been disposed of. Remind me, when these good people have gone, to mulch my palm before I go to bed. Her hormones aren't what they were, the sweet old hairy thing.'

'Mulch ado about nothing,' muttered Mr Porter, who was feeling furious that his stored up thunder was being stolen. It was he who should be lecturing the Fruit-drop.

He and his deputation had not come to Clôs de Joi in order to be stared down at from a veranda by a little fat man who pinched children, and broke up their sand-castles and behaved like a cad at Miss George's funeral.

He took a deep breath and struck an attitude, forgetting that it was getting too dark for his stance to be fully appreciated, and he was on the point of rallying the deputation with the kind of crisp, incisive delivery for which he had once been noted, when yet again he was thwarted, for Mr Rice and Major Havershot both began to speak at once.

'After you, Rice,' said Havershot.

'After you, Havershot,' said Rice.

Mr Pye turned his beaming face from one to the other and back again.

'I think you were just before me, old man,' said Havershot.

'Not a bit of it,' said Rice. 'You were well away.'

'Well, if you insist,' said Havershot.

'I *do*,' said Rice.

'Yes, he does, you know,' said Mrs Rice, who was standing squarely on her short, powerful, utilitarian legs. 'I know when my hubby is serious all right.'

'True enough, old man,' said Rice. 'Fire away!'

'Right ho,' said Major Havershot.

There was utter silence.

'Do you know,' he said at last, 'I can't for the life of me think what I was going to say.'

'Come, come, old chap,' said Mr Rice after a few tense moments. 'Put your thinking cap on, as we say in Sark.'

'No, we don't,' said a voice out of the gloom. It might have been De la Moo, or it might have been old Bleu de Nonce, or it might have been neither.

Someone began to laugh near the bamboo clump.

'Oh, yes,' said Havershot, suddenly, 'I know what it was. Now take Russia....'

'Oh, no, no, no. Not at a moment like this, my dear major. There are times when it would be just the thing to take Russia, and there are times when no one wants to take her. Let us keep to the point, shall we? Of course we shall.

'Now I have heard what you have had to say, ladies and gentlemen, and I see exactly what you mean. It has been most stimulating, not to say moving. Indeed I would go so far as to say I am proud of you, one and all. You have behaved just as I would have wished you to behave. How could you, my dear deputation, ever have guessed the reason for my irrational behaviour over the last month or two? How *could* you? And how could you know that I was only waiting for such a moment as this to unroll the secret parchment.'

'What parchment is that?' muttered Mr Porter.

'I am speaking metaphorically,' said Mr Pye. 'If you wish to hear what I have to say I suggest that absolute silence is observed. You will forgive me, Porter, but this is no time for interruption.'

He turned his face to the offender, and raised his eyebrows, and smiled down with his charming, quizzical, self-depreciating air.

'You must all realize that what I am about to tell you is in no way a form of defence on my part – in no way an attempt to justify myself or my actions. Oh, no. It is something very different. You have come to *me*, remember. I have not come to *you*. But I have *waited* for you. For weeks I have waited for you, longing for the time when you would have the courage to approach me. I have been testing you.'

Mr Porter ground his malacca cane into the red gravel at his feet. 'Tommy rot,' he muttered to himself, and began to poke at the gravel again irritably.

'Mr Porter,' said Mr Pye in a voice as gentle as the cooing of a dove, 'do you know whose gravel you are mauling? It is Miss Dredger's. What you are doing only gives more work to someone else. The gravel cannot rake itself, you know. Now can it, Mr Porter? Be truthful.'

Mr Pye tilted his head on one side, but he kept his eyes on Mr Porter, until that gentleman shook his head sourly.

'No, of course it can't,' said Mr Pye. 'Someone has to rake it. Just as someone has to tidy up our souls. We all need raking, don't we?'

'We do! We do!' cried Mrs Porter in a voice so out of normal register that everyone turned to look at her. She had risen to her feet.

'You speak with feeling,' said Mr Pye, 'and so do I. Without feeling we might as well be dead. Sit down, my dear. I have not finished.'

Mrs Porter, turning to do so, caught sight of several faces

peering through the laurels that divided Miss Dredger's garden from the road.

She pointed at them, and every head turned. It had happened so quickly that the eavesdroppers had had no time to duck their heads.

'Welcome! Welcome!' cried Mr Pye. 'There is room for you all. I have so much to tell you. All of you. Residents, islanders, and even visitors. Whoever you are, my friends, you are truly welcome.' He spread his arms. Pushing each other forward and hiding behind one another as they shambled shamefacedly up the drive, a brood of Norman issue came to a halt in full view of Mr Pye and Miss Dredger aloft on their veranda, and the seated residents. But Mr Pye never gave them a moment in which to be ill at ease or hesitate, but waved them in one after another, and made them sit down on the grass.

The news of the deputation had, of course, swept across the island at least a day before the residents had decided to form one – and similarly it had become known that they were to meet Mr Pye tonight, long before a date had been fixed.

There was consequently a formidable stream of islanders moving up the drive and before long the front garden was filled.

Thick dusk was falling when at last Mr Pye was able to continue. As he stood with his hands on the railing, and gazed down at the sea of faces, rapidly becoming more and more blurred in the dusk, Miss Dredger got up from her seat beside him.

'One moment, chief,' she whispered hoarsely.

Mr Pye raised his eyebrows.

'What is it?'

'Candles,' said Miss Dredger, 'it's getting dark.'

Mr Pye raised his hand, and all talking and muttering ceased in the garden below him. The ugly old palm tree rubbed its dry fronds together, but apart from this there was complete silence until Miss Dredger reappeared through the door of the upstairs bedroom with a lighted candle in each hand. After turning the candles upside down so that they dripped on to the railing on either side of Mr Pye, she stuck them upright in the soft warm wax. Then she sat down and lit a cigarette, but Mr Pye, turning to her, frowned gently, and she knew at once that this was neither the time nor the place for a smoke.

'I can hardly see you,' said Mr Pye, gazing down at the merging faces, 'but I know you are with me so let us, without wasting time, get down to the question that overtops every other question in this island – or indeed in the Channel Islands generally – and farther. Let us put it this way: There is a certain Mr Harold Pye, late of England. He has, in the course of his evangelical life, shed all fear of ridicule, all personal advantage, all cowardice, and all restraint, and thrown in his lot with the great Apostles. His passionate desire to promote the happiness of those with whom he is in contact led him to Sark where, upon a small canvas, he hoped to complete a picture to its last brush-stroke. That again is a metaphor, Mr Porter.'

Somewhere in the darkness below the veranda, Mr Porter blew his nose. Farther away and to the left a lady tittered.

'Whoever *that* was,' said Mr Pye, leaning on the veranda railing and clasping his hands before him – 'whoever *that* was, should be glad of the darkness that hides her from our scorn. Even a cat would know that this was no moment for levity.'

Mr Pye drew out his little tin box and took a fruit-drop. Miss Dredger eyed her chief. If fruit-drops, she wondered, why not cigarettes – but she dismissed the subversive thought as soon as it had entered her head.

'And so this Mr Pye,' he continued, clasping his lapels again, 'did what he could to bring love to Sark. He brought to the island all his spiritual knowledge: he spared himself not a whit in his battle to re-generate the living soul that was struggling to free itself on this storm-swept rock. He brought the Great Pal into the very homes of the islanders – and, after a crusade that left him tired but proud, he felt that this Alcoran, this Ly-King, this Vedas, this Purana, this Zenavesta, this Shaster, this Zantama, this Mormon, or, as Mr Pye would call him, this Great Pal, was accepted – and a stream of love began to flow throughout the island.

'But what happened? Ah! Now we are coming to it, my friends. Now we are coming to it.'

'And about time too, I should bloody well fink!' cried a callow voice from behind the laurel hedge. It was young Pépé who, having no notion that his callow and unpleasant accents were manifestly recognizable even in the dark, was out to impress the five members of his gang who crouched trembling with excitement in the gloom. In particular he was anxious to impress the boy with the birthmark on his nose the shape of Australia, for that young man was out for leadership, and young Pépé knew it.

Mr Pye, when at last he spoke, seemed to be talking to himself.

'That would be the infant Pépé,' he mused aloud. 'The infant Pépé from the Groumière. What an ugly voice the dear child has got. And what ugly words he uses. I am sorry, deeply sorry for little Pépé. The love of God means little to him. I will have to talk to him tomorrow. Poor little fellow with his pungent odour. Poor little fellow indeed.'

Mr Pye had been speaking in so abstracted a manner that it had sounded as though he had been intoning in a church, a candle flame on either side of him, and so when his last words ebbed into the dark air, they were echoed involuntarily by a couple of ex-churchgoers. 'Poor little fellow indeed.' – Then the silence came back and the palm tree rubbed its tired fronds together in a gritty monotone.

'My friends,' said Mr Pye. 'A lot of time has been wasted, but I know you will bear with me a little longer. I will be as brief as I can. I will take you so completely into my confidence that there will be no need to explain. I shall simply *state*.

'At the height of our mutual understanding, when the Great Pal lay athwart the island like an invisible power, so that you and I, my friends, were able to loll in his shade, or braced by his occult presence, stride forth upon our missions – at the height of this – what happened?'

Mr Pye listened for a moment to know whether young Pépé or one of his pards proposed to interrupt with some facetious answer – but no. So shattered had been the Pépé gang by Mr Pye's recognition of their leader's voice that they had taken flight and were now skulking unhappily in a field behind the 'Seaweed'.

'What happened?' repeated Mr Pye. 'This. Now listen carefully. It will grip you. I suddenly realized that loyal and true as you had been to me, yet there was something missing.

'I knew that if you saw me at the lowest ebb of human conduct; if you saw me despoiling the castles of children; or parading myself shamelessly before Miss George's grave and behaving in a hundred mean and obnoxious ways, then surely you would say to yourselves, "This man is one of us – only more so." "This man is no saint" – you would say – "he is of the earth earthy." And then, I said to myself – if, worse than this, if I were seen, my friends, with a hump upon my back, then the island would not only hate me, but they would fear me.

'And all for what? For what? Why did I make a wire cage upon my back so that my cloak hung down in ghastly swathes? Why did I invite this scorn and horror?

'For this reason, my dear friends. It was because I realized that until I knew what it was like to be suspected, loathed, and feared, how could I understand how to comfort and to bless those that (in their lesser way) were equally afflicted by sin and weakness.

'I am now no longer the armchair missionary. I have no longer any theories. I have only knowledge. Naked knowledge.

'This, I submit, was no easy thing to come by. From now on as I work for you I work as a man who has tasted both good and evil, and tasted them to the dregs. Goodnight, my friends. Be gone. Your wives await you. Once more the Great Pal shines above us like the Great Bear, or Orion, striding the sky, and with one eye at least, of all his million eyes, focused, you may be sure, on this pregnant island.'

TWENTY-SEVEN

On the following day Mr Pye awoke with a sensation of buoyancy as though his bones were filled with mercury and that there was nothing that he could not do. The world lay at his feet.

He sprang out of bed, and slipping on his dressing-gown he skipped down the stairs and surprised Miss Dredger in the kitchen.

'Sailor!' he cried. 'Good morning to you, dear.'

'Chief!' she gasped, for the sight of Mr Pye had sent the smoke down her lungs in too great a volume, and she was forced to cough uncontrollably for a few moments, the cigarette still sprouting from a corner of her mouth.

'What are you doing down here, at this hour?'

'Oh, I'm an unpredictable fellow, sailor. You should know that by now.'

'Those bites on your forehead don't seem any better, chief.'

'Out damned spot! Out I say! One ... two ...' cried Mr Pye.

'Your voice is happy,' said Miss Dredger. 'It is happier than it has been for a long time. You have tried to hide your sorrow, chief, but you couldn't fool yours truly.'

'You have stood by me, sailor. You deserve every moment of

the rich and happy days that lie ahead. Last night I cleared the air. Today I breathe it.'

'You were not quite truthful, were you, chief?'

'What is that, my dear?'

'You said your strange behaviour was because you wanted people to know that you had plumbed the depths. It wasn't that really. It was the wings, wasn't it?'

'Sailor,' said Mr Pye. 'There is a difference between the small, mean falsehood that is for personal gain, and the wide clear lie – the reverberating lie that like a wave washes all guilt and pettiness away – that is for the benefit of others. A lie can be salutary and profound. What you do not like, my dear, is the *word* – not the effect. What *is* a "lie"? It is a thing of three letters.'

'I suppose so,' said Miss Dredger. 'And I know that your wings are a secret, but I am sorry that you should have had to tell a fib.'

'You have obviously not understood a word that I have been saying, sailor,' said Mr Pye. 'If you were hiding your grandmother from murderers, and locked her in a cupboard, and if the murderers arrived and demanded to know whether she was in the house, would you say "Yes she is", or "No she isn't"? You would say "No she isn't". What a fib *that* would be. Perhaps it would be best for you to leave matters of conscience to me.'

'Of course, chief.'

'Then what's for breakfast, dear?'

'Scrambled eggs, I thought,' said Miss Dredger.

'Delicious,' said Mr Pye. 'You thought perfectly.'

'Where are you going, chief?' (Mr Pye had opened the back door of the kitchen.)

'I'm going for a few turns round the house. But before I go – tell me, have they absolutely gone, my dear?'

Miss Dredger knew exactly what he meant, and as Mr Pye half removed his pyjama jacket she was able to say – 'All but absolutely, chief. Just the merest nothing. Isn't it topping?'

'I can certainly *feel* nothing,' said Mr Pye, and he tiptoed to the back door again in his bare feet and then skipped out into the garden and began to prance, such was the renewal of his vitality, round and round the house. Miss Dredger could hear snatches of his singing, as he flickered past the kitchen windows.

> 'Dare to be a Daniel,
> Dare to ...'

which half a minute later had melted into:

> '... Greenland's i-cy moun-tains,
> From India's coral strand
> Where Afric's ...'

and later on when the scrambled eggs were all but ready,

> 'From earth's wide bounds, from ocean's farthest coast,
> Through gates of pearl stream in the countless host ...'

In spite of Mr Pye's gaiety he was not forgetful of the terrible time he had passed through. He had set his black sails upon a drastic course, and by any standards he had sinned considerably. But what other course could he have taken? Whether he had been right or wrong, it was now for him to throw himself upon the mercy of the Great Pal, that omnipresent essence, whom he had flouted: but flouted out of necessity and with no will to sin: flouted with the intelligence rather than the heart, so that at the earliest opportunity he would be able once again to draw the island into the vortex of his love.

It is true that there was that hideous *beckoning* from Dixcart Valley, where the grey goat stood tethered nightly; it is true that he had gone too far and had acquired a taste for evil, but Mr Pye was no weakling, and he locked the door of his room, and for an entire day he gave himself up to contrite meditation, and on the following night he walked smartly through a downpour to the Eperquerie, where he stood by the old cannon and watched the rain bouncing off its corroded barrel. He had not been there since that day of acute anxiety when the wings had first pushed through – but now, in his new-found freedom he listened, smiling, to the sound of the sea – and a surge of faith arose in his breast and a deep sense of the renewal of his mission.

'Have faith in me,' he whispered to the Great Pal, who glimmered in every drop of the moonlit rain. 'Have faith in me, and forgive me, and nothing can go wrong. I am no tyro in your service.' He wiped his glasses. 'You called me and I came. But you must remember that I am only flesh and blood and that I am unable to give of my best when you upset me. What can I do when you weigh me down with plumage and confuse me with riddles so palpable, so enigmatic? If it has been a punishment for some sin I have committed – then I have surely paid. Tomorrow is a new day in your service. It will be a full one. And so goodnight to You – goodnight to You.' And as Mr Pye walked smartly home through the rain he knew himself to be richer and stronger in his love than when he stepped ashore four months ago, so brash, so fresh, so confident in his zeal.

When Mr Pye woke the next morning the wings had disappeared completely, leaving no trace, but, as though to take their place, or to fill some vacuum of the spirit he was aghast to discover on raising his face to the bathroom mirror, that his full and intelligent brow was the seat of a more frightful manifestation. Two small horns had, during the night, pushed their way painlessly through, and there, at his temple, in the light of the bathroom window, they glinted, no larger than thorns.

Instantly he raised his hand and drew his index finger towards the sharp and sinister tips hoping it would pass unhindered across his forehead and prove to him that what he saw in the mirror was an illusion. But no. His finger was brought up against the 'thorns'. They were real enough.

The shock was more severe than might be expected in a man who had already been seasoned in so dire a school of sickening incongruity and alien growth. It might have been supposed that his experiences with the unsolicited wings would have hardened him to such overt manifestations – and in a sense this was true.

But the shock he sustained was of another kind, for it is one thing to find yourself on the road to paradise, however embarrassing, and another to find yourself heading for hell.

It was no longer a case for embarrassment, it was a case of fear, primordial and dark.

He had gone too far. His sensitive, and naturally noble nature had been shaken by the spate of his misdeeds and somewhere inside him some delicate structure had collapsed. A pendulum had been swung – and although he could not (being so close to himself) feel or see any difference in his nature (for he had banished the goat from his mind, and the rest of his sins were *calculated* and in no way a part of him), yet a change nevertheless had taken place.

He leaned his face against the cool mirror, trembling and perspiring. But he had overloaded the delicate scales with darkness. What was he to do?

Was he to spend the rest of his life in trying to balance his morals, to balance them in so exact a way that neither the wings nor the horns could find a way out? Was he, at this very moment less in the hands of the Great Pal than in those of the Great Goat?

'Brekker!' cried a voice from the hall far below. He heard it as in a dream. 'Are you ready, chief? Brekker up!'

Some time later when he opened the kitchen door, Miss Dredger, wondering why he had been so long, was surprised to see what looked like an illustration of a pirate out of a story book for infants. It was as though a publisher had exacted from the illustrator a promise that he would not make the pirate-chief the least bit frightening. The pirate-chief must on no account be liable to give the children nightmares. He must be a gentle, round-faced man, and in no way grotesque, although the artist could, if he really wanted to, give him a pointed nose or something like that. Colours; yes. Ear-rings; yes. Bandanas; but nothing horrid.

Mr Pye had not gone in for ear-rings – or particularly bright colours. But he was wearing a bandana, knotted behind, in true pirate fashion. It was fairly loose across the forehead and pulled well down in front, the eyebrows barely showing.

'Good God, chief! What's the idea?' said Miss Dredger.

'There comes a time,' said Mr Pye slowly, 'when we must break our habits, whatever they are. It is not that there is necessarily anything wrong with what we may be doing at any given time, but it is wrong to go on doing it automatically. I have been coming down to breakfast all my life without a hat on. It is deadening. Just as it is deadening to always shave, or always put on shoes. It is wrong to keep on smoking as you do. One must break one's habits, on principle, until the very breaking of them has in itself become a habit, and then one can start again where one left off – refreshed.'

Miss Dredger watched him as he took a fruit-drop.

'Oh, poppy-cock!' she said.

'It may well be,' said Mr Pye. 'It may well be. But that is how I feel about it.'

'Well, chief, you can carry on. Come down as a Red Indian tomorrow; or King of the Esquimaux; or – or – a unicorn! It's up to you. Do what you want, chief. It may be right for you, but not for me. No thank you. Not for "yours truly".'

'I suppose not,' said Mr Pye, staring at the tablecloth. But what he saw was no tablecloth but a vision of darkness, of the darkness in Dixcart Valley and the sound of the leaves and the secret track he had worn between the sycamores; and the clink of a chain in the maw of the night; and at that moment, as Miss Dredger stared at him and while he traced a circle on the cloth with a fork, the long and bearded face of God's enemy leered at him.

TWENTY-EIGHT

HE could not tell her. He just could not. Loyal and dependable as she was, there were, nevertheless, some things which even a mandrill would keep hidden. She had proved herself true as steel, and no doubt she would go on proving herself so, whatever befell her chief, but other thoughts would inevitably cross her mind directly she saw the little horns; thoughts not only of the peril that lay in wait for her chief, but of the peril in which she might conceivably find herself. She would suppose – how could she help supposing? – that there lurked behind the bland façade of her mentor some terrible thing long hidden from her, a secret so diabolical that it had forced its way through into the open.

No! No! he could not tell her.

And yet his urge was to do so. The last month had set so great a strain upon him that even his buoyant spirit and elastic vitality had been tried to their limits. His final triumph over his wings had proved to be no triumph. His joy had turned to ashes. He was again in the merciless and incalculable hands of the supernatural forces and he was immeasurably lonely.

But he was not one to brood; no, not even supposing he had been a weaker character would he have had time to waste on any such thing.

He must now *give* whatever was in his power to *give*. He must act and act with imagination.

But what could he do? What could he do that, at one fell swoop, would purge his system of the sprouting evil and, before they strengthened on his brow, send back the foul horns, like wild beasts into their lairs?

From his past experience he knew – and this was his only comfort that results *were* possible: that the supernatural *did* respond to his efforts. If the wings could be forced to retire, why not the horns? That his life would become unbearable and desperate if it resolved itself into a ding-dong battle between the warring forces of horn and feather was something he dared not contemplate.

There was, at this terrible and immediate juncture, like a weak star in the void, this knowledge that the horns might well withdraw themselves were he able to make some selfless decision.

While Mr Pye turned the whole thing over and over in his mind he redoubled his efforts to put himself at the disposal of the island and to do what he could to give help and counsel to those in trouble. From morning till night he toiled unremittingly, and in an atmosphere that had lost its faith and brilliance. For one can never return. To make a come-back is always a confession.

It seemed that he was no longer needed, for the gap that had once yawned in the breasts of the islanders, and which he had filled so full with love and wisdom, had emptied itself of all his teaching and had closed.

The gist of his speech to the residents, with its explanation of the peculiar change in his nature had, of course, in various forms, been spread by word of mouth to every quarter of the island. It had cleared the air and he was looked upon with more tolerance than seemed possible a few weeks earlier, but the magic of his pre-plumage days was gone – the radiance had fled.

Late one evening, three days after his dire discovery in the bathroom, Mr Harold Pye lay upon his bed with his eyes closed, and his nose pointing sharply at the ceiling. His horns were now about an inch in length and he had taken to wearing a large basque beret when in public. It went against his nature to wear a hat in the houses he visited, or at the Pal Club (now upon its last legs), but there was no alternative. The beret was on the bed at his side, and as he lay quite still he seemed like a plump child, with lines beneath the eyes, a child with a pointed and unchildish nose, but with toy horns curling – all ready, it would seem, for his part in a pantomime.

There he lay exhausted from a day of philanthropy. He had given out so much and had returned with so little. He thought of how different everything had been in those earlier days – in the spring of the year – that now seemed a hundred, a thousand, a million years ago.

He opened his eyes and gazed at the ceiling. It appeared to bulge and was blurred for he could not see without his glasses. Then he shut his eyes again and turned over in his mind the happenings of the day that was now ending.

What had he done since seven in the morning when he had risen to pump the water into the attic tanks and to put in an hour of housework before he prepared the breakfast for Miss Dredger? What had he done to halt, if only by a few seconds, or by a millimetre, the progress of the damnable horns? It all seemed now, in his survey of the day, too ordinary, too feeble. He knew in his heart that to have left the anonymous packet of fifty five-pound notes in the vicar's porch with the block-letter note to the effect that it was to be spent on the church roof which was sagging dangerously – to have done this was a laughable nothing in the face of his predicament. It did not hurt him. Perhaps to give away all his money and go barefoot for the rest of his life would have had more potency in frustrating the devil. But even so sweeping a gesture might well be looked on as mere self-advertisement. He had stood at the Colinette on the low stone wall, and a crowd had gathered round him to hear him describe the wide and golden vistas that lay in store for those who were willing to search for the Great Pal.

There had been a cold whistling wind, but colder than anything was the silence in the air as he had spoken. He was now no longer the mercurial, heart-stirring stranger: he was, to them, the oddity, standing there with his back to the distant foam-flecked sea, and Jersey like a strip of tin on the far horizon.

He had not spared himself. Like a true evangelist he had moved to and fro across the island, his neat, emphatic little feet pattering along the rough lanes until he came to some new vantage point where the cottagers or the passing visitors, or the tittering day-trippers, surrounded him once more as he preached the gospel of love and laughter, and spoke of the Great Pal, that composite God, while, all the time, his terrifying secret lurked beneath the folds of his basque beret.

He had not spared himself – but now as he lay meditating he knew that there was more that he could do. He had not touched the fringe of self-denial. It was not enough to be good or even saintly. He must be hurt and humbled. He must so strengthen the fibres of his will that he could bear to abase himself and shed the last sweet foible of his pride. Pride; was that it? Had his life been built upon vanity? Was that why the Great Pal had mocked him with wings? Was that why the powers of darkness had taken him to themselves, and furnished him with their foul insignia?

Aghast at this idea, Mr Pye sat up in bed.

Was it wrong to enjoy working for the glory of the Great Pal, and to chat with the Great Pal as though with a friend? But perhaps he was not working for the Great Pal, but for his *own* delectation.

He tried to recall any moments of true humility, or mortification, but he could think of none. The wings and horns had not brought him any such thing, but merely anxiety and concern lest he should be humbled in the sight of *man* – that he should be ridiculous, in *man's* eyes.

At the first light tapping of this thought – at the first light touch of its finger-tips, he rose upon his knees on the crumpled bed.

Had he ever loved the Great Pal at all? Was it not possible that his nature had revelled in the idea of the human soul and in the idea of netting it as fishermen will net the mackerel? Was it possible that his very charity was suspect – that he was a merchant and that Love was his trade?

A voice – Miss Dredger's – called through the door. 'Chief ... are you there?'

'Yes, my dear....'

'Are you all right, chief?'

'Of course ... of course, sailor.'

'But tired? ... you're tired, aren't you? I can tell by your voice....'

'Somewhat way-worn, sailor ... somewhat....'

'Then I'll bring you something up to your room, chief ... if you'll go straight to bed.'

'Oh, no, no, no! My very dear sailor – no! Why should you? I am not too tired to come down. Not that I can *eat* anything, I'm afraid – but some hot rum and milk would be splendid.'

'Yours truly will tackle it right away, chief. Tintagieu is in the garden, with the artist.'

'Our garden, dear?'

'Of course.'

'Well, I'll be blowed,' said Mr Pye. 'I haven't seen *them* for a long time. Have they come to see me – or you – or both of us – or what?'

'Well, I don't know exactly, chief. Both of us, I expect, and you in particular.'

'Tell them I'll be down very soon, will you?'

'Of course I will, chief, and take your time. I'm worried about you.'

'Oh, I'm all right, dear.'

'Yes, chief. See you soon.'

'That's it,' said Mr Pye.

He walked to his window and gazed into the dusk, and the dusk reminded him of the Dixcart Valley, and the memory of the valley made him shudder, and his gorge rose.

Turning back into the room he walked smartly to a small bookcase and drew forth the seven books on magic which had once so fascinated him and dilated his brain with occult and sinister fancies. He wanted to destroy them now. He wanted to make some gesture. He wished to fling a gauntlet into the devil's face, for he now knew that he had never loved the Pal and this had now, within the last few moments, become his burning purpose. He no longer admired Him : or feared Him, or even wished to praise or worship Him. He only longed to love Him.

But he knew that it would be a stronger thing to do to replace the volumes on the shelf and to destroy them at leisure, than to stamp on them and tear them apart and hurl them through the window into the darkness. For the first time for a long while he felt vigorous and full of power, and he put the books back, hating all that they stood for, and as he was doing so his face within its circular outline grew strangely luminous and beautiful. He knew that it did not really matter now whether he had horns or wings or scales or a dragon's tail – something had come to him, a rare knowledge that blotted out his own particular heart and left him fearless of all save that he might fail to love the great Fountain-head, not as a child loves his father but as a father loves his child.

Deep in thought Mr Pye descended the stairs, which were still without banisters as a result of Miss George's plunge.

As he reached the lowest tread there was a knock at the front door.

For a moment he drew back, but then, not knowing what it was that made him pause, he walked smartly to the door and opened it.

Before him stood the young man who had been sent to the Guernsey asylum a few months previously. He had shown himself to be quite harmless and he had been persuaded that his story of having seen the shadow of a man with wings in Miss Dredger's house was an hallucination. He now no longer believed it himself, but this did not prevent him from stiffening from head to foot at the sight of Mr Pye, and from dropping the bottle of methylated spirits which Miss Dredger had ordered, with a crash to the ground so that the purple fluid spread freely about his boots.

His eyes were fixed, not upon Mr Pye's, but were focused above them, and as Mr Pye's small hands moved upwards involuntarily to his temples, the fated youth opened his mouth to scream – but no sound came, and with a convulsive effort he turned his back on the apparition and scampered away into the night.

Next day he was put aboard the Guernsey boat for the second time and within a matter of hours was back among the familiar faces, the doctor with the blue chin, and the two squat nurses who spent every moment of their spare time in cutting out pictures of European royalty and sticking them into enormous scrapbooks while they discussed the private lives of even the most obscure of the crowned heads, nudging one another as they turned over the pages.

When the bottle of methylated spirits fell and was smashed on the doorstep, the painter jerked his head in surprise at the noise and his thin little beard trembled. Tintagieu thrust out her lower lip and raised an eyebrow. They had been left in the sitting-room by Miss Dredger, who had retired to the kitchen to prepare the rum and milk. The oil-lamp had been lighted and was standing on a table in the centre of the room.

Mr Pye, turning on his heel in the doorway, skipped nimbly up the stairs again and put on his basque beret. He was curiously unaffected by his absent-mindedness. It seemed to him that he had reached a stage in his spiritual development where things of this world were of no account. Nevertheless he was not prepared at that moment to expose himself unnecessarily. There was still such a thing as rashness. It was still true that there was a time and a place for everything. And so he put on his beret, and descended the stairs again and entered the room.

'Tintagieu,' he said, 'I am glad to see you. Last time I saw you was in the front garden when you would not have a cup of tea, but turned your back on me with an air of distaste as though you did not like me at all – nor *did* you – and I imagine that as we have not met since then, you are *still* allergic to me. But that is as it should be. Please sit down.

'And *you*, Mr Artist, how are you? I remember that you *did* stay and you *did* have some tea, and that we talked much of art and of what it is all about, and that we came, as all honest men must come, to no conclusion at all – for who in the world wants a *conclusion* unless he is a gross materialist? But enough of this: good evening to you, old chap. Sit down, and you too, Tintagieu, sit down and let us relax a little – I have had a tiring day.'

'I know,' said Tintagieu.

'Do you now,' said Mr Pye. 'What do you know?'

'I know you are ill,' said Tintagieu. 'Bloody ill.'

'That's true enough,' said Thorpe, stroking his little beard.

Mr Pye looked at them in turn. Then he took off his glasses, polished them, and re-set them on his nose. He was about to speak when Miss Dredger came in with the rum and milk and a pot of coffee.

'Tintagieu,' she said, 'I know you won't mind.'

'Mind what, Miss Dredger?'

'Letting Mr Pye have your chair, dear. He always sits in that chair. He's rather tired.'

Tintagieu got up, and when Mr Pye refused to take her seat lifted him up and carried him a few paces and deposited him with great care in the chair she had vacated.

'Really, Tintagieu!' said Miss Dredger.

'Really, my famished *foot*!' said Tintagieu. 'He's poorly.'

'It is strange you should say I am poorly when for the first time in my life I have begun to love my Maker,' said Mr Pye. 'I have found my path, though Satan haunts me.'

'Drink your rum and milk, chief. It's getting cold,' said Miss Dredger.

'You may have found your path,' said Tintagieu, 'but you have lost something else.'

'And what would that be, dear?'

'I know what she means, Mr Pye,' said Thorpe. 'You have

lost your sparkle. You have lost your hold on the island. As you know, I don't care much for religion. It never suited me. I am a cubist – and even so I'm pretty obsolete. I can't paint anyway. I'm a thing of thwarted genius – and it's better to have no genius than to have it stillborn – my paintings are like dead children or blue babies. I've got a "blue period" too.' He laughed in a hollow and rather silly way.

'I thought we were talking about Mr Pye,' said Miss Dredger.

'I'm getting round to that,' said Thorpe. 'What I mean is this: although *I* think the whole thing is a racket, Mr Pye – your Great Pal included – yet Tanty and I can't bear the way you are being talked about. We can't bear to see you making your speeches and then hear the stupid laughter after you have gone – and we've come to advise you to lay off.'

'Lay off, my friend?' said Mr Pye.

'Yes,' said Tintagieu. 'Lay off. I didn't like you. You are quite right. When the whole of the island was licking your boots I laughed at you. Now that the island is laughing I want to help you.' She turned to Mr Pye. He was far away in a world of his own. He had lost touch with the conversation. On his lips was that famous smile – so gentle, so distant, and so private. Tintagieu turned to Miss Dredger. 'What is the matter with him?' she said.

'I have never discussed my chief,' said Miss Dredger, 'and I don't intend to.'

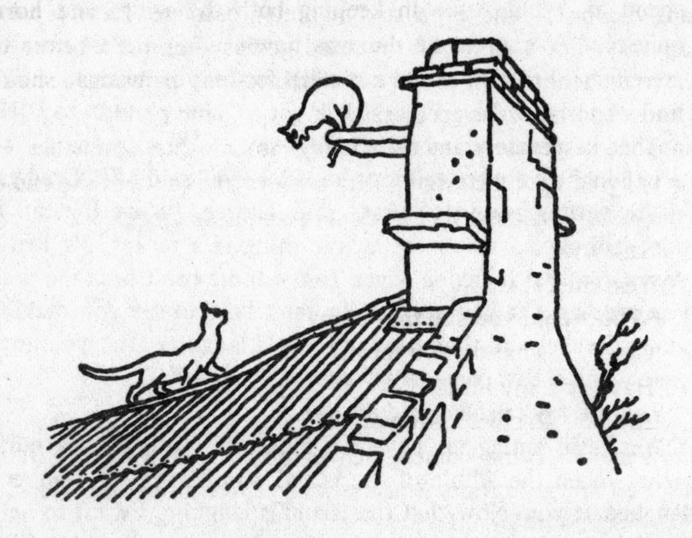

TWENTY-NINE

For the next fortnight Mr Pye was forced to walk the tight-rope of his brain, and as the days went by the strain of so exquisite a balance became overpowering.

All things else had to be set aside so that this new fantasy, this pendulum of the occult, might be controlled in its operation. Never before in his life had the days burned up the hours with so fierce a speed – and so mad a purpose. For events had taken a quite unpredictable turn.

Something he had done, Mr Pye had no idea quite *what* – had sent his horns back like the heads of tortoises into their shells: But before he knew that they were gone the itching at his shoulder-blades had started again and he was forced to do some mean little act to keep them at bay. But as it was quite impossible to measure sin as though it were a liquid in a measure-glass – there was always either not enough of it or too much.

Mr Pye was now in a state of extreme tension. The whole process of growth had been speeded up, and he was forced to spend his whole time in keeping both the wings and horns quiescent. Whatever he did was now having almost immediate effect so that he could not sleep for fear of what he should find when he woke up.

This desperate state of affairs was palpably untenable. He was living upon his nerves, and one evening towards the end of the month he knew that he could stand it no longer.

'Sailor.'

'Yes, chief?'

'Who would you say that I am?'

'Chief ... what do you mean?'

'Have you any idea?'

'Are you ill, chief? Are you ill?'

'Very ill – come, come – answer me.'

'You are my friend. You are Mr Pye, from England. What is it? What is it?'

'What indeed ... what indeed....'

'I think I will ring the doctor, chief.'

'I do not advise you to. Oh, no, sailor. There is no doctor wise enough in all the wide and multitudinous world.'

'Lie down on the couch ... chief ... stretch yourself out.'

'I have no desire to rehearse what, after all, needs no rehearsal, sailor. There will be time for that ... soon.'

'You frighten me. It isn't fair, chief.... What is it? You must tell me.'

'I cannot tell you. I do not know myself, save that I am the plaything of the gods.'

'Chief! Chief! Is it those wings again? Tell me. I will never let you down.'

'I am tired, sailor.'

'Lie down.'

'I must go somewhere....'

'Go somewhere? Where?'

'It may be to a cave.... I don't know. I don't know.' Mechanically he took out his little box, but when he had opened it and stared at the coloured fruit-drops, he closed the lid again without taking one.

'Have you ever seen a goat?' he said.

'Of course, chief.'

'With horns?'

'Yes.'

'What other beasts have horns?'

'Is this a game, chief?'

'What else have horns? Answer me. Haven't you heard of the giraffe? the antelope? the rhino? Haven't you heard of the narwhal, and the Old Man himself? – but, my dear sailor, I must be getting along. You have been *so* kind. So kind.'

Before Miss Dredger could think what had happened he had left the house. Her lips trembled. A cloud crossed over the setting sun and a voice, as though from very far away, sang faintly:

'Pull for the shore, sailor,
Pull for the shore....'

Stupefied, Miss Dredger stood for some while, her hands on her hips, her feet astride, staring sightlessly before her. In her mouth, the cigarette she had been smoking had gone out.

When she recovered she dropped her hands and then clasped them together behind her and drew back her shoulders so that her shoulder-blades were all but touching. Then, realizing that it was now or never if she wished to catch the chief, she ran down the drive and through the gate. To left and right the darkening road was empty. She cried out: 'Chief! Chief!' but there was no reply.

Remembering how Mr Pye had spoken of the caves she turned to the right and ran up the road as far as the ruined mill. There she came to a halt, panting. 'Chief! Chief!' she shouted, but again there was no answer. A cold silence lay over the island like a film of ice. Away to the west, the strung-out lights of Guernsey twinkled through the branches of the Sark trees.

What was she to do? Was she to inform the constable? Was

she to let the island know, for the one meant the other. No. Not yet. Not yet.

She ran back down the road to Clôs de Joi, her back very straight as she ran, her head held high in the air, her chin forward, her mouth set in a straight, almost lipless line.

As she stumbled through the door, panting, she knew what she would do. She would phone up the de Plavés who lived near Tintagieu and ask them to send the girl along, for Miss Dredger felt an overpowering need to speak to someone who was, above all, earthy and solid – someone who was not merely on the island, but of it. Not one of the English residents crossed her mind – not a man or a woman among them all – it was Tintagieu alone whom she wanted. Not necessarily to talk to – but to have at her side, Tintagieu, crude, sensual, and trusty, with her throat of gravel. When she had phoned up the de Plavés, controlling her voice as best she could, she hung up the receiver and as she turned into the room she saw that Mr Pye was kneeling in the shadows at the far end. After some while he got to his feet. He turned to her as though he had never left the room. 'Hopeless,' he said. 'I can make no contact. This is my last effort. If it fails then I will give up. I am tired of Him.'

'Oh, chief! My own friend!'

'He's no help at all....'

'Who, chief?'

'That Great Pal. That abstraction. That vapour. I am afraid I am making you unhappy. I have deserted you and I have been deserted. I found myself outside the Manoir just now. Someone was filling his bucket at the well. I knew that I was pitying myself. So I returned at once. I have no more strength. They are growing very fast. But I will not pity myself. You must put me up, you know – as though I was your guest. The last bus has gone, you see. Hasn't it? You have no option but to put me up. I am going to let them grow. I am tired of stopping them.'

'Chief... is it the wings?'

'The wings are drowsy.'

'Drowsy?'

'They are having a nap. I have done something wrong. I don't know what it was, but the wings have disappeared. It's the others.'

'The others? What do you mean? Oh, damn it all, chief – damn it all, why must you torture me?'

'But I will make one last tremendous gesture,' whispered Mr Pye.

'Your riddles are nothing but cruelty – cruelty!' Miss Dredger cried. 'I cannot bear it. You are no longer yourself. What do you *mean*? What do you *mean*?'

'Shall I tell you? Shall I tell you what I believe? Shall I tell you that I am beginning to understand the harshness of God? Shall I tell you how my heart has yearned for Him and how He has despised my love? It has been too soft. Too loving. Fires are needed and the edge of knives. He does not even answer. He does not say if He is listening. He knows my love is tainted with pride and that until I am nothing in man's eyes and in my own, nothing, and worse than nothing – He will cause me to be flung from pole to pole – half seraph and half devil. And I know what to do, sailor. I know exactly what to do. I am ready for the final humiliation. I shall expose them.'

The door opened and Tintagieu came in.

'What is it?' she said. 'What can I do?'

Mr Pye turned to her. He was standing with his back to the mantelpiece. The light from the Aladdin lamp cast a subdued glow of colour across his face. His hands clasped the lapels of a beautifully-cut pepper-and-salt suit. His glasses shone, reflecting the light of the lamp. Upon his face was an expression which neither Miss Dredger nor Tintagieu had seen before. He was obviously in another world. The fact that he spoke to them did nothing to reassure them that he was with them.

'You may wonder why I wear this panama, my dears. I will tell you. It is because it is so *capacious*. And why should I need such *capacious* headgear? Because I have a large head? No. It is not particularly large, is it? You would not say I had an inordinately bulky head, would you, Tintagieu? Would you, sailor?

'No, of course you would not. Then what can the reason be? Shall I tell you? Shall I?'

He turned first to Miss Dredger and then to Tintagieu, but his eyes stared right through them, just as his words seemed to drift from his mouth.

At that moment the doorbell rang and then the door must presumably have been opened, for a rather high and unmelodious voice stuttered out: 'Sorry to be a n-nuisance – but are you there, Miss Dredger – sorry and all that, b-but I've lost Tintagieu, and I wondered ...'

'Yes, yes, yes!' said Miss Dredger, who had marched into the hall. 'Can't you ever do anything without her?'

'Is it the paint-box?' growled Tintagieu. 'What does he want?' She followed Miss Dredger into the hall. 'Why don't you go away, dear? You're like that bloody shadow in the poem "that goes in and out with me" ...'

'That's it, Tanty! That's it!' said Thorpe, who was delighted that he had found her.

'Shut up!' said Miss Dredger.

Both Tintagieu and the painter looked at her with surprise.

'I gather you have come to find your friend and not to visit Mr Pye.'

'Well, both, you know,' said Thorpe.

'Really? Then you had better come in.'

As the three of them turned to the sitting-room door they were surprised to see how dark it had become, and a moment later to the accompaniment of a series of popping sounds, the Aladdin died for lack of oil and the room was in complete darkness. Out of that darkness came Miss Dredger's voice.

'Have either of you a torch?'

'No.'

'No.'

'What was that?' It was Miss Dredger again. Something had skimmed through the air between their heads and had landed in the hall. It must have come from the direction of the mantelpiece.

'Chief!' cried Miss Dredger. 'Are you there?'

'Of course.' The voice was clipped and abstracted. 'Of course I am here.'

There was a small scraping sound as of a match-box being opened. 'Tell me who is in the room, sailor.'

'There are three of us, chief. Myself, Tintagieu and the painter.'

'And the l-last of the three is getting a dose of the w-willies, if he may say so,' said Thorpe, feeling around in the dark for Tintagieu as he spoke.

'Shut up,' said Miss Dredger again.

'Haven't you got another lamp alight anywhere in the house?' said Tintagieu. 'What are we hanging around like this for?'

'Sailor, Tintagieu, and the young painter. What could be better? Are you all quite comfortable?' It is an odd thing to be asked whether you are comfortable when you are standing, but they had no time to reply, for at that moment Mr Pye struck a match and there was a little spurt of fire.

Mr Pye must have been holding the match well forward of his body for at first all that could clearly be seen was the bright honey-coloured light on the knuckles of the hand that was holding the match. Then as he drew the flame towards himself and lifted it to the level of his head, the three spectators saw his face light up, at first from below, and then from the level of the eyes so that the deep shadows shifted their positions. When his hand stopped moving, and the steady flame of the half-charred matchstick made of his face a strange and circular island that appeared to float in the darkness, the three who watched him, in absolute silence, were perplexed to see, above the glow of his face in the dark air an inch or two above his head, two points of light which they could in no way understand. It was plain that he had discarded his panama, and Miss Dredger remembered how something had sailed into the hall. But what were those two points of light that glinted in the glow of the failing flame?

The charred head of the little match-stick was twisted and bent upon one side like the head of a hanged negro. It moved yet higher and closer to the forehead, and in a terrible and icy silence, while three stomachs turned over and six hands trembled, and a cold sweat began to pour down three faces, the flame died from the black match, and a moment later there was a heavy thud upon the floor. Thorpe had swooned and fallen headlong to the ground.

THIRTY

'FIRST things first!' cried Mr Pye out of the velvet darkness. 'Come along now, come along. Something has fallen, and I don't blame it. Where are you, sailor? – out of the door with you! Lamplight ahoy! Into the kitchen with you – lights ho! We have three more lamps: they can't *all* be empty, and if they *are* there's paraffin in the larder! And candles! Candles, Tintagieu, for I presume it's the painter on the floor. It's no good telling *him* what to do. I'll see to him myself. There's brandy in the cupboard. I'll deal with that, and him. Find each other. Have you found each other? No? No? Mind your heels. You may be walking on the poor boy's face – have you found each other yet? ... what? ... what? ... yes or no... ? Answer me!'

'Yes ... ch ... chief.... Yes, my ... friend. Oh, my poor darling ... and you never *told* me.'

'Enough of that, dear. Over the side with you, sailor. Feel your way, dear. Have you got hold of her? Tanty doesn't know the house as you do. Tiptoes does it ... off you go. I'll get this genius to the couch – if I can find him. Poor thing. He can gulp down Goya by the quart and wallow in Heronumus. I've seen him at it. But when it comes to my poor little effort, what does he do? – he collapses like a rotten floorboard. Where are you, young fellow? Really, with that beard of yours I wonder *you* weren't chosen.'

While Mr Pye continued to talk to himself, for the other two had left the room and were lighting the lamp, their eyes wide with an amazement of horror and their tongues dry as leather in their mouths, he heard a kind of moan and then a faded voice. 'It's a . . . racket . . . Tanty – the whole thing's a racket. I had a filthy dream – that was a racket too. I feel as sick as a pig in a pram . . . where are you . . . for God's sake?'

Mr Pye, moving gradually towards the voice, was not long in finding him. Kneeling down he held the young man beneath the arms and dragged him gently along the carpet. He could hear feet in the hall and a light glowed in the doorway.

'Come along! Come along!' cried Mr Pye, and Thorpe, who had swung back his head to see who was holding him, leapt like a fish and fell back with a long scream into Mr Pye's arms. He had seen them again, silhouetted against the lamplight in the doorway – silhouetted with a sharpness and blackness quite terrible in its intensity. Thorpe was by no means an exceptional draughtsman, but he was good enough to be thrilled, even while terrified, by a superb piece of drawing when he saw it – the inevitable curvature of these deadly spikes. They were like two sweeps of a Chinese brush – spontaneous, fierce and inevitable. While his loins weakened and his throat contracted with fear, yet the other side of him leapt in gladness and in praise as, with eyes as wide and round as pennies, he stared, as he lay, at the apparition.

'One, two, three, and *up* we'll put you, Mr Artist,' cried Mr Pye. There was something almost hectic in his gaiety. 'Come along now, sailor. You have never been one to hang back – nor you, Tanty. Come along now, one of you must hold his feet and we'll have him on the couch in a jiffy.'

It is perhaps a blessing at such moments as this, when the supernatural is in the house, and the ordinary values and beliefs are torn to shreds before the eyes, when the heart pounds, and the sanest of mortals is found to stand upon the brink of madness – it is perhaps lucky at such times to have no option but to *do* something – in this case to answer a request and to move across the lamplit room towards a man with horns, and to help the man with horns to lift a painter on to a couch, and this is what Miss Dredger did, while Tintagieu, seeing that the lamp was smoking, turned down the wick.

It is a blessing also when the supernatural can talk with not only the voice of a mortal but a voice so familiar in its rapid delivery, and so gentle in its tone.

'Now, you two ladies will do as I tell you. I know you will, because I know you trust me, in spite of these extraordinary spikes. Ha, ha, ha, ha, ha, ha! It is such a relief to show them to you, my dear friends. I cannot think of anyone else I would like to show them to. On the contrary, I would probably die of shame. Because they're not exactly *pretty*, are they? – and I suppose they mean I'm some kind of a devil – if not *the* Devil. Ha, ha, ha, ha, ha, ha! But where was I? Ah, yes. I was telling you that you must do just what I tell you, ladies. It won't be difficult – in fact it's only *this*. You must sit down. That's all. Sit down. I see our young painter friend is sitting *up*. That is good. But you must sit *down*, for that is better still. And why? Why? Because I am going to fetch a bottle of old wine. If this is not a moment to drink wine, then the grape can turn to vinegar and the famous vineyards wither from the face of the earth. Sit down, my dears. Do not be afraid. I will not be long ... I will not be ...'

'Oh, chief.... Oh, my dear chief....'

'Calm yourself, sailor ... my dear ... my trusty one ... I will be back in a moment.'

He left them, his head, out of habit, cocked a little on one side, and with the old jauntiness in the way he pattered from the room. The lamplight was reflected from his polished shoes, from the buttons at his cuffs, from his white collar.

When he had found the wine, a Château d'Yquem which he knew Miss Dredger was fond of, he got down the long narrow cut-glass beakers which he had given her in the pre-plumage days, and holding them in turn before the light (for Tintagieu had lit a lamp for the kitchen) he washed them one after another, dried them with care and polished them until they sparkled. Then he caught sight of himself in the mirror that hung by the window and he almost dropped the glass he was holding, for his horns during the last five hours had made awesome progress.

Gone were the callow, gently curving spines, two knuckles long. In their place were horns; mature and dangerous, the length of a span. Had Mr Pye not flung away his panama, it would by now be perched clear of his head, upon the arrogant points. The last hour had brought them only a kind of compound interest. It was obvious that some profoundly selfless gesture must be made, and made very soon if he were to stem the speed of this horrific up-surge. Some gesture that must be more than a gesture. Some deed that would so hurt his pride, so humble him, that the gods or whatever power it was that was now so darkening his life, would have no option but to end the torture.

It was lucky for Mr Pye that he knew exactly what would place him in a position of extreme ridicule. A position from which there would be no recovery. He knew in his bones that there was now no hope for him, in the sense that his life was over. This wing–horn, horn–wing business was fatal. There could ultimately be no medicine for so ghastly and fundamental a disease.

But he knew that he would go down fighting. If the Great Pal had forsaken him, he would not forsake the Great Pal. If God kicked him he would not kick God. He had sinned. He had dabbled in the Black Craft, but only to free himself from madness, not to gain it. He had been gay. Was that a sin? He had brought hope to many – was *that* a sin? He had enjoyed himself in doing so. Was *that* a sin? Evidently. Evidently.

He would with every ounce of energy left in his body, and with the last iota of strength that his soul possessed, confound himself before the island that was once to have been turned into the Garden of God – expose himself as a warning against – against what? – against what? – save pride. Surely it could be nothing else but pride.

As he stared into the kitchen mirror, while these thoughts raced through his brain, he gloated, all of a sudden, in his terrible loneliness and in his decision that if anyone was to be let down, it would be he, Harold Pye, and not his Maker.

He also knew that he was free. For the little sins no longer counted in the face of his decision. Were he to kiss the ghastly lips of the grey goat – what would that be but play-acting? For his soul would all the while be bare in the cold wind of ignorance. He would be deserted and alone. Alone as the last man to be left alive in a great city when even God had died.

He placed the polished beakers on a tray and carried them into the lamp-lit sitting-room. The three were sitting bolt upright in their chairs. The painter had moved from the couch. He felt less vulnerable sitting between Miss Dredger and Tintagieu.

'My dears,' said Mr Pye. 'You are being truly kind. You are helping me so much by keeping a grip on yourselves. I know how frightened you must feel. And I am frightened too. Bear with me, if you can, for a little while.'

'My darling ...' whispered Miss Dredger. '... Oh, my darling....'

'Sailor,' said Mr Pye, 'I don't know what to say. You have been my right hand. Tomorrow it will all be over. I will not say you will then be free of me and therefore happy, for I seem to have brought more misery than anything else to the few people I really know on the island. But you will live in an atmosphere less likely to tear the nerves to bits. Tanty..." He turned to Tintagieu, and as he did so, he began to pour out a little wine into his own glass. He raised his round face to the ceiling and pursed his lips at the taste and then tilted his head on one side, like a bird. Then he smiled, and all the horror, for a moment, died out of the room and the three who watched him spellbound, found that somehow their hearts were lightened for an instant by the radiance of his smile – for it flashed from his gentle, indomitable face with so rare an outpouring of love – so sweet a conflagration. 'Oh yes, yes ... yes ... I *think* you will enjoy it,' he said. 'I *do* hope so,' and he turned his head to Tintagieu again, and raised his eyebrows as though for permission and, when she nodded her head slowly, while two tears gathered at the lids of her huge eyes – he poured her out the wine.

Miss Dredger's glass shook in her hand as it was filled, and it was no easy matter for Mr Pye to pour the wine without spilling it over her wrist. But not a drop was lost: pouring a little, then ceasing from pouring – pouring a little more and then ceasing from pouring, he patiently filled her glass.

'And now for you, artist. I have never really known you very well. Perhaps I do not understand art very well. Does the one imply the other? But paint on, my good friend, paint on when I have left this island – for I will leave it – for prison is a thing I *do* detest. No, ladies, I have never *been* in one – but I can imagine how it feels to have one's wings clipped . . . in the bud. There's a really mixed metaphor for you. What? What? Perhaps I am a metaphor – and one day I'll fit the thing I'm metaphorising. Now there's a word for you. I seem to have a certain inventiveness today. Ha, ha, ha, ha! A certain inventiveness. There we are, my dear painter. I have only to charge *my* glass and we will drink a toast. What shall it be?'

'Chief!' the voice was harsh and broken. 'Put down your glass!'

For the first time the eyes of Tintagieu and the painter turned from the horned man to Miss Dredger, who had risen to her feet.

'Put down your glass,' she said again.

Mr Pye put down his glass.

'We drink,' she said, her gaze moving quickly from Mr Pye to Tintagieu and from Tintagieu to Thorpe and thence back again to Mr Pye – 'we drink to a gentleman: to the finest gentleman this island ever saw: to the finest gentleman who ever left England – to *you*, Oh chief; Oh chief; my darling! Some cad is torturing you!'

Miss Dredger, in her agony of spirit, had forgotten for the moment that she was proposing a toast, but now, while the glass trembled she raised it again, while Tintagieu and Thorpe followed, lifting their glasses to their lips together.

Mr Pye stood quietly and watched them. 'Thank you, sailor,' he said at last. 'And I drink now to you, the staunchest friend I ever had. And to you, Tintagieu, my jungle child; and to you in the name of Bosch, my dear Thorpe. One day you will prove yourself, my friend, in amazing pigment. Neither of you have said a word and that is as it should be. There is nothing you can say. In me is being fought an enormous battle. An experimental battle – but enormous none the less. The legions of the damned are at war with the seraphim, and my poor body is their cockpit – that is if there's enough room in a cockpit for such a surging mob of preternaturals – it certainly *feels* as though the whole lot are here, and flourishing their spears of midnight steel. But the extraordinary thing is that I feel utterly apart from this titanic *mêlée*. My heart is nowhere touched. Miss Dredger will explain – won't you, dear – when I have gone? It is right that you should be tongue-tied. Words at such times make little sense and what sense they do make is nonsense – of which, incidentally, I was once particularly fond. I used to write it once – at board meetings while others doodled. How did that one go . . .? That particularly good one that I wrote on the back of a procedure form? Ah yes . . .

'O'er seas that have no beaches
To end their waves upon,
I floated with twelve peaches,
A sofa, and a swan.

'With flying-fish above me
And with cat-fish all around
There was no one to love me
Nor hope of being found—

'When, on the blurred horizon,
(So endlessly a-drip),
I saw—all of a sudden!
No sign . . . of any . . . ship.'

Mr Pye had closed his eyes as he had recited the verses. Before he opened them he spoke in the most authoritative tone of a man who was used to being obeyed.

'Sailor.'

'Yes, chief?'

'I do not wish you to be alone in the house tonight. Heaven knows what I will look like tomorrow morning, or how I will behave. Well – I trust and believe. Nevertheless you are to make up another bed in your room for Tanty. You will also make a bed for the artist in the small west bedroom. Tomorrow is the island cattle show. We must be up bright and early. It is to be my day of days. You will now, all three of you, leave the room. Do not speak to me. Your silence has been eloquent enough. I say this in the utmost sincerity. I am more than usually sensitive to atmosphere. It has been charged tonight – as charged as our beakers of good wine – but it has not been charged with any more than fear. There is no crime in fear. What was missing was antagonism. There has been no antagonism and I thank you for that from the bottom of my heart.

'Now run along – all of you – and not a word. Just as I have not flinched from parading my poor head before your eyes – so, tomorrow I will not flinch from my last gesture. We will see whether there is a sense of mercy, and I must add, fair play, in that realm above the sky that children dream of.'

Of the four of them only Mr Pye slept well. His conscience was clear. He knew, now, at the eleventh hour, what to do and what form his penance should take. It was to take, had come to him, the basic ignominy. There was no need for him to fret. All responsibility now lay with the Great Pal. With his brandished horns he would be, to the island at large, if not the Devil himself, then one of the devil's closest relatives. A wicked thing now brought to heel, and a warning to all men.

The painter, when at last he fell asleep after a night of supreme doubt as to his own sanity, dreamed of roses filled with dew. Inside the roses sat fairies with wings of standard gauze. Each fairy had on a tiny panama hat. Their eyes were huge like Tintagieu's, but this was rather spoiled by the fact that they were all smoking 'Three Star' cigarettes like Miss Dredger. Every now and then they'd sing in chorus, their voices thin as the cry of gnats:

'He'll never be an artist! ha ha ha
He'll never be an artist, ha ha ha.
He's too thin. His beard's all wrong,
Tanty doesn't want him—ha ha ha!
He'll never be an artist, poor old thing.
Goya, yes! Heronumus, yes!
Michelangelo, yes! Hiroshiga, yes!
Picasso, yes! but poor little paint-box
No—no—no.'

And then the fairies would all change places and start all over again until a huge goat trampled its way into his dream with cloven brogues on its feet and a purple busby on its head with slits for its long ears to stick through, and opening its hideous mouth, eat up the lot of them.

Long before the sun rose he knocked upon Miss Dredger's door. It was opened by Tintagieu and Thorpe came forward into the room like a caricature of himself, every idiosyncrasy of gait and appearance ridiculously intensified.

Miss Dredger and Tintagieu were still in their clothes. They had not been to sleep. They had not even rested their heads on their pillows.

No one said good morning. Thorpe sat next to Tintagieu, who was now perched on the side of the bed. She continued to bite her nails in the darkness before dawn. Thorpe ruminated how women are able to be so self-contained. When in trouble they never came to him. It was always he who went to them. Miss Dredger was standing by the window gazing out at the darkness, in the depths of which she could make out something even darker that scraped its hands together with a sound as harsh as the shovelling of cinders. It was the ugly palm tree with its dry hands, and Miss Dredger's mind skipped back to an earlier age when a man squatted sprucely at the base of the palm and mended her mowing machine with such happy brilliance while he sang that little hymn that now was like the echo of an echo.

Pull for the shore, sailor...
Pull for the shore....

She remembered their duet on that cloudless morning – and how it had ended with such bubbling gaiety:

There'll be toast galore—
Not to speak of coffee, sailor
Pull for the shore....

and how, from then on, he had called her 'sailor'. It was too much. She turned abruptly from the window, her fiftieth cigarette burning itself away between her stern, trembling lips.

THIRTY-ONE

In vain they had entreated Mr Pye to do no such thing. But he had only smiled and thanked them for their concern.

'Perhaps the Great Pal is ashamed of Himself,' he said, laughingly – 'see – they have not grown in the night.'

This was true. They had not, although they were big enough in all conscience.

'But I cannot let you go – I cannot,' said Miss Dredger. 'They will laugh at you and then they will be frightened and then they will send for the Guernsey police. I have thought it all out. That is what they'll darned well do.'

'You are absolutely right, sailor. I have thought it out too, and I have come to the same conclusion. But do not forget that it takes time to get the police over. At least an hour. And when they *do* land over here they are not very nimble on the rocks.'

'On the rocks,' said Tintagieu. 'Oh, but why should you be on the rocks? They'll trap you there between the tides.'

'You can hide at my place – if you should ever care to, sir,' said Thorpe.

'I won't be hiding exactly, dear boy – and I *do* thank you for the thought. It is just that I am anxious to give them a run for their money. After all, if one cannot fail with a smile one might as well not fail at all. Failure *is* glory, you see. It is success that looks so tarnished and jaded the next morning. It is failure that keeps its freshness. Failure is the thing. Success is finite, but failure is infinite. It is all rather wonderful, really. What is the time?'

'Eleven o'clock,' said Thorpe, 'and you are a great man, sir. It frightens me that you should be like this – but you are a very great man. There's a dirty racket somewhere, sir. I never believed in religion anyway, and this more or less . . .'

'Quiet,' said Mr Pye, 'you are drivelling. Eleven o'clock, eh? They will be there by now and I must say good-bye.'

He shook hands with each of them in turn. There was absolutely nothing to be said.

Turning from them he walked smartly down the drive twirling his silver-headed cane through his fingers. And a few minutes later he could see in the distance the great field where the cattle stood tethered in long lines and the Sarkese as they moved to and fro among them or stood at the door of the refreshment tent, or sat upon the grass in groups, or prodded the cattle with their walking-sticks, while the distance that divided them from Mr Pye diminished momently.

And then, all at once he was among them and a kind of rhythmic throbbing filled the summer morning.

The effect upon the Sarkese was to root them where they stood. The effect upon the cattle, and particularly the heifers, was to create such a restlessness in their breasts that the poor things strained at their moorings, and in some cases tore the iron spikes out of the ground and fled, trailing their chains. The four enormous bulls were bellowing, without ceasing, and the mooing of the distaff side was pitiful to hear.

Through the noise of the cattle and the motionless silence of the Sarkese, Mr Pye threaded his way. He had chosen to wear his city suit with its beautifully cut black jacket and striped trousers. His little feet were immaculately shod, a diamond point of light on either toe-cap. His fawn waistcoat fitted over his paunch as neatly as the feathers on a wagtail's breast. His high, stiff collar was peerless. His rounded face shone with a purity of complexion as translucent as to give the impression that all other mortals were, by contrast, grubby. His glasses shone in the sunlight. His long horns sprouted from his brows, their curled tips sharp as knives.

But it was the air with which he walked! His every gesture was a kind of abdication. It was the way he spread out his small gloved hands at his sides, his palms facing the way he was going. It was the subtle tilt of his head – all cockiness gone and in its place a token of almost unearthly renouncement. His whole body was a token. It was a *word*, just as a poem resolves itself into one word. A word that is not found inside the poem, but is the result of what's been written down. As Mr Pye moved over the grass his form spelt *failure*. It was as though he were opening the doors and windows of his house that all might see how derelict it was. How *monstrous* it was. How ghastly – in spite of the fresh paint upon its outer walls.

'Here I am,' he seemed to say. 'Here I am, the missionary who came to convert you. See what has happened to me. I have been adopted by the Devil. See – I have horns. Perhaps I *am* the Devil. Take warning from me, gentlemen, take warning from me and continue as you were before I came.'

All this was expressed in the way he moved to and fro through the frozen crowd. And yet in the heart of the humiliation there was a native dignity he could not lose. He knew nothing of it. It was simply *there*.

When at last the tension was broken by that terrible cry from Mrs Du Palmé, that cry of profound horror which rang grotesquely across the fields and sped, bounding and echoing, down the lanes to Dixcart Bay, where it stoned itself to death in the shallow caves – then, like a motion picture that has stuck only to start again with a jerk, the cattle-field erupted, as it were, with feverish movement.

With an instinct akin to that of starlings when they wheel in the sky, every bird veering at the same moment, so that it seems they have no leader but share a single brain; so the islanders all of a sudden found themselves standing in a solid mass outside the refreshment tent. Compact, agape, licking their parched lips, and trembling with the thrill of their alarm, they gradually grew braver by being able to feel one another's shoves and nudges. They had converged from every quarter of the wide cow-avenued meadow at a pace hardly credible.

Taking courage from the fact that he was standing in the centre of the mass and was all but invisible, someone suddenly shouted: 'Where's the constable?' and immediately his cry was taken up by the whole congregation: 'Where's the constable? Where's little Pee-wee?' 'There he is!' 'Here he is!' 'Arrest him!' 'What are you waiting for, Pee-wee?' 'Where is he?' 'Where's the constable? Where's the constable?'

A small thin figure was pushed forward out of the crowd. He was very pale. He stood wiping his face with his handkerchief. Then he sank gradually to his knees and was sick.

Another voice shouted: 'Keep your distance, Mr Pye!' And another: 'If you *are* Mr Pye.' And another: 'Get to hell from here, Mr Pye!' And another: 'That's where he comes from – he ought to know the way!' And a woman's voice: 'God save our little children...!' And a man's: 'Some of them, anyway!' And another man: 'God help our crops!' And another: 'God help the lobsters!' 'The cows are ruined!' 'He's b...d their milk!' 'He b...d the summer visitors!' 'Keep your distance!' 'He's b...d my nerves!' 'Where's Pee-wee?' 'Where's the constable?' 'He's no bloody good.' And then a huge voice: 'Cut your cackle, you fat and bloody cods! Phone Guernsey!' And then everyone shouted together: 'Phone St Peter Port, phone the police! Phone the police! Phone Guernsey!'

Mr Pye advanced slowly, his head bent in shame. He went down on his knees, as though before his masters. But someone shouted:

'Bloody missionary!'

'He's a goat!'

'He's the first goat.'

'He's the king of goats.'

'A goat with a walking-stick!'

'A goat with spectacles!' and then a huge voice again:

'Silence! You bloody, ignorant fools. He'll horn your guts out. He'll put a bloody spell on you. He's the Old Man. He'll drink your blood.'

There was a terrible silence and in that silence a gull could be heard crying from Brequhou. And then that slow, heavy voice again: 'He'll drink your blood.'

'Oh no he bloody won't!' It was a new voice. It was husky, and every face was turned from Mr Pye to Tintagieu. She had walked across the field unseen and as she had come she had heard the voices.... 'Guernsey.... The police ... the police ... telephone...' She had seen six youths race from the field, and knew that by now they would be ringing through to the Chief Constable. She knew that it would take some while before he decided against it being a practical joke, but once he knew there was anything serious he would commandeer a speed-boat immediately, which would carry at least a dozen of his men and land them in Sark harbour in under forty minutes. There was no time to be lost. She had left Miss Dredger prostrate on her bed; indomitable as ever, she was yet so struck to the heart that she could not move, but gazed angrily at the ceiling, a dead cigarette in her mouth. Thorpe had promised that he would sit by Miss Dredger's side until Tintagieu returned.

'Oh, no he won't!' shouted Tintagieu again. 'Mr Pye won't drink your blood, my dears. Will you, darling?'

Mr Pye shook his head.

'And you'll do just what you are told, won't you?'

Mr Pye nodded his head.

'And you won't butt anybody, will you, dear, with those lovely bright new horns of yours?'

Mr Pye shook his head.

'Or be any sort of a naughty little goat... ? Because you love me, don't you?'

Mr Pye nodded.

Tintagieu had struck the only chord. The only chord to flatter and seduce the crowd into a sense of superiority and safety. They were immediately off their guard. They were convulsed. The devil had suddenly become a plaything; a laughing-stock. The compact mass of the congregation began to disintegrate – single figures working themselves loose from the parent body, legs and arms breaking away from the pack, as the laughter rose into a great gale.

'Now I'll tell you *what*,' shouted Tintagieu. 'We'll have a game with him. Have any of you heard of hide and seek?'

From the noise that followed they evidently had. Cat-calls followed, and every kind of ribaldry, and then a strange, high-pitched voice: 'And he was such a *good* man.'

'Now get up, my love,' said Tintagieu, and as Mr Pye rose to his knees, 'Do everything I tell you,' she whispered, 'They'll jail you if you don't. I will hold them here. Make for the prison. Here's the key. I stole it. Lock yourself in. Four short taps on the door. That will be me – an hour after sunset.'

'Look at him,' she shouted; 'the devil is such a pretty boy,' and she stroked his face. 'You wanted to be *humbled*, didn't you?' she muttered, while she stroked his horns and winked at the crowd. 'Why, I don't know, but you wanted it, didn't you?' And then: 'Oh, such a pretty boy,' she cried again, her voice as hoarse as a raven's.

At this moment Mr Pye experienced an extraordinary sensation – a dual sensation – for a positive wrench at his shoulders had coincided with a contraction of the temples, which left him shuddering. 'Oh, my dear ... my dear Tanty,' he whispered.

'Quiet,' she said, and then she turned to the islanders again. 'Listen to me. He can eat out of my hand, my dears. I can do what I like with him. Can't I, Beelzebub?'

Mr Pye nodded. His face was red with shame. Another spasm at the temples brought tears to his eyes, and at the same moment he could feel yet again that something was happening between his shoulders.

'Ladies and gentlemen, *and* darling Mr Missionary Pye,' said Tintagieu, striking an attitude, 'I would like absolute silence *if* you please.' After a great deal of shouting and laughter there was an absolute silence. She continued: 'We are gathered together to discuss what we had best do to fill in our time between now and the arrival of the police. For the cattle show is over, is it not, my dears? How could any cow expect a prize after seeing Mr Pye?'

'You had better be bloody careful,' said the heavy-voiced man, who was also owner of the best cow; 'it's a dangerous thing to play around with devils, however they behave. He'll have your liver out of you. You wait and see.'

'Just forget my liver, George, if you will,' said Tintagieu, 'and concentrate, dear. Now we live on an island and there's no escape for him. The tide's out and he has no boat. The police will soon be here and will take him away and we'll never see him again.' She turned to Mr Pye. 'You *did* say you loved a good romp, didn't you? You did say hide and seek, didn't you? That's right. And *how* long did you say you'd like to be given? Ten minutes? Is that all? Well, well, well. He can't go far in ten minutes, now can he? No, of course he can't. Now listen carefully, my little dears. We'll all go into a nice tight clump again and we'll all look the other way, and when I say so, we'll shut our eyes to be doubly sure, and when ten minutes are up I'll give you such a shout it will jerk the hearts out of you, and then, *away* we'll go, and I don't mind betting a pound to a penny that we'll have him within the next fifteen minutes. Now here we go. . . .' and without a pause in her monologue, and giving no opening for argument, but sweeping the thing along through pure velocity and a curious magnetism, Tintagieu cried out in a voice all husk and passion: '*Turn!* Turn in your tracks! Yes, *turn*, Mrs de Coop. Yes, you and *you*. Yes turn, Harry Portiner, turn, my darlings, and shut your bloody eyes. . . .' And when at last she had got them all to face the opposite way, she signalled to Mr Pye, who, with his forehead and his shoulders in turmoil, ran nimbly from the field and was within a minute half-way to the prison, skirting the avenue, on the Jersey side. Not a soul did he meet. In his hand he clutched the key. When he reached the door of the stone loaf he plunged the key in the lock and at the third attempt it turned with a grinding sound.

Withdrawing the key he entered the prison and, closing the door and locking it behind him, he sat down upon the cold floor. It was littered with dead leaves and scraps of paper with faded messages which had at one time or another been pushed through the small barred window.

He had been abased. He had made his gesture. If the Great Pal didn't absolve him now, from any hint of pride, then that Deity was no longer a Pal or very Great. But it seemed that He *was* at work. So much so that Mr Pye, after sitting quietly for some while in the gloom was forced to take off his black coat and then his fawn waistcoat, for the feathers, as though they were old hands at the game, pushed their way confidently forth into the prison darkness.

And at the same time his horns were dwindling. For the first time in his life he had a foot in either camp. Neither the angels nor the damned entirely owned him.

And then he heard the shouts of his pursuers. The cries and counter cries. The single footsteps running past the jail, and the heavy-footed packs as they clattered down the stony road to the Manoir. The far hullo-ing across the fields. They were everywhere. But no one thought of looking in the prison.

An hour after sunset the island was still searching. The Guernsey police were not amused. To begin with it had been very choppy round the point of the island, and four of them had been sick. No one had remembered to have a carriage waiting for them at the harbour and they had had to toil up the hill. All they found at the top was that an absurd game was in progress – explained to them by the few children they came across, and by an old woman too old to join in. The game had already been named and called 'Catch a Pye-Goat', according to the children who had drawn a blank in Derrible Bay.

'But has the gentleman really got horns, my dear little chap?' said the angry Chief Constable in a thin little extra voice which is often reserved for cats. He mopped his brow and put an enormous hand on a small child's head, and while wishing he could use it to whack the infant's bottom, he showed his teeth in a repellent smile. 'Has he really and truly got *horns*, my little fellow?'

'Course he bloody has,' said the sweet little boy. 'And he aren't a gentleman. He's old Horny Satan, all right, he is. Don't *you worry,*' and the irritable Chief Constable found his big hand suspended in mid-air, for the sweet little boy had gone.

Tintagieu, an hour after sunset, moved stealthily through the shadows like a great cat. Two hours earlier she had lured the policemen to her cottage, where she had heated their blood and then locked them in. For some while they had simmered gently and then the cold wind of reality chilled their loins as they recalled their assignment. Apart from the policemen who had not yet escaped from the trap, the whole island was still searching. To those who suggested to Tintagieu in varying tones that her idea of hide-and-seek had been, to say the least of it, 'a mistake', she merely raised her huge black-fringed eyes and answered: 'I *know*, dear, I *know*, but then where *can* the naughty little beast have hidden himself?'

She tapped gently four times and Mr Pye unlocked the door from the inside. Tintagieu entered immediately and the door was locked again.

'I have brought you something to eat,' said Tintagieu, 'and a bottle of your wine. Miss Dredger made the sandwiches. She sends her love, dear, and so does the paint-box. They know it would be dangerous for you if they came to see you, although they want to, chief dear.'

'You've never called me chief before,' said Mr Pye.

'Haven't I?'

'Never.'

'I suppose because it's really Miss Dredger's name for you, dear.'

'The brave old sailor.'

'Not so very old.'

'No – no – of course not – a fine type.'

'Am *I* a fine type?' said Tintagieu.

'Of course you are, Tanty. You are a very fine type, but of course, an altogether different type ... of type.'

'Sounds rather confusing, dear. Look; I've got a torch, but we'd better block the window first.'

It had grown a little chilly in the prison and Mr Pye had put his coat over his shoulders. The wings prevented him from putting it on. They were growing much more rapidly than in the old days. It was as though Mr Pye had so thoroughly expiated his sins by the humiliating penance he had voluntarily undergone that the wings were doing all they could to prove to him that he was forgiven.

'Tanty,' said Mr Pye, 'here's my jacket – "black as the night that covers me".... Will you fold it neatly, dear, and place it in the window? It was well cut. I had a good tailor – but I will never wear it again and it'll fit no one else, so let it perform its last and most significant duty – to free us from the eyes of the island.'

'And the ears too, for that matter,' said Tintagieu; 'we must talk more quietly.'

'Here is the coat,' said Mr Pye. 'When you switch on your torch you'll get a shock, but you are probably shock-proof by now, eh, Tanty?'

'All but,' said Tintagieu. She forced the black city jacket into the little prison window and then switched on the torch.

The first thing that she noticed was that the horns seemed shorter. The supernatural powers were wasting no time, and Tintagieu grasped Mr Pye by the arm.

'They're on the run,' she whispered. 'They've got the breeze-up, dear.'

'I know, Tanty, but there's no escape. Were you ever given one of those toys which, when you pressed down, for instance, a wooden donkey's tail, it lifted its head, and when you pressed its head down to its knees, the tail shot up again? That is what I have become. I had hoped that the Great Pal would free me altogether. These things are almost worse.'

'What things, my darling?'

Mr Pye turned his back on her for a moment.

The silence in the little stone prison was pressed against her forehead and hummed in her ears. It was for only a moment that Mr Pye turned from her, but her blood ran cold, and the seconds as they passed were big with horror.

'Ah! no, no, no. Ah! my poor one!' She put out her hand and touched his arm.

'It's all right,' said Mr Pye. 'Don't worry. I've had them before, and very high-class feathers they are indeed. I couldn't have chosen a better pair for myself – no, Tanty, not from the poshest store in Paradise – or the brush of Raphael. The only trouble is, my dear, that I don't *want* 'em. Ha, ha, ha, ha. . . .'

'You are very brave,' said Tintagieu. 'I will never forget you.'

'Oh, but *I* will,' said Mr Pye. 'That's exactly what I *must* do, and the sooner I forget myself the better. Now what about the wine and these splendid sandwiches? Bless the old sailor; she has never forgotten what I taught her about the sandwich – that splendid conception.'

Tintagieu poured the wine into the two glasses she had brought. Then she put down the bottle on the prison floor, her hand shaking. 'What does it all mean? Do you understand, Mr Pye? – are you safe? Are you safe? What can I do for you? We cannot hide here for ever. Sark is alive tonight. The island is after you. No one will go to bed. We must think.'

'Not yet,' said Mr Pye, 'it would spoil the wine.'

'Horns were bad enough, chief – but they were something I could understand, somehow. But wings? Wings are . . . unfair.'

'They are certainly unfair. Have they grown at all?' said Mr Pye.

At that moment something shook the door of the little prison, and then a voice within a few feet of where they sat together in the silence told them that the shoulders of one of the searchers had struck against the moonlit door, and that someone had sat down upon the flagstones and leaned back heavily. 'If I haven't walked the soles off my feet, I'd like to know what I've been bloody well doing all day, I would,' said the voice.

'It was her flaming fault,' said another voice. 'I'll skin that Tintagieu.'

'I'd like to see you,' said the first voice again. 'She'd eat you.'

There were more footsteps and in the distance the rumbling sound of wheels on the stony road, and a third voice:

'She wouldn't eat *him*,' it said with scorn.

'Why not?' said the second voice again. Its owner was evidently in a muddle. On the one hand he felt insulted that his friends thought so little of his strength that they imagined he would allow himself to be devoured by a woman, but on the other hand he saw no reason why they should think he would prove unpalatable.

'Did you say *why?*' said the third voice. 'Because you're so bloody "ripe", that's why. A flipping vulture wouldn't eat you, friend. You're a disgrace, you are, like rotten fish, I shouldn't wonder.'

The gentleman who was being so severely criticized was very angry, but he had no wish to fight, contenting himself with a string of horrible imprecations. These were interrupted by the arrival of two carriages. Inside the prison the sound of the wheels and the creaking harness and the hooves of the horses as they struck the ground sounded horribly close. And then to outdo these noises, a cacophony of shouts and oaths filled the air, and one maudlin voice kept on telling the company that when Irish eyes are smiling it is like a breath of spring. Judging by the endless reiteration of this sentiment it might have been imagined that the singer was indulging in a brand of masochism as potent and as tedious as that enjoyed by the sons of Erin.

And then another carriage rolled up and someone shouted:

'He's nowhere to the north.'

'That's what I said, anyway....'

'Old clever guts.'

'...Scared me stiff. Thought I saw him over the bloody hedge near the Clos-a-jaon. Thought I saw him, I tell you. Turned my belly over. Wasn't the Fruit-drop at all. It was Harry's cow with her horns against the moon.'

'He's nowhere to the north.'

'The tide's too high for the caves.'

'Bloody *vanished*, my old cock.'

'When Irish eyes are ...'

'Oh, shove 'em somewhere.'

'Woa! there....'

'Tie her to the railings, Freddy.'

'Where's the rest of us?'

Then another voice, an authoritative and strident voice, began to call from the road above the Manoir. It was impossible for either Mr Pye or Tintagieu to distinguish what he was saying, but a few minutes later, they could hear a word or two quite clearly. It was the man who had insisted that Mr Pye had turned into a blood-sucking goat and was Satan's nephew.

'Get on your feet,' he cried, 'you lumps of stinking conger! Get out your jack-knives! Tie up your horses. We've got him by the short and curly ones!'

'You've *got* him, did you say, Pawgy?'

'Every house and bloody cottage has been scoured, and so has Dixcart Valley. The caves are all under water. Little Sark's empty as a bloody drum. I've had two hundred of you work across from Rouge Terrier to the Moi de Fontaine, from Port Gorey to Venus Bath; from the Coupée to Vermandee.'

'What about the silver-mines, mister? He could hide in the silver-mines.'

'So could your aunt with the yellow itch,' said the unpleasant Pawgy. 'But they're as empty as your skull, my friend.'

'What about the police, mister?'

'Well, what about 'em?'

'Where are they, mister?'

'Working across from Havre Gosselin. Two more boatloads of the suckers, with great torches.'

'Don't need torches in this moonlight, mister.'

'What a clever b...r you are,' said Pawgy. 'Now listen to me. The coast's been combed, all the way round. There's not a hiding place left. We've had fifty men, women, and children from Coupée to the Butts. Another fifty from the Butts to Brecqhou; another from Havre Gosselin back to the Coupée – and the police on top – and there's only the centre of the island left. In fact, where we're standing – and all about us. We've searched Miss Dredger's. If she's hiding him, it must be in a matchbox. She don't know what she's doing. Spends all the time singing about someone bending the oar.'

'That's right, Pawgy,' someone shouted, 'I've heard her – *and* seen her. Standing at the window she is, in the flaming moonlight – singing all the time – "Pull for the beach" – or something like that.'

In the hollow darkness of the little prison Mr Pye grew suddenly very cold and he trembled so that Tintagieu gripped his arm.

'Sentries are posted all around the top,' continued the man they called 'mister'. 'They are forming a ring and will close in like, at a signal.'

'Where'll we put him when we catch him, mister?'

'What do you think this prison's for? You've got a brain like bloody Solomon's, I wouldn't wonder. Now, join the ring. In half an hour the signal will be made, and then every house and cottage and pig-sty of these last forty acres will be rooted out. I want to see him dead! He's no good to the island. He's a bloody horror. He's unnatural. He's dangerous. I've always said so – that Mister Harold Pye. You mark my words, they'll string him up in Guernsey.'

'Or sell him to a circus,' said another voice.

Tintagieu, in the prison, drew Mr Pye's small hand to her lips.

'Leave the horses tethered. The carriages will only be in the way. Up with you. By God, you need the stick, some of you. Do you want your children to grow up with horns? Eh? Eh? Let 'em all help. Maybe it takes a child to catch the Devil.'

'I think that God would like that all right, eh, mister? Catching the Devil, eh, mister? God would be pleased, I bet.'

'Shut your long mouth, and get your thick legs moving.'

There was a sound of shuffling, and the creaking of harness, and then after a few minutes the sound of feet grew fainter as the searchers moved away in the direction of the church and the Seignorie road.

Removing Mr Pye's coat from the window, Tintagieu peered out into a scene of unbelievable brightness. A full moon was flooding the island as though with phosphorus.

Turning from the small barred window she saw at first no sign of the Mr Pye she knew. He was plunged in the prison darkness. What she *did* see was where the moonbeams, streaming through the window, lit up with dazzling whiteness a wing the size of a swan's. Across this moonlit wing that had grown with such secret rapidity, the bars of the prison window cast their narrow parallel shadows.

'Chief! Chief!' she whispered vehemently. 'Listen to me! If you have never listened to me before, listen to me now! Your wing! Can you see it – and the size of it? Oh, Mr Pye, do you see what I mean? It is growing every moment. Don't you see that you'll be able ...'

'My darling Tanty. I know what you are thinking – but where, where, where? – save in the moonlight.'

'Perhaps you were made for the moonlight, chief. ... Perhaps you ...'

'I must comfort the Sailor.'

'I will comfort her, chief. You must go. Now. Now. It is your chance. Can you beat them?'

Mr Pye stood very straight, his head raised, his sharp nose pointing at the roof, his eyes closed.

'I don't know ... Tanty ... I don't know ... dear.'

'Oh, try, my love.'

In the darkness, in the silence, in the chill of the little stone prison the shape of a sea-chest, while the moonlight glowed beyond the walls, and the Sarkese waited to draw in from every quarter, and while the sea lapped at the weird indented coastline of the island, Mr Pye, grasping his hands together beneath his chin, called upon all his physical and spiritual resources and, as he did so, in that moment almost of dedication, a power, not his own, entered him; and the muscles across his back, contracting in a splendid rhythm, lifted his wings to the height of his shoulders with a strength he had never known before in those far-away days when they had driven him through hell to Harley Street.

'Do what I tell you, chief.' Her husky voice sent whispering echoes along the walls of the hollow prison. 'There is no time to lose. Sooner or later when they gather here again, one or other of them, and there are hundreds of 'em, will think of the prison. They only think of it now as the place where they will put you. But that can't go on for ever. You must jump a carriage. The best horse is the black. He's fast and he's strong. In a minute I will untie him and turn him, and then when I whistle, out of the prison with you, chief, and up into the driver's seat with you, oh, my dear one, and then away with you. I will comfort the Sailor. Have you a message for her – or anything?'

Mr Pye drew in his breath with a slow and profound shudder.

'Whatever she wants of mine is hers, of course,' he said. 'But that's not much use to her, is it? There's my gold watch in my waistcoat pocket, Tanty – but all that sort of thing is so tactless. I don't know what she'd like – if anything. I don't know what to give her – except my love.'

'Your love, Mr Pye. Can I tell her that?'

'I think so.'

'That is what I'd hoped for most, Mr Pye. But you must not stay, you must not be captured. What will happen we don't know, but you must gallop her. Make for the Coupée. Where else is there but the Coupée, at a moment like this?'

'The Coupée,' whispered Mr Pye, and his mind flew back to that first night in Sark, when, in the storm he had stood on the narrow ridge and heard the waves thrashing the rocks three hundred feet below, and the wind beating on the face of the cliff.

He shut his eyes again and he could see in his imagination how the land narrowed: how Big Sark dwindled to the perilous isthmus: how it seemed as though two great forces were joined together by the Coupée as though it were the cord that joins the unborn child to its mother, or like that moment called *life* that links the dark domains of the womb and of the tomb. He knew that Tintagieu was right. He must make for that place – the wasp-like waist of the island he had come to save from itself.

'Good-bye, Tanty.'

She gripped his hand and then, moving to the door, turned the key. Opening the door a fraction she let in a tall spear of moonlight. There was no one. The only noise came from one of the tethered horses who had flung his head back and set some metal jingling at its brow. She walked to it rapidly and untying the reins, turned it about in the road so that it faced to the south. As the wheels revolved on the stony road it seemed as though all Sark must hear – and it is possible that the sound of the wheels *was* heard and was the cause of the long-drawn note of a police whistle that rang at that very moment across the island. What is more likely, however, is that the signal was at that instant due, and at once, voices from across the fields on every side began to punctuate the moonlight.

Mr Pye, hearing the whistle, stepped out at once, and climbed smartly on to the driver's seat. For a moment he sat there erect as a little guardsman on the high perch. His horns had all but gone, but what was left of them twinkled. He withdrew a little box from his trouser pocket and took a fruit-drop and popped it into his mouth.

'Thank you, Tanty.' He turned his face to her. In after years, Tintagieu, in recalling that expression on his face when he looked at her for the last time, suffered so sweet a pang in her breast – a pang of such pure affection – that no one who only knew her as Sark's least virginal of daughters, could ever have believed.

'Away with you,' she cried in a voice as hoarse as a raven's.

'And away it is!' shouted Mr Pye, plucking the whip from its mouldering scabbard and cracking it above the horse's head, so that the black beast rose on its back legs and then began to lurch violently down the short decline. For a moment it looked as though it were going to flatten out the pump of the Manoir well and wreck the carriage, Mr Pye, and itself, in the hollow beyond, but turning dangerously upon two wheels it headed up the hill past Rosebud cottage while Mr Pye, his wings beating at his sides, cried out encouragement to the black charger. This enormous brute was striking sparks from the rough road with all four of its iron shoes, and up the hill she snorted, tossing her head and rolling her eyes. Rosebud Cottage moved by on the right and then Mr Pye saw the painter. He was standing at the gate and looking, in the moonlight, like something from a Byzantine niche in some cathedral, or like Ethelred or Egbert, in a history primer.

'Ars longa, vita brevis!' shouted Mr Pye, as his carriage rattled past the gate – but Thorpe had no power to answer or even to wave his hand. His eyes were half out of his head. All he saw was a moonlit seraph with Mr Pye's face, a seraph in striped trousers, a seraph aloft an ancient chariot with a whip in his hand. No, he could not answer, nor could he close his mouth, into which the moonbeams poured.

Then suddenly, with the old mill in sight, everything seemed to happen at once. A whistle blew from behind a hedge. Three figures appeared at the top of the mill and one of them screamed. The second figure could not release his grip on the railing he was holding, and it was lucky for him or he might have shared the fate of the third of the look-out men, who missed his footing and fell down the precipitous spiral of the stairs, and was dead before he reached the bottom.

Three Guernsey constables suddenly appearing out of the night were forced to leap for their lives into the ditches on either side of the road. By now a score of cries broke up the night. The road was now level, and the black horse began to gallop, and at the moment it did so the ground became alive with dogs. Somehow or other the island, like a sounding board, had drawn the hounds together from every quarter, and like a pack they surged around the galloping hoofs of the black horse, yelping and snapping and bowling one another over in the madness of the race.

Turning the right-angular corner and into the long Coupée road at the speed at which the black horse was moving was a feat that could, on paper, be proved impossible. There was no logical reason why the horse and the carriage and Mr Pye were not destroyed. The walls of a cottage rushed at them: the horse had its head all but through a broken window when it reared: the carriage shook itself like a dog when it leaps ashore from the sea: the hand brake screamed, the wheels rattled or spun like tops in the air. Mr Pye aloft in the driver's seat threw out one of his wings to steady himself and then beat it rapidly in the air until balance was recovered. A dozen islanders appearing from the door of the 'Seaweed' gave a great yell that brought out a dozen more. A pony, tied by a rope to one of the great stones with holes in them that act in Sark as horse-anchors, broke its tether and sped whinnying down the road towards Petit Beauregarde, the whites of its eyes flashing in the moonlight. More whistles rang across the fields, and men on bikes began to pedal furiously in the wake of Mr Pye. Somehow or other the whole island knew what had happened. The devil had become an angel. It was the rarest night in the annals of the island. The chase was on. Every carriage was miraculously filled with the pursuers, and a score of wheels rang and rattled down the Coupée road. Those without bikes or horses ran. Those who could not run, being too old or infirm, tottered. The dogs, galloping in the wake of the apparition, yelled themselves hoarse.

The three leading carriages of the pursuers raced in the wake of the dogs, jolting and bounding up and down on the rough stones.

Five boys on stolen bicycles skidded madly among the carriages, and behind them again, were dogs, and behind the dogs a single carriage that had lost its driver but was full of human freight, and behind this carriage were more bikes, and a young man who ran like a deer with a fixed expression in his eyes – and behind all these were more of every kind that had for some reason or other been delayed, or had suffered accident.

Overhead, as though they had got wind of something unusual, a great cloud of gulls wheeled and veered, screaming over the heads of the pursuers.

Mr Pye was now in the hands of the Great Pal. He had ceased to assume any responsibility for what was happening or what he did. He had shut off that part of his mind which made decisions. He had made his gesture. He had humbled his pride. If the Great Pal wished to torture him further that was up to the Great Pal. For himself, he knew that he was clear of it all. He was already in another world. What happened didn't matter very much. His conscience was free and he felt a kind of radiance of the heart.

As he thundered down the road, and as the Coupée grew momently closer he never ceased to beat his wings. They now spread farther than his outstretched arms. His face was transfigured, and when for a moment he turned on his precarious and bounding perch, and shot a glance over his shoulder at his pursuers, they were dazzled as though a burning glass were trained upon them. They were chasing the apparition like a horde in a dream. They had no option but to pursue. A kind of mass compulsion drove their wheels. Their eyes were wide with speculation. Their brains dizzy with conjecture. Their tongues loose with fear, for they yelled as they swept by down the long moon-illumined road – woven with the dogs and gulls. It was no longer revenge, or fear, or hate – it was dementia. Amazing, silent, serene, and winged – Mr Pye, at the plunging spearhead of madness, was a mere ten yards ahead of the fastest of his pursuers. He sat perfectly upright, yet perfectly relaxed while the great hoofs thundered below him. As the ground began to dip he drew forth his soul and tossed it skywards to his God.

'Oh, catch it, if you care to,' he cried, and he beat his wings in an earthless exultation, and as he did so the horse below him stumbled as it poured its hoof-beats down the sharp and narrow decline, between the pink and ashen walls of rock and there, all in a flash, was the Coupée curving like a white snake – but only for that one instant, for at the next the black horse, rearing in the shafts, veered to the right of the track and, catching the carriage wheel in the railing, tore it off the body and the next moment the carriage, losing balance, was toppled bodily over the rust-red rails. It tore them apart as it swayed monstrously and fell, dragging with it the black horse, so that together they plunged, a hideous conglomeration, down, down, down, vaulting horribly as they descended in giant arcs to the shingle far below.

And what of Mr Pye? At the moment of the crash he was hurled from the driver's seat and high into the air. Three hundred feet below him as he hurtled was the wide and sweeping bay, the Grand Grève, where he had once dispoiled the castles of the children. From the reflecting shore the wet face of the moon shone up at him.

For the first few moments, as he sailed through the night, the violence of the impact against the Coupée railings had all but stunned him, and when he recovered his faculties he found himself in mid-air and about to fall like a stone.

It was at that moment also that the vanguard of his pursuers reached the Coupée where, almost within the time it takes to tell, an interwoven mass of horses, dogs, and bicycles had begun to form while the forerunners of those who had no means of conveyance but their own feet were already arriving. As the moments passed, the Coupée filled until the islanders stood like a caterpillar, taking the curve of the isthmus.

All shouting had ceased. There was no more movement now than there had been at the cattle show when Mr Pye had turned them into stone.

The lapping of the water far below them and away at the fringe of the sea where the ebb tide drawled, was clear in their ears. Even the gulls had ceased to scream, and hung in the air watching.

And what they saw, and what the Sarkese saw, when Mr Harold Pye reached the end of the long hurtling flight was this. They saw him begin to fall, suddenly, like a dead-weight, but then they saw, as he fell, a movement of the wings and, all at once, they were stretched in a great span on either side so that the speed of his descent was checked, and he hung suspended. And then they saw his first attempt to fly.

It was a never-to-be-forgotten sight. There was beauty in it, with those ample wings of dazzling whiteness that bore him to and fro as he tried to learn how best to manage them: and there was pathos – for he looked so solitary – adrift in the hollow air. And there was bathos also, for it seemed incongruous to see his city trousers and his small, black, gleaming shoes.

And the Islanders saw how he had already mastered his wings and was beginning to soar in slow wide arcs, and how he was now far out to sea and dwindling until he was only visible to those of keenest vision, and then, even to these he was lost, and the island was suddenly empty – and was nothing but a long wasp-waisted rock.